YOUNG MEN ON FIRE

A Novel by Howard Hunt

SCRIBNER

NEW YORK   LONDON   TORONTO   SYDNEY   SINGAPORE

SCRIBNER
1230 Avenue of the Americas
New York, NY 10020

SCRIBNER and design are trademarks
of Macmillan Library Reference USA, Inc., used under license
by Simon & Schuster, the publisher of this work.

For information about special discounts for bulk purchases,
please contact Simon & Schuster Special Sales:
1-800-456-6798 or business@simonandschuster.com

Designed by the Author

Set in Adobe Garamond

Manufactured in the United States of America

1   3   5   7   9   10   8   6   4   2

Library of Congress Cataloging-in-Publication Data
Hunt, Howard.
Young men on fire : a novel / by Howard Hunt.
p.   cm.
I. Title.
PR9619.4.H86 Y6 2003
823'.92—dc21   2002042779

ISBN: 978-0-7432-4173-1

In fond memory of the Vanderbilts

YOUNG MEN ON FIRE

INCOMING

Four days before the World Trade Center was destroyed by terrorists, Jim Troxler caught a United flight from Los Angeles to New York. This was September 7, 2001. Bad things had not yet happened, so it was business as usual in the land of the free. Bush had proved tough on third world racism and the environment, Tiger Woods was on the cover of *Time,* and the Regis Philbin gameshow, *Who Wants to Be a Millionaire?* had briefly captured the heart of America, spawning the catchphrase "is that your final answer?" which was deployed with much rueful humor in financial circles ever since the Nasdaq took a dive and showed no sign of bouncing back.

Troxler had been awake for fourteen hours. The previous morning, he had boarded an intercontinental flight from Melbourne, Australia, where he had lived for the past five years, and flown to Los Angeles via New Caledonia. A hellish stopover at LAX, then six more hours in the air to New York, most of which were spent listening to a cunning rock spider of a woman named Joyce, who trapped him at the start of the in-flight movie and didn't let up until the plane was on the tarmac. Joyce, it transpired, was an alcoholic who had not touched alcohol in fifteen years.

Troxler's visit to the States was motivated by a series of urgent email messages from his younger brother, Martin, the meat of which concerned their father, a practicing alcoholic from the old school of two-fisted, unapologetic alcoholism, who had finally succumbed to cancer and was understandably pissed-off about it, to the point of demanding a closing ceremony with fireworks at the old family home in Fern Grove, Fort Lauderdale. Exactly why this necessitated a flight to New York instead of Florida was something of a mystery. Despite their urgency, Martin's emails had been cryptic. The brothers needed to talk. Some heavy shit was going down. Interestingly, the heavy shit quotient of these messages was referred to in a kind of frantic subtext; the main subject of Martin's emails being the performance specs of the brand-new Audi Quattro he had recently acquired, and the course of action he was proposing (and which Troxler had provisionally agreed to) was that the brothers hook up in New York and drive down to Fort Lauderdale. The old man would be discussed. The heavy shit would be resolved. A road trip. In the Audi. Which was, apparently, Heaven on Wheels.

The United flight was half empty, the plane a Boeing 767. Standard three-four-three seating configuration. Plenty of seats to go around. Anticipating a clear view of Manhattan, Troxler had secured himself a window seat at the right-hand rear of the aircraft, his little porthole unobscured by wing. He had his blanket and pillow. He was savagely tired. And here was Joyce, peering around from the seat in front of him, talking through the headrests, then actually getting up and switching rows. A big woman. Midwestern. Her name was Joyce, she was sitting beside him, and—

"Why do you consider yourself an alcoholic if you haven't touched booze in fifteen years?" he had asked.

A twelve-step litany ensued. Alcohol had brought Joyce to the brink of ruin. Alcohol, in fact, had taken Joyce beyond the brink. Way, way beyond. She had been out there. On the slippery slope. Drinking drinking drinking. Joyce could have been anywhere between forty-five and sixty. She described the alcoholism of her past in practiced soundbites. She was a bad wife, a bad mother. She did things, bad things. The details were hazy, not that Troxler needed details – his dad, after all, had played for the majors – but the odd thing about Joyce was that she didn't let up. There was no end to her badness. No point in the narrative where she saw the light and quit. Fifteen years had passed, and yet here she was, on the verge of tears, reliving the halcyon days of her old life as a booze hound. How very strange. On the projection board in front of them, the War in the Pacific played itself out, and it looked for all the world like the U.S. Navy was winning. The carnage was high-gloss and cinematic, the scope of production affording director Michael Bay the opportunity to blow things up on a truly epic scale, and as the film progressed, many great, gouting fireballs of destruction blossomed like flowers on the video screen.

The Manhattan skyline was somewhere to their right. The plane had banked above Long Island and was curving down into Kennedy. Joyce was still talking, her voice husky with use, imploring Troxler to look at her, look at her, not the New York City skyline which would still be there tomorrow. She had stayed in his face for several hours, punishing herself for his benefit, and yet the true, harrowing sadness of her account came with the shuffling of tray tables and the fasten seatbelts sign, and the sudden realization that fifteen-year-old alcoholism was all Joyce had to offer. Nothing of interest had happened since. Alcoholics Anonymous had given her the courage and the script, Jerry Springer the belief in the importance of her story. It was self-help in the truest sense. She had debased herself in the eyes of a stranger. The effect was cleansing. It was time to move on.

"And what about you?" she asked. "What brings you to New York?"

They were standing at the luggage carousel. Troxler's bags had appeared and he was tracking them.

"Good question," he replied.

The airport lighting was surreal. Uniformed black guys guarded the handcarts, the idea being that they would cart your luggage for you if your luggage required carting—presumably for a tip. Joyce was smiling at him, her eyes wide open, blinking in the slow rhythm of someone chewing gum. It was a distancing gesture. The wide eyes and slow blinking meant "please go away now," and Troxler was happy to oblige.

"Here's my luggage," he pointed out.

"You're a very perceptive and intelligent young man," Joyce said warmly. "It's been a real pleasure speaking with you."

Jim Troxler was thirty-six years old. Unlike his younger brother, who had inherited the old man's swagger and charm, he had channeled the family genes into his work, and had developed a quiet intensity that kept him somehow in the background. You switched him on, he hummed like a refrigerator. A reassuring noise you noticed only when it stopped. In the five years he'd lived in Australia, this was the first time he had returned to the States, for the simple reason that the work demanded it. He too had been out there. On the slippery slope. He was one of those guys who took karate to relax.

This business with his father, then, was something of a wake-up call, because there was no way the old man would willingly concede to death. That would involve losing, and his dad never lost. His dad – who both sons considered to be one of the more interesting and colorful and frightening people on the planet; who continued to astonish and excel at a disparate range of careers (highlights including insurance salesman, race-car driver, security consultant, and, of course, bartender), the whole time taking down an inhuman amount of booze – was something of a legend when it came to not losing. He never gambled (gambling was for losers), borrowed money, or went to church (for losers), took shit from his bosses (a pack of losers, many of whom he had set straight over the years), or died, the idea of death being as inconceivable as some big midwestern woman on a plane wanting to talk for three hours about life off the wagon. Yet here it was. Tough old Alan Troxler from Red Hook, Brooklyn. Ass-kicked by cancer. So now it was time to take stock of the legacy: the clapped-out house on the best street in Fern Grove; the impressive but clapped-out collection of cars; the devastatingly beautiful but hard-boiled and defiantly clapped-out former Miss Miami, Dottie Troxler (née Harris); and the semi-famous younger brother, Martin, who, despite assurances that he would be here at the gate, was not at the gate. Which was no surprise, really.

A billboard-sized photograph of Steve McQueen in his *Le Mans* racing gear covered an entire wall of the arrivals area, and as Troxler carried his heavy bags past it, he couldn't help smiling at the thought of his dad. Two Corvettes in the driveway. Fabulous windblown hair. And yet like McQueen, especially in his *Le Mans* period – *Le Mans* being an out of control vanity project that cost many people in seventies Hollywood their jobs – what it came down to was the *idea* of fast-lane living. McQueen had no clue what his film was about. All he knew was that it revolved around a famous car race in France, which he would presumably win on account of being the hero, and that it gave him occasion to wear a cool-looking outfit. Plot, character development, story arc, believability: these things were not important in the case of *Le Mans*. It was McQueen. In an outfit. Squinting at the camera in a portentous but otherwise meaningless collection of iconic moments, one of which the Tag Heuer people would freeze-frame and blow up a quarter century later, displaying it prominently on an airport wall as a symbol of success.

Was the old man successful? If McQueen was the role model, the answer was yes. McQueen was bigger than *Le Mans*. He had walked from the wreckage, leaving a stunned and bankrupt pit crew to quell the flames behind him, and he had looked damn good walking. There was something heroic about the way he left the site. In much the same way, Alan Troxler was a legend in Fort Lauderdale. He was an expert at walking from wreckage. Years of disaster had not only untouched him, they had somehow enhanced his thrillseeker cachet. He felt zero remorse. You did business with him, you were basically employing him to take your risks, which meant you were too much of a pussy to take them yourself, which put you somehow in his debt. This was the logic, take it or leave it, and, oddly enough, the phones kept ringing. Despite evidence to the contrary, people didn't just believe; they wanted a participatory role in Alan Troxler's mythic life. And thus *Le Mans*. Old man Troxler and his cars, his beautiful wife, and a forty-year career trajectory that was one huge racing skid from Brooklyn to the Sun Belt. Twisted metal and glass. The inevitability of collision. The engine whine and freefall. Seconds, hours, days before the crash.

This book takes place in that moment of freefall, in a similar environment of zero remorse. The crash we were expecting occurred in April 2000, and it was routinely huge and horrible. The dot-com economy imploded. Many people lost their shirts. In New York, the wreckage was largely metaphoric, resulting in a lot of would-be millionaires not becoming millionaires, and a lot of on-paper wealth disappearing overnight. It was different in the heartland, where houses and farms had been mortgaged on technology, but this wasn't the heartland. This was big city USA. All the great players had walked from wreckage; the hallmark of true greatness being the ability to predict a collision and keep driving toward it, increasing acceleration and reaping profit all the way, and then selling like mad at the point of impact. Like U.S. foreign policy, the economic big picture was driven by so many short-term agendas and high-risk plays that the resulting crash was not only inevitable but necessary (and, if you listen to the rationalists, desirable) in terms of creating the kind of supercharged environment in which a global rethink might be possible. In which we stopped, by virtue of the accident, and went, "People are getting hurt here. Perhaps it's time we slowed down."

The old man's closing ceremony was symptomatic of this – the onset of death being a particularly good conduit for change – although Jim Troxler could no more imagine the old man sitting up in bed and saying, "Jim, Marty, I've been wrong all these years," than he could the Tag Heuer people going, "That McQueen movie sucked." And yet these emails from his brother . . . impossible to decipher, but very much in the language of mortality. His brother sounded spooked. Five years of scant communication, and suddenly these long, rambling, confrontational emails that really did suggest some kind of crisis of belief. His wheels had left the tarmac. He was in freefall. And, in sharp contrast to his dad, who had crashed and walked so many times that the act of crashing and walking was nothing new, Martin Troxler had yet to hit the wall himself. Dot com hadn't touched him. He was there for the crash, but it wasn't his crash, so he got to hang loose and party guiltlessly in the wreckage. Party being the operative word because the truly creepy thing about the economic flatline was that there was still a lot of money around. Share prices had fallen, but there were millions of dollars of as yet unassigned venture capital and company assets to play with, and if you were remorseless – that is to say, if you figured all those people in the heartland were a bunch of fucking pussies without the wherewithal and guts to make their farms work themselves – it was an easy job to make this money disappear. From the top to the bottom of the food chain, enterprising New Yorkers squirreled wealth from the wreckage, the mentality being that if they didn't, someone else would, and why should that someone else get all the breaks? Dog eat dog world, pal. Can't stand the heat, get out of the kitchen. Is that your final answer? Yes it is.

September 7 was a Friday, the big party night in NYC. Young men and women would soon be suiting up and preparing to hit the clubs. Booze would be consumed. Drugs taken. This was a typical night out in the final days of dot com, and yet for Jim and Martin Troxler, the evening would prove significant in ways that had less to do with money and more to do with their given outlooks on life. Jim the idealist. Martin the pragmatist. Both in freefall as a result of their dad, and both on the verge of a serious flameout. The old man's DNA was combustible. Both sons were pushing their respective envelopes, and the next fifteen hours would turn the evening white hot. In the next fifteen hours, the environment would turn critical and a directional change would somehow be achieved, but not before the younger Troxler had set himself on fire. Martin Troxler would hit the wall, there'd be wreckage galore, and the old man's demons would stand grinning in the flames.

The question, then, was whether to face them.

Whether to stay at the site and hose those demons down.

LEGENDS OF THE FALL

Martin Troxler was struggling to explain the New Cynicism above the noise of a Chinese restaurant–turned–sports bar in the financial district of Manhattan. The bar was not located on Wall Street, but it was a well-known broker hangout. The noise level was ridiculously high. An enormous twelve-console widescreen hung down from the ceiling, alternating Super Bowl footage with rapid-cut highlights from the Extreme Sports Network. The soundtrack was one big guitar squeal.

"You get out of college in the eighties–early nineties," he was saying. "You size up the workforce. The old trades. Architect. Doctor. Lawyer. Whatever. The old trades are hierarchy-based. You start at the bottom and work your way to the top. The top is what it's all about. And there are people ahead of you. Doing it. You with me?"

"Sure." Jim Troxler nodded.

"These people at the top. They paid their dues. It's a competence and respect thing. You learn from your competent superiors. You respect them. Someone is incompetent above you – or, godforbid, your competent superior screws up – you take his job and move on. This is the workforce in the eighties–early nineties. You can get to the top. But it takes time. And time is good, right?"

"Sure." Jim Troxler nodded.

"Okay. So now you get out of college in the late nineties–early naughties. You go straight into e-biz. Doesn't matter what you're studying. E-business will take you. Anyone with a computer can be a convergence analyst. A website developer. An e-commerce VP. Anyone with a spark of an idea and an MBA can get venture capital. Float a company. Get to the top in no time. And no time is bad."

"Why is no time bad?" Jim Troxler asked. "I would have thought getting to the top in no time would be great."

"It is great, except you have no guidelines. No competent superiors to show you the ropes. You wouldn't believe how many thirty-year-old CEOs there were in Manhattan with like, twenty mil VC in their accounts, going, 'What the fuck do I do now?'"

"I imagine you'd buy a lot of real estate," Jim Troxler said.

"The money's on paper. That's not the point. The point is, there's no value to this kind of success. It wasn't hard fought for. It meant nothing. The dot-com economy was built with smoke and mirrors. All this money appeared. Companies overdeveloped like crazy. And even before the crash, the question everyone was ignoring was like, where the hell is the revenue coming from? Do we know? Does anybody know?"

"I have no idea," Jim Troxler said.

"Nobody knew. Ergo the New Cynicism. The whole thing could fall apart at any minute, so let's greenlight that project! Let's spend the venture capital! You're the New Media VP at Nissan, I'm the e-biz dude from Young and Rubicam, let's develop your web presence! Let's fit you up with an e-tail facility even though no one in their right mind is going to buy a Nissan from you without sitting in it first, because we could both be laid off in a week! Lunch at the Four Seasons? Oh you betcha!"

Troxler talked like this. He was a Gatling gun of absolutes. He spoke from a position of authority on everything, especially things he knew nothing about, and got away with it because he wrote hi-tech lowbrow for a range of magazines. People respected his opinion because his opinion was published in *Esquire* and *The New Yorker*, and it was a kind of Dave Barry opinion, only younger and meaner. Since 1996, he had authored two popular books of social criticism, and had a third book scheduled for a Christmas release. Everything he said was completely obvious, but delivered in an incredulous tone that made you doublethink his meaning. He straddled the terrain between Coupland and Rushkoff, and had a sportswriter's knack for delivery and punchline. On the rare occasions when he was feigning interest in someone else's opinion, he had this aggressive habit of rapid-firing the questions, leaning into the person's body space like Holyfield fighting Tyson, parrying each answer with a new question until the conversation quickened into a flurry of data. Faster and faster. And somewhere in the speed of repartee, he'd lose interest and politely disengage. This is not to say Martin Troxler was an asshole. He was actually very charming when it suited him to be.

"So what's the difference between the New Cynicism and, you know, just plain old cynicism?" Jim Troxler asked.

"Old Cynicism is the result of non-success. You're promised the American Dream and it doesn't happen? Someone less qualified gets the job because they play golf with the boss? Old Cynicism. New Cynicism is the result of success-not-earned. Where you don't believe in what you're doing, but profit regardless. It's all there in the galley proof. Not that I expect you to read it."

Outside the book contracts and the magazine articles, Troxler made serious money as a "youth consultant" to Fortune 500 companies. His field of expertise was the shifting landscape of youth consumerism. He spotted trends. Explained markets. He was suit-friendly in the sense that he could work a room full of outstandingly wealthy but creatively inert businesspeople without seeming smug or condescending, and his wardrobe was an intimidating closet of hipness. Right now, he was wearing a fussily tailored Italian-style suit – in Tony Nova, a statement in itself – and this visual dynamism really worked in the boardrooms, even more than his one-two punch of obviousness and incredulity. Conference planners fought to book him. His praise appeared on the back of work by much better writers. His own jacket art was stylish and conceptual, and you could tell that a great deal of time had been spent on the author photographs, which were contrived to look as though they had been snapped on the fly, but were obviously the result of a professional shoot.

"Of course I'll read it," Jim Troxler said.

Troxler's latest book was titled *The Slum Lords*. It examined the Silicon Alley boom in turn-of-the-century Manhattan, and held it up as a microcosm of the economy under Clinton. Lust and guilt. The loss of the father figure. All those thirty-year-old CEOs, money in the bank, keening. Chapter excerpts had appeared in *Forbes* and *Wired*, and Troxler was sunning himself in the public glow. He'd written an amusing piece for *Men's Journal* and done a fashion shoot for *Rogue*, the webzine of the moment, and his brother's question floated down out of nowhere, almost inaudible above the sports roar overhead.

"So which cynicism are you? New or old?" Jim Troxler asked.

Troxler studied his brother's face, looking for the insult. There was none. It appeared to be an innocent question. He leaned forward on his stool, tilted his head into three-quarter profile, and threw a dangerous smile up from under his eyebrows.

"Post," he grinned. "I earn my money, same as you."

C. C. Baxter returned from the bathroom and collected the first round of drinks from the bar. Baxter, whose first name was Greg, had acquired the C. C. initials after the character Jack Lemmon plays in *The Apartment*. As per the movie, the moniker was quickly busted down from "Buddy boy" to "Bud," which was Baxter's nickname of renown in financial circles.

"Yojimbo," he said, setting tall glasses in front of Troxler and his brother. "Samurai who has lost his master. *Ronin*. I salute you."

Jim Troxler studied the drink. It was sunset pink and fluffy, like there could be an egg in there somewhere. He took a cautious sip and recoiled at the taste.

"I actually wanted an Amstel Light," he said.

"I made you for a beer drinker because of the accent? And the tan?" Baxter said cheerily. "But you're in Manhattan now. You're on my turf and I tip huge to have these babies put together, so take the fucking drink and stop complaining!" Baxter had clearly been hitting the smoot in the bathroom. He stood on a footrail, hoisted himself high above the other bar patrons, and snapped his fingers at the waitress.

"A beer chaser for the gentleman," he ordered. "What you drinking, sport? A Foster's? Australian for beer?"

"No one in Australia drinks Foster's." Jim yawned. "I'd like an Amstel Light, please."

"Tab it," Baxter said grandly, waving the waitress and Troxler's money away. "No one in Australia drinks Foster's? *Don't go there!*"

"It's an export beer. Foreigners drink it. The locals do not."

"Do not *go* there!" Baxter exclaimed.

Jim Troxler took another sip of his cocktail. "This tastes like suntan lotion," he pointed out.

"Yesh," Baxter rumbled in the voice of Sean Connery. "Yesh it doesh, but itsh not the tashte that mattersh."

Baxter was the founder/CEO of a formerly huge online advertising agency. He'd been in the Audi when Martin turned up at the airport, forty-five minutes late and full of excuses, and had wasted no time in making his presence felt adversely. "Yojimbo" was the first stage of a familiarity campaign he would run up various flagpoles and kick around all night, and his manner was so abrasive and gleefully vicious, it was possible the crash had affected his sanity. Too few paying clients and too much time on his hands. A young lion in winter. Cardinals cap, slimline Randolph shades, talking a whole bunch of nonsense in the back of his brother's car. All these nightclubs they were going to visit. All these girls they were going to . . .

What Jim Troxler didn't know – what he had no way of knowing – was that his brother and Baxter had been planning this for weeks. A homecoming parade. An underbelly trawl through glamorous fast-lane Manhattan. Welcome home Jim was the theme of this party, but it had as much to do with Jim as it did the old man's cancer. It was Martin's show. The renovators had just finished work on his loft, he had bought himself an expensive car, and he had long-standing family business to attend to. His status in the family was negligible, the result of a competitive tough love program engineered by his dad, and as a consequence, his relationship with his brother was inwardly fierce. Here he was, kicking it, in the City That Never Slept, and he was still that kid in the movie who never got to drive or fly or shoot. He'd been on *Letterman*. He was about to start a legitimate ten-city book tour. What an interesting career he had managed to have. But interest from the old man? A guest slot behind the wheel? His dad like Batman in his cave, waiting to rush out and wreak all kinds of havoc, but a quick trip up to Gotham to see Boy Wonder in action? Too goddamn hard. And now the prostate. Too late to have more sons, so the existing sons will have to do, but no prizes for guessing *which* son the old man calls first.

As a big-eyed, willful little boy, Martin Troxler had negotiated the many disappointments of childhood by buying himself presents on festive occasions, and the release of his new book was no exception. The launch wasn't due for another couple of months, but his advance check had cleared and he was robust enough to underwrite a big night of drinking in celebration of himself, and the convergence of family brought about by his dad was actually quite convenient in that it gave him the chance to drive/fly/shoot the pants off his brother. Something he'd wanted to do for a very long time.

To do Martin justice – given that we know his night will end badly – it would be good if we could break from narrative convention for a moment and concede him the competitive edge at the outset of this battle. Right now, his desire to outfly outdrive outgun his brother just sounds like boring sibling rivalry, which is really not the case. Yes, the old man lay at the heart of everything, and the evening's clash of values would be fought in his name, but what we're looking at here is different perspectives on success. We're on Martin's turf; this is Martin's night out; Martin's our man in big city USA; so why don't we concede him the high ground and let him come down from there, and put Jim in the background, at least until the battle lines are drawn. Baxter has already been sandbagging the terrain, calling Jim "Yojimbo" – the samurai hero of a Kurosawa film – in a sardonic tone of deferential respect, so why don't we tune out Baxter's irony and accord Jim this role. The quiet outsider. The one through whose eyes we will follow the story. Yojimbo's particulars will be revealed in time, but it's Martin's career path we need to gloss over now. His faultlines are of the same topography as his environment, and are thus informed by the deep core seismology that lurks at the heart of metropolitan life.

Like anyone who has ever had the privilege of being styled, photographed, and written about in a glossy magazine, Martin Troxler had an appetite for star treatment that, once whetted, became insatiable overnight. His first two books, *The Uncanny X-Men* – an obvious/incredulous look at the "cultural commentators" who made serious money explaining the youth brand to marketing firms and advertising agencies – and *Totally Wired* – an anthology of e-biz-related articles and profiles commissioned and published by *Wired* magazine – had both been well received, leading to the usual chat-show and magazine offers through which he would vault himself into the public arena. By the end of the nineties, he was a neophyte celebrity in the sense that he could get a table at most restaurants and was invited to a few of the important movie premieres, but he was nonetheless tarred by the ugly brush of journalism. At no stage did he feel the city's Big Embrace. He wrote obvious/incredulous things about people more famous than he was, and was thus lumped in with the paparazzi in the eyes of such people, regardless of his word-play, his author photos, his striking jacket designs. He hadn't harpooned the Zeitgeist, coined a phrase that would linger in the collective memory, or even written a book in an unusual tense, and it was just as well the economy imploded when it did, because his attempts to crash the A-list were going nowhere.

Around the time of the crash, he had been experiencing a lot of turbulence uptown, the result of a seemingly harmless "Shouts and Murmurs" column he had written for *The New Yorker,* deconstructing the "new" Steve Martin by pointing out that the new Steve Martin was exactly the same as the old Steve Martin, humor-wise, and that the comedian-turned-playwright's French and high art–sounding *Picasso at the Lapin Agile* was, in fact, a kind of goofy conceit featuring a slapstick turn by a character named Schmendiman, the likes of whom could have easily turned up in any of Martin's early films such as *The Jerk* or *The Man with Two Brains*.

The column's thesis was fairly straightforward, but Troxler had laid on the incredulity with a trowel. Without rehashing the particularly damning paragraphs, the article's tone was deemed to have crossed the line of respect, and was quietly reviled in the very staterooms of influence the writer had been trying so desperately to access.

Bad news for a neophyte.

But nothing compared to the hideous embarrassment of running into Steve Martin a few weeks later.

The chance encounter with Martin was mercifully brief, but Troxler had the misfortune to be eating a messy hors d'oeuvre at the time, and was deprived of an equal footing with Martin, appearancewise. They sized each other up at a Park Avenue fundraiser; the comedian/playwright in tasteful Prada, the columnist/pontificator in a Vilma Mare plastic suit, trying to contain a mussel/crab/thousand island dressing grenade that had gone off in his hand, and if there was any one moment that conveyed to Troxler the enormity of the gulf between celebrity journalist and celebrity celebrity, it was that ten-second freeze-frame right there. Not a word was said, but Troxler could feel the stench of Princess Diana lingering around him. He felt shifty. Predatory. Responsible for the bloodshed. Fingers dripping with viscous fluid as his eyes darted wildly in search of a napkin, and of course there was no napkin and there was no escape route and there were no sympathetic faces he could appeal to in a jokey, tension-relieving way, so he had no choice but to stand there in extreme discomfort, containing the flow, until Martin moved on.

After Martin moved on (and Martin never really moved on –
Martin is still in Troxler's head, staring across the room at him with
a perfectly blank expression that could contain any number of
hidden meanings and nuances if you were to play the moment over
and over like Zapruder footage: something Troxler doesn't want to
do but can't stop himself from doing), Troxler collected his coat and
caught the first cab down to Wall Street. There was a drinking
scene down there. An as yet uncharted scene where you could deal
yourself in to the humiliation fury of dot com by slapping money on
the bar and trading lines of smoot and bullshit. A rough scene.
Non-stateroomly. No smiling old dears in their palatial apartments
with their antique furniture and actual wealth. This was the once-
scrappy paradise of other people's money. Money that hadn't actu-
alized. Money that had gone. A pyramid scheme of prospective
wealth was what it was, and the incredible thing was that so many
people bought it. All these superbright people with their expensive
degrees, and they may as well have been peddling tupperware for
all the good it did them. Three or four years of subsistence living,
waiting for the good times to roll out of escrow?—Sorry no. The
Nasdaq took a dive and it was party time on Wall Street; in the
canyons of finance; from the World Trade Center to the hi-tech
shantytown of Flatiron. The Nasdaq was dead, and like the disco
ghouls of *Thriller,* the entire lower echelon of stock-and-wage-
earning trenchworkers – the programmers, production managers,
sales and marketing staff, designers – crawled out from their graves
to shake what booty they had left. A rough fucking scene. Couple
of bars down there you wouldn't walk into. These were the places
where the wingless gods of e-biz came to sell the office hardware and
drain their corporate accounts. And drink. This is where the down-
wardly mobile came to drink, and Troxler was of a mind to get
righteously loaded.

The drinking hole he washed up at was suitably roughhouse

and exclusive: the back room of a Chinese restaurant in Hanover Square. Prior to the crash, the restaurant part of the restaurant had been a popular lunchtime eatery, waggishly known around the traps as Zero Sum. Post-crash, it was Sum Zero. Where the New Cynicism percolated blackly. Where C. C. Baxter and his henchmen held court. They served corn chips in straw baskets until ten, and after midnight it was standing room only. All kinds of stuff going on in the bathroom. The shameless wholesaling of goods in which people's needs were bluntly stated and addressed without the usual preamble of lineage and backstory. Certain moral constraints had loosened up as a result of the Faludi backlash and the surge of badboy culture as championed by *Rogue* and *Maxim*, and it was the kind of bare-knuckled, sweaty atmosphere of service where it all came down to money. Sum Zero. It was here in the back room the free market lived large, and where Troxler would first grasp his concept of *The Slum Lords*.

"You want to know how this works? Here's how this works," he was saying. "That guy sitting behind you. The unfortunate-looking gentleman with the volleyball-like face, who, for the purposes of this conversation, we will call Wilson. Shiny-faced Wilson has the heart of a criminal. He didn't cause the crash. He wasn't selling tupperware. All he did was found a company that built a state-of-the-art system for tracking banner ads in websites. Three long years at the coal face. Leveraged buyout. Equity deal. Corner office with view. Things are humming along nicely for Wilson until the parent company sends a couple of career counseling dudes to see him, and here they are in his office, admiring the view, wanting to know where he sees himself next. Which is nowhere, because he's mortgaged to the hilt. He's overdrawn. He's maxed. He's on the slippery slope. The counseling dudes, it turns out, were once in dot com themselves, and a lot of self-congratulation takes place in Wilson's office as these condescending fuckers on the company payroll explain that, in these difficult times, you need to be proactive, you need to think outside the cube. Which Wilson does. His brother owns a van. The following day, something like forty brand-new, market-fresh, sleekly ergonomic and commercially desirable Macintosh G4s (retail price: $4,799) disappear from the two floors of Woolworth Building the parent company leases. There are a million stories in big city USA, and Wilson's is—"

"—wait wait wait. Back up a second."

"Pourquoi?"

"Correct me if I'm wrong, Marty, but at the end of the day, what you're talking here is stolen property."

"Oh please." Troxler shuddered.

"Yojimbo. My friend." Baxter smiled into his cocktail. "What we're talking here is the interesting process by which a new meritocracy of wealth is forged in the glowing embers of ruin. We're talking evolution."

"Excuse me?"

"Forty Macintosh G4s. Property of the liquidators. To be sold in auction anything up to eight months after the closeout, by which time their street value has depreciated to fuck-all. A 336 MHz, two-gig G4? I can pick one up now for less than a grand. Back in September 2000, when Wilson's severance comes through, they're trading at two-five. A two hundred grand purchasing order becomes a hundred grand street deal. Six months later at auction? Forty grand if you're lucky. So. On a negative scale—"

"I understand depreciation," Yojimbo said wearily. "My question was more a question of ownership."

"Your brother is kidding." Baxter whistled in amazement.

"My brother is not kidding." Troxler grinned.

"Your brother . . . *is* the weakest link. The ownership question. Jesus, Jim. Not for you the little details. Poor old Wilson and his forty G4s, no no. You're a Big Picture man. You want the answers."

"He's like this."

"You want to go global. See the little lights a-flashing. An Intel server here, a couple of Pentiums there, of no interest to you in your quest for truth, hey Jim. For you, it's war surplus. It's Vietnam. It's the hardware of Nam you wish to account for. Who signed the purchase order? Who owns the shit and how do we get it back to them? Am I right?"

"You're asking me this question?"

"Not really, no. America owned the shit. We, the people of America. It was a cluster fuck, it should never have happened. But hey. The war drive. Trillions of dollars spread hither and yon. More shit than we knew what to do with. More guns than we had soldiers—"

"And now it's Macintosh G4s instead of M16 rifles. Is this what you're saying?"

"The war has come to us, my friend. We're fighting a war in this country."

"Oh really?"

"Oh yeah."

"So helping Wilson unload his G4s is . . . what? Part of the war effort?"

"Part of the recovery."

"We're the good guys in this story, bro," Troxler said reassuringly. "We're putting food on tables. Helping families in crisis. How's your Amstel? You want another Amstel?"

"I'm okay for the moment," Yojimbo replied.

"We're like those lovable guys from *M*A*S*H*. I mean, look. You've drunk your Amstel and you're refusing another one out of pride. You'll do without, like poor Tom Joad loading up the old truck, and see, you don't have to do this! All you have to do is *ask* me for a beer! We're here for you! We're here for the little guys like you and Tom Joad!"

"By Tom Joad, you mean the *Grapes of Wrath* Tom Joad."

"*Grapes of Wrath* Tom Joad is correct."

"Interesting choice of metaphor there, Marty. I was under the impression the reason the Joads had to load up the old truck and head out to California was because the Depression had bled the country dry. The money was in the cities, along with the war profiteers and organized crime."

"Don't go there!"

"But hey. You want to buy me something, buy me a coffee. I said I'd come out for a few quiet drinks, and I'm holding up my end. But don't push it, okay? I'm not in the mood."

"A coffee for this gentleman! Standard NATO? Extra black?"

"A plain old filter coffee would be fine."

For the latter part of this conversation, Baxter had been rocking on his stool, weighing up the pros and cons of a return trip to the bathroom. War profiteers? Organized crime? *The Grapes of Wrath,* which was one of his all-time favorite novels? Baxter was cursed with a razor-sharp intellect and a profound love of the superior swordsmanship of argument, and the disappointing thing was that there were very few people with the courage and wit to match him in battle. He was a monster, yes, but this was really no excuse. It all came down to the mediocrity of others, and, like so many seriously bright people driven mad by boredom, he had taken to dulling his blade with a smorgasbord of drugs. Yojimbo was on his feet and ambling toward the bathroom, so the question of a return trip was temporarily answered. But time was of the essence. Because Big Guy, with his heavy armor plating, his turrets and guns and camouflage paint, would be walking through the door in the next fifteen minutes, and it was Baxter's practice to fling back the curtains and flood the room with sunlight before his gloomy friend arrived.

C. C. (Bud) Baxter. Founder/CEO of Hike-It Hut Hut Hut.

The first of the Porsche-driving, Silicon Alley millionaires to buy a townhouse in the Village and float a perfect IPO. Romantically linked. One of the original cyber sixty. The prankster. The warehouse party maven. The guy who bought that hideous Schnabel. A Bowery Bar regular, one of those ironic guys who drank themselves silly so they could stagger outside and actually *be* on Skid Row, whose e-biz celebrity rose to truly epic heights after Monica Lewinsky crashed one of his parties a couple of months after she blew into town.

Lewinsky was apparently on flirting autopilot ("You can see the attraction" is Baxter's stock response to anyone asking him to describe her in depth), but he dutifully took her number, called her back, and showed her the sights for a couple of weeks, collecting her bizarrely garrulous phone messages on his answering machine and posting them as sound files on the web. By far the best cut in the collection was the now legendary "Hello . . . you!" drunken phone ramble in which Monica satirizes herself in conversation with the Big Creep, a portion of which would be sampled and remixed by Junior Vasquez, played at a million raves and dance clubs throughout the country, and turned into the unofficial soundtrack for Hillary Clinton's New York senate campaign.

In the face of the ensuing controversy (Where did these sound files come from? Who could possibly be responsible for such a betrayal? How is Monica holding up? What is Monica wearing?), Baxter shamelessly stonewalled the press, denying all knowledge of any messages or sound files, but with the right amount of irony and poise to let everyone know that he was in on the joke. The Lewinsky site had been set up via a Swedish porn rerouter, and whoever had coded and scripted it had taken the precaution of not disclosing his identity to anyone directly. When the dust had settled and Monica was back in Washington where she belonged, he might eventually take credit. But now was too risky. Especially in light of all this *war profiteering*. (It should be pointed out that Baxter's the kind of guy who, for as long as it takes for the subject to bore him, will not only start incessantly referring to his activities as "war profiteering," but will somehow manage to transmute this idea into the local sociology. Unless something drastic happens to divert his sway of influence, the midnight to four shift will soon be using this term ad nauseam, and, rather than resenting Yojimbo's muted accusation, he actually admires it. The last person to raise the ownership issue of all these orphaned computers he's been helping relocate . . . well, the last person with the guts to do that was Martin Troxler himself.)

Troxler and Baxter had circled each other warily in the early trading days of Zero Sum. Their reputations preceded them. Column width for column width, photo for photo, Troxler's press wedge was as fat and colorful as Baxter's, and he had the clippings with him if you wanted to take it further. Paparazzi, you say. He'd traded quips with Rudolph Giuliani! This was him looking modest in *Vanity Fair*! The guy who did those super-quick but eerily accurate pen-and-ink caricatures in *The New Yorker* had done one of him and here it was! He was unencumbered by loss, unburdened by liquidators, had revenue streams that yielded actual revenue, and for some reason found himself on the receiving end of a lot of less-than-complimentary bar talk, catching flak from all sides like every other FNG. His Letterman status meant nothing to the slum lords, and Baxter was quick to let him know it. It was Baxter's scene, and if you wanted in, you had to deal yourself a game at Baxter's table. Humility was not an option, so Troxler went for the throat. He picked fights. Made his presence felt. Went after Baxter's henchmen with a nihilistic zeal. You couldn't help but admire his technique. It was business. He'd kill you in argument and then slip you his card. In the prisonyard hierarchy of the Zero Sum back room, Troxler wasted no time in slapping the bitches.

And he could drink.

He could really knock back the booze.

Baxter appreciated this last fact more than Troxler's bravado, because Baxter at heart was a cheerful drunk, and cheerful drunks need company. In a moment of kingly inebriation, it was Baxter who staggered over to Troxler's place at the bar. Who stuck out his hand and welcomed the writer to the fold, thus facilitating the pitch, package, and sale of Troxler's latest book. It was Baxter who made it happen. Who personally dialed up, charmed, negotiated access to, calmed the nerves of, screamed at where necessary, and ultimately assembled the impressive roll call of former e-biz legends you can see behind Troxler in his latest jacket shoot. It was Baxter who made *The Slum Lords* possible, on the Catch-22 proviso that the author be his friend. And the author went willingly. Signed up for the full tour. For beneath the bombast, despite the sea of reserve, Troxler liked nothing more than to sharpen his wits on a professional bullshitter, and Baxter was a master of the form.

His *"Don't go there!"* for example, was delivered in a self-referencing bleat designed to convey the idea that the person exclaiming "Don't go there!" was not Baxter, but some poor fool completely unaware that the phrase "Don't go there!" came and went in '96. The linguists call this practice "speaking in parentheses," and Baxter spoke in hardly anything but. He could float the quotation marks like nobody on earth, adopting and discarding personalities and accents, scaling the heights of the Spalding Gray/Eric Bogosian school of solo performance, and always hanging in until the end of the tab.

He was a piece of work, old C. C. Baxter, old Bud.

Troxler couldn't wait to turn him loose on his brother.

THE NEW CYNICISM

"Step up to the plate, Marty. I'm hefting ice here."

"You heft that ice. You *heft* that ice, you badboy. Excuse me, over here? Another round? Two sum zeroes, one coffee, one Amstel?"

"One Amstel for Mister Sobriety."

"One Amstel for Tom Joad and the poverty he stands for. So what are we packing?"

"DOA. Six tabs," Baxter murmured. "Big Guy's good for smoot. You want to get the paperwork out of the way?"

"Yeah, sixty do you for two?"

"Sixty's good. You buying for your brother?"

"Nah. Keep it together around him if you can. And keep Big Guy on a leash."

"I hear you. You want to start now, or you want to wait until Uzi?"

"Start now. I'm thinking one now, one on the boat. I'm also thinking about the bunny situation. If we want to cut one in."

"Do it with smoot. You think you'll be able to handle a bunny? With your brother in tow?"

"Probably not. Depends on the bunnies, though."

"As always. *Na zdorovie,* my friend."

"Fire in the hole!"

Yojimbo had just returned from the bathroom when Big Guy billowed through the restaurant, a workout flush still pulsing through his cheeks. He made a show of switching off his cell phone, tossing it into his gym bag, and slinging the bag beneath the nearest bar stool.

"Yobigguy! Whatup whatup?"

"Buddy boy. Legend."

"Hey, Big Guy. This here's my brother."

"Dude," said Big Guy.

"Big Guy," said Yojimbo.

"I bring news from The Prairie," Big Guy announced. "The cowgirls want us back."

"Yee-hah!"

"You're kidding. Because we tip huge, right?"

"Reading between the lines."

"Oh that's *funny.* We should go there now."

"Who'd you talk to, Wendy?"

"Nah, Dave Silverberg rooms with Crack Whore, who's tight with Irene, remember?"

"Irene as in Pravda Irene?"

"Yeah."

"Oh cringe. Oh kill me now."

"I can't even *remember* that night. But it was ugly, right? Bouncers and shit, I seem to recall."

"Don't go there!"

"And how is Crack Whore these days? She keeping well?"

"Crack Whore sends her regards. The *fatwa* is still upon you."

"Ah yes, the *fatwa*. No sign of it letting up then?"

"No. I'd say she's still serious about the *fatwa*, Marty. I'd be inclined to watch your back, wear disguises in public, that sort of thing."

"Bummer."

"So let's map out the evening. Are we slumming or what?"

"Slumming. Club bunnies. On a boat."

"Boat party! Haven't done one of them in a while."

"Kickoff at midnight. Some kind of bar trawl beforehand."

"We could go to The Prairie! I miss the cowgirls. I *miss* them."

"Never happen. We have the pharmaceuticals?"

"Pharmaceuticals are go. And no, we are not going to The Prairie."

"I'm gunning for Uzi, myself."

"Uzi's good."

"So we're heading east. So I have time to change."

"Yeah. Kill that and we're out of here."

"I gotta powder my nose."

"I gotta powder my nose too. You okay there? You want another drink?"

"I'm fine," said Yojimbo. "Take your time. Enjoy."

An awkward silence settled in beneath the widescreen. Big Guy leaned into the bar, studying the wood grain like a carpenter at a lumberyard. He took his time acknowledging Yojimbo, and when he did, he either suffered from some kind of mild myopia or else had a straight-up eye contact problem. Whatever it was, he was staring at Yojimbo and his gaze was slightly off. He said nothing, but his eyes seemed to veer to the left or the right, like they were filtering him out of their field of vision. Yojimbo stared back politely, taking in Big Guy's meaty biceps and barrel chest. Big Guy's body had been sculpted in the gym, but it was the wrong kind of body for sculpting.

His shoulders sloped into arm muscle and his buffed-out stomach merged with his hips and ass, making his body seem tubular beneath his clothes. The pec-work had overloaded his torso. He wore the kind of wristwatch an alligator wrestler might wear.

"So what do you do?" Yojimbo asked.

Big Guy frowned, his eyes skewing slightly to the left.

"I can tell you what I *don't* do," he said. "I don't ask people I've just met what they do. Conversation 101. You want to establish common ground, that's cool, but 'what do you do?' is strictly for the little leaguers. People who ask 'so what do you do?' at parties deserve to be taunted cruelly. No offense. Just sharing the wealth of knowledge, as it were."

"Right. So what do you do?" Yojimbo asked again, this time with the cold steel of zero bullshit tolerance in his voice.

"I buy and sell content." Big Guy sighed. "On the web."

"Really. What kind of content?"

"Does it matter?"

"I imagine that would depend on whether you're the person producing the content or not."

Big Guy shrugged. "I deal in news. I buy news and sell it to companies who have news links on their sites, but no news gathering facilities."

"What kind of companies?"

"Any kind. You go to the Nike site, they'll have a news link. They don't need one, but it's there to keep you on the page."

"So what, is the news on the Nike site footwear-related, or is it news news?"

"News news. AP, Reuters, shit we buy from news groups. Sifted down into a customized format. We don't do Nike. This is just to give you an example."

"Do a lot of companies do this? Recycle news?"

"You say it like it's a bad thing."

"No no. It's just . . . I'm trying to get my head around the idea of news as a tradable commodity. What you're saying is that there's no real difference between the news you pull off the wire and sell to a company like Nike, and the news *The New York Times* would pull off the wire and publish in *The New York Times Online*?"

"None whatsoever."

"Except that *The New York Times* lends to its news a credibility a company like Nike may not have."

"Ah." Big Guy smiled grimly. "You're one of those guys who's big on credibility."

"Not really. I'm just trying to see the point of a footwear company having a news link on their site."

"We don't do Nike. I told you this."

"But anyway—"

"There is no point. It's *business*. It's a cheap way of value-adding a website. You're now going to ask me the hard-hitting question of what our ethics would be in the event of Nike getting busted for a labor law infringement, right? Oh my God! Will they run the story? Give me a fuckin' break."

"You're way ahead of me."

"I buy and sell content. That's it. That's all she wrote."

"Gotcha."

Big Guy's eyes were definitely glaring, but they were glaring into space. For some reason, Yojimbo had a mental flash of an old college roommate disciplining his cat by tapping it on the forehead with his finger. The roommate was textbook passive/aggressive material. He had this thing worked out where he'd berate the cat in an assertiveness training voice while whacking it repeatedly between the eyes with his middle finger, and this would go on three, maybe four times a week, because the cat was a nervous wreck and had taken to pissing on the roommate's bed with monotonous regularity. Yojimbo had once broached the subject with the guy, suggesting there might be a correlation between the bed-pissing and the forehead-tapping, and the roommate had come back at him with a cat lover/humanitarian tirade that was not dissimilar in tone to Big Guy's description of his work. Yojimbo's jetlag was such that he wasn't really interested in making conversation with anyone, let alone someone who reminded him of a sicko cat tormenter, so it was his turn to throw a weary gaze across the bar.

"See these three drinks lined up in front of me? I'm only going to drink one of them," he said. "The Amstel and the pink drink are up for grabs."

"Oh yeah?"

"Yeah. Help yourself."

"Thanks dude. Don't mind if I do."

As Big Guy and Yojimbo nursed their drinks in silence, Yojimbo's attention was drawn to the MIT signet on Big Guy's right pinky. Had he been less groggy from the flight (and had Big Guy been more accommodating in conversation), he might have been inclined to say, "So you went to MIT?" instead of glazing over and waiting for his brother to return, and this is a shame because the MIT/NASA story is one of the truly interesting things about Big Guy, if you choose to ignore the whole business of "the transformation" and the improbable amount of sexual traffic he has managed to attract in the three years since his long-term girlfriend dumped him.

Two things a casual interactor needs to know about Big Guy are (a) he aced his computer science master's and is considered "brilliant yet troubled" by the faculty at MIT, and (b) the anti-depressant wonder drug Prozac really did give his personality that miraculous lift you read about in magazines, but unfortunately not in time to stop the long-term girlfriend from moving to an undisclosed city and leaving complex screening instructions with her family and friends.

Reeling from shock and unfortified by Prozac (the happy union of Big Guy and Prozac would take place some years later, in New York), Big Guy signed on for the highly classified, sensory deprivation chamber work environment of an unnamed research and development firm in Houston, Texas, where he punched code for NASA, authoring a role-playing game for astronauts simulating the effects of deep-space travel.

The astronauts in question were testing the body's ability to function after prolonged periods of suspended animation. Science-fiction aficionados will no doubt be familiar with this concept, as most of the spacecraft built on Hollywood soundstages these days tend to favor the "cryogenic freezer unit" solution to deep-space travel, over the more cartoonish and logistically implausible "hyperspace thruster" model, made popular by the original *Star Wars* trilogy.

The "cryogenic freezer" device, as employed by movies such as *Alien* and *Aliens,* tackles the deep-space issue (as in, "How the hell do we get our heroes into deep space without a hyperspace thruster?") by using existing technologics as a starting point for futuristic conjecture. In the *Alien* films, the heroes are already *in* deep space when the narrative begins, and we are introduced to them via an awakening process, where we see them under the glass of some kind of cryogenic pod, frozen for the journey, and then the little lights come on and the unthawing mechanisms kick in and some grizzled space marine says, "You're damn lucky to be alive, kiddo. You could have been floating out there forever." Whereupon we learn that the film's protagonist has been in a state of suspended animation for fifty-seven years.

Right now, a scenario like this is within the realm of human capability. NASA has the technology to cryogenically freeze and unfreeze astronauts at whim. Assuming you had a very fast spacecraft, you could, as per the *Aliens* scenario, shoot a platoon of space marines across the galaxy in a state of suspended animation, but before you could even think about unfreezing them in time to duke it out with the big-headed monsters, you would first need to figure out some way of stopping their muscles from atrophying in the event of the journey lasting more than three days. Around the time Big Guy graduated from MIT, the atrophy question was high on the list of NASA's priorities, and was being studied via a battery of R&D tests in Houston that required groups of would-be deep-space travelers to simulate suspended animation by climbing into a faux cryogenic pod and being encased in styrofoam for a really long time.

Big Guy's access to the astronauts was minimal, so he's not in a position to comment on the findings of these tests, but suffice it to say that there would be no Nam-style muscle flexing and two-fisted banter at the end of the journey into deep space, because the astronauts' bodies were wasted from inactivity, and the men themselves were depressed and stir-crazy from all that sitting around, day in, day out, doing nothing for months on end.

To lighten things up around the test site, NASA (via the unnamed research and development firm) hired Big Guy to write and produce a voice-activated role-playing game for the astronauts to occupy themselves with while their muscles turned to jelly. Computer game development was Big Guy's specialty. He had authored a couple of role-playing sims in his graduation year at MIT, and the scouting guys from NASA came around and sized him up, nodding approvingly at his grades, his buffed-up physique and astronaut-like intensity, and pretty much offered him the R&D gig on the spot. His office in Houston was in the basement of the building, out of the way of most of the scientific traffic, and he was free to keep his own hours, do the work however he saw fit, and stock the room with whatever wildly expensive computer hardware he figured he might need. He had an Ikea desk, an Ikea chair, an assortment of ergonomic wall racks and modular lighting, and he could play his stereo as loud as he liked.

It was the perfect place to stage a nervous breakdown.

Had the NASA scouting guys been a little more switched-on, they would have seen telltale signs of Big Guy's epic wrestle with depression. Even before his girlfriend dumped him, he was kind of morose. He worked hard, drank hard, worked his horn in traffic. Stared into space with those weirdly skewed eyes. In Houston, he drank coffee by the gallon, traded his Brooks Brothers ensemble for a confronting range of cowboywear, and took to stalking the hallways in lizard skin boots and tight jeans augmented by a soupbowl-sized belt buckle he had bought off an aging rodeo champion. For no reason at all, he would throw his head back and laugh like Jack Nicholson, scaring the hell out of the Mexican women who served food in the canteen.

His work ethic, however, was beyond reproach, and an early prototype of the NASA sim was soon ready for testing. The astronauts were outfitted with little microphones to speak into, and greeted the challenge of the game with some enthusiasm.

The exact point of the game (dubbed "Game Over" in the wake of the fiasco, for reasons that will become obvious later on) remains hazy. The six astronauts were isolated in little cubicles and networked to each other via computer screens that replicated the view from their individual space helmets, complete with breath fog and aural static. They appeared to be marooned on a moonlike planet, and their oxygen supplies were running out fast. No actual game rules were provided, but the unspoken idea was that the test group had to "work together as a team to survive." The crew would start the adventure inside a landing module, disembark onto the lunar surface, then make a twenty-minute low-gravity trek across the dunes and craters to a *Chariots of the Gods*–style pyramid that dominated the skyline. Access to the pyramid was determined by a series of hieroglyphic puzzles that were carved around the massive stone doorways and fortified by a variety of primitively lethal booby traps that would snap out and take your head off if you stayed too long in the one place or touched the wrong hieroglyph by mistake. Astronauts unfortunate enough to find themselves decapitated or shot through with arrows or dropped into pits filled with poison-tipped spears etc. would be automatically transported back to the landing module, whereupon they would have to make the low-gravity trek back to the pyramid once more, usually in time to witness the spectacularly gruesome death of one or more of their teammates.

The complexity and elegance of Big Guy's programming and rendering skills made the game's difficulty factor tolerable at the outset. The six astronauts ventured out to the pyramid and dutifully studied and discussed the symbols and icons like the NASA-trained scientists they were. A couple of people in the group had serious big brains and linguistic experience, and a lot of post-accident time was spent in the landing module, trying to crack the hieroglyphic code.

Hieroglyphs aside, the other significant factor impeding the astronauts' access to the pyramid was their limited supply of oxygen. The twenty-minute trek across the planet's landscape, which was fun at first, but quickly became a tedious chore, drained roughly one-fifth of a crew member's air tank, and it was soon deemed not worth the while of a recently decapitated or disemboweled astronaut to make the return journey to the pyramid after a certain time period had elapsed. One of the big-brained scientists, prior to being crushed by a block of sandstone the size of a bus, had detected a slight movement from the north-facing doorway, apparently activated by a couple of group members simultaneously touching the same icons in a hieroglyphic cluster, and was firmly of the opinion that teamwork was definitely the key to solving "the mystery of the pyramid." It was thus determined that in the event of a casualty after the collective air tanks had drained past the three-quarter mark, the surviving astronauts were better off cutting their losses and killing themselves (the game started afresh only after the whole team had been eliminated), and then launching a renewed assault from the landing module.

As the death toll piled up and the suicide rate climbed into the low three figures, the attending staff noticed a severe downswing in the test group's morale. Even the most robust crew members were showing signs of clinical depression, and there was considerable anger and bickering within the team, especially back at the landing module when the whole group faced the unhinging prospect of yet another trek across the exact same terrain they had been trekking across for the past couple of months.

By the time Big Guy finally broke down and revealed that there *was* no solution to the hieroglyphic puzzles; that the long-term girl-friend's departure had accelerated his depression along suicidal lines to the point where he had been killing himself vicariously through the astronaut test group, everyone who had participated in the experiment was a basket case, and would never work for NASA again.

This all resulted in the inevitable lawsuit and countersuit. Threats were issued. Big Guy's reputation was righteously smeared in the appropriate circles, and it was only a matter of time before he was on the couch in New York, pouring his heart out to the Fifth Avenue shrink who would eventually introduce him to Prozac. (The interesting footnote here is that bootleg copies and actual test carnage from "Game Over" became highly prized and collectible in San Jose and Seattle, resulting in a barrage of job offers from hip, edgy software companies that somehow missed the point. The new, happier Big Guy admits to being tempted by the money, but a new career as a content salesman had presented itself, opening up an important avenue of exploration: promotional trade shows and the women who attend them. He had no trouble at all saying no.)

"Marty. Your brother."

"My brother, Big Guy. Love him or leave him."

"Love him or leave him, take your chance—

"*—don't deceive him—*"

"—*yes you do* (sniff). *You do you do you do you do you dooo*—"

"*Waa waa waa.*"

"That was great. You guys are professional."

"We rock. We rock like gods."

"We rock like Norsemen. We *are* Norsemen!"

"Oh christ, not again."

"From the fjords of Scandinavia!"

"I seem to recall this being the thing that got us in all that trouble back at The Prairie."

"And they want us back. What does that tell you?"

"Uh, that we dropped two grand on champagne alone?"

"It's the Scandinavian way! We honor them with money!"

"Do we have time for another round?"

"No!"

"Yes we do! I disagree with your desire for another round, but I will defend with my life your right to have one!"

"God you're a suckhole."

"That's why they pay me the sick bucks."

"Make the call. I'm settling up. Excuse me! Can we have the check?"

"Have my Amstel."

"Can we have the check, please? Over here?"

"Nah, I'm good. You okay?"

"Fine. So what are we doing now?"

"Going to, uh (sniff)? Hang on—"

"Uzi. For a few warm-up drinks."

"East Side first. I gotta *change.*"

"Over here!"

"I thought these were the warm-up drinks."

"Marty. Your brother."

"Oh *yoo hoo!*"

UZI, NINE MILLIMETER

Uzi, Nine Millimeter was a Los Angeles–theme bar with an eighties/nineties futurist aesthetic. It occupied two floors of a former warehouse on East Eleventh and Avenue D, and conformed to every cliché of LA-style nightclubbery as depicted in movies such as *Strange Days* and *The Terminator,* where the idea is that we are slightly in the future (i.e., the late nineties) and the prevailing fashion has veered toward an edgy fusion of punk rock and big-haired gothic. Chain-link fences dominated the space, encircling the mosh pit and rippling strobe light all the way up to the high mezzanine and associated VIP rooms, which in turn overlooked a brightly lit stage at the back of the warehouse where a hardcore band could be seen grinding away behind two sheets of double glazing. The band was purely a visual effect. You couldn't hear them. They were dangerous wallpaper, nothing more.

"Is this great or what?" Troxler bellowed above the techno.

"I didn't think places like this actually existed," Yojimbo bellowed back.

"Oh they don't. That's the whole point of the chain-link fencing. Uzi exists in homage to the art directors and set designers who visualized the chain-link fence as the future of nightclubbing interior design."

"I always wondered about that."

"You'll also notice a lot of people here are sporting the same kind of outfits and hairstyles as Fred, the sidekick character to the character Nicholas Cage plays in *Valley Girl*."

"The buffalo guys with the blue spray-on hair?"

"Yeah. The Fred character is like the prototype of this whole aesthetic."

"I thought he was just an LA punk."

"No no no! He's an LA punk as visualized by a bunch of Beverly Hills studio execs who had never *seen* an LA punk before they greenlit the film."

"Ah. I see where this is going."

"Exactly! The whole thing is *wrong*. You can construct a whole world from these misconstruences. A bizarro universe of bad fashion and unconvincing drug addiction. Robert Downey Jr. as a perkily unauthentic crack addict, turning tricks in his jockey shorts with his hair gelled to perfection in *Less Than Zero*, versus the real-life Robert Downey Jr. as a skeevily authentic smack fiend, falling asleep in various houses and gutters, violating parole, etc."

"And this is all in the book?"

"Uh huh."

"So how come the club is playing techno? Shouldn't we be listening to, I don't know, the *Pretty in Pink* soundtrack or something?"

"No, that would be cheesy and retro. The point is not to re-create a specific filmic moment. The point is to visualize the future as per the filmic guidelines put out by cheesy Hollywood, and then project yourself inside the framework as though you were the kind of person who would actually go to a club where someone like Andrew McCarthy could be found having blue-lit public sex with a lesser celebrity against a chain-link fence in the back room."

"Sounds like an awful lot of work."

"Depends how seriously you take it. It's like anything. You check it out, you work it out, you move on."

"I get the impression Big Guy takes the whole thing very seriously."

"His place is a trip, huh?"

"Yeah, I'm still not sure I completely understand what happened back there."

The group had cabbed it to Big Guy's East Village apartment on the way to the club: Troxler and Baxter sniffing and riffing in the backseat, Big Guy up front giving directions in a manner that could only be described as "brusque" and "thuggish." The driver was one of those Indian guys who usually put up a fight when you try to push them around, and Big Guy had just rolled over him, taking on the affect and demeanor of a South African policeman, complete with accent and girth and threatening vocal cadences to the point where Yojimbo actually got the chills in the backseat listening to him. This was merely Big Guy warming up for the evening, but Yojimbo found himself completely reappraising his earlier conversation with the content salesman. Was Big Guy South African? Had he suddenly become a whole lot bigger in the cab? It was uncanny. His shoulders seemed enormous and his neck had become thick and bullish and very, very hairy, and he was saying ordinary things, like—

"Take the next left and turn right onto Houston"

—but with a meaty inflection that conjured up all kinds of

images from the stationhouse in Jo'burg, and it was all Yojimbo could do to tune the bastard out. Baxter was still hardwired into "we are Norsemen" mode, but he had lapsed into a Connery accent and was somehow doing Connery as a Nordic warrior by way of dialogue lines from *Highlander* and *Zardoz*. He was obviously having a wild party in his head; the kind of party that spills out onto the street and keeps the neighbors up and would in all probability result in someone beating him so severely that he would shy off booze and drugs for the rest of his life, and the combination of him and Big Guy in the taxi were enough to make Yojimbo seriously regret not checking in to a hotel as he had originally planned.

The Audi ride back from Kennedy had set the tone for the evening, and Troxler had adjusted the balance and fiddled with the EQ all the way home to his Franklin Street loft. A spare bed had been made up with brand-new linen, and Yojimbo's luggage had been hustled in around it. Presents had been exchanged. The really expensive bottle of Glenfiddich had been unboxed, and a crackling four fingers had been pressed into Yojimbo's hand.

"It's good to see you, bro."

"It's good to see you too, Marty."

"Watch it with the Marty, Jim. You know I hate the Marty."

"You hate the Marty?"

"You call me Marty, I kill yo' ass."

"Well, I guess we won't be calling you Marty then."

"I bust a cap in yo' ass, gnomesayin?"

"Settle."

"Settle?"

"Australian for 'calm the fuck down.'"

"Very precocious. Mind if I steal it?"

"You do that. I'm going to jump in the shower."

"Yeah, freshen up. We have a big evening planned."

"We do? I don't think I'm going to be able to handle a big evening, Marty. I'm knackered from the flight."

"Knackered?"

"Knackered. As in, I-must-go-to-sleep-very-soon."

"Oh really?"

"Yeah. Really."

The Jetlag had been discussed. The hotel option was overcourteously extended. Like bait. Weary as he was, Yojimbo could sense that his brother's end of the old family dynamic had been polished up to a high gloss. His newly acquired dealmaking skills were frighteningly impressive. Whereas an argument like this back in Fort Lauderdale would have culminated in the usual cursing and wrestling and rolling around on the floor until the old man staggered over and put the boot in, the younger Troxler merely laid out his terms like the businessman he'd become. One all-night executive Manhattan club trawl in exchange for a hassle-free trip down to Fern Grove. We bury Dad like grown-ups. No club trawl, no grown-up burial. You make the call.

As he walked down the stairs to Big Guy's apartment, Yojimbo ran through his options one last time. He could call his brother's bluff and see what happened. Check in to a hotel. Make his own arrangements. Fly to Florida and sort things out on his own. The gauntlet thrown down in the Franklin Street apartment was unexpected and annoying, but there was also an honesty in it that Yojimbo found touching. Instead of sustaining a success veneer, playacting the celeb, or affecting the kind of big-league New York lifestyle most people find intimidating, his brother had chosen to inflate or explode the myth in one night. This is my life. We're on my turf. I have the advantage, just as you will have the advantage in Fern Grove.

You're my older brother.

Let's see you deal.

So on to Big Guy's apartment. Big Guy had himself a basement apartment on Stuyvesant, one of the most coveted streets in the East Village. It was railroad-style, with a bedroom, a study, and a large square-shaped lounge, and Big Guy must have been dropping incredible rent on the place, because it had been recently renovated and the parquetry floor had been restored. There was a shoe rack just inside the doorway, and Troxler, Baxter, and Big Guy shuffled out of their boat-shaped Kenneth Coles and padded up the hallway in their socks. Yojimbo kicked off his Blundstones and followed them into the living room.

"Drinks," said Big Guy, pointing to an Art Deco tea cart overloaded with liquor. "Beer in the fridge."

He caught Yojimbo staring at him, trying to work out whether the South African thing had actually happened in the cab, and he broke out a boyish smile that actually cracked his dimples.

"Get you something to wear?" he asked.

"Sorry?"

"Something to wear. A suit? I have a kevlar vest that would actually look great with those . . . were they work boots you were wearing?"

"I'm okay, thanks."

"I'm serious about the vest. It's a Gaultier. I have the riot pants that go with it and everything."

"You'd look a riot in those pants," quipped Baxter.

"You know, I'm quite all right in my nerdware," said Yojimbo. "But really. Thank you so much for your concern."

"Dude. *Mi casa es su casa*. I'm going to throw on some clothes and I'll be out in a second. Make yourself at home, okay?"

The DOA Troxler and Baxter had taken at Zero Sum was obviously starting to kick in, because their eyes were bright and shiny and they were responding to light and shadow as though they were exploring a cave in the Utah desert. Yojimbo wandered over to Big Guy's fridge and checked out the stunning array of Czech beer – the Gambrinus and Staropramen, the high-quality, don't-fuck-with-me import Budweiser – and then closed the door and crossed the room on impulse, leaning down to study the liquor tray. The collection of gins, bourbons, scotches, and vodkas was similarly enigmatic. All top-shelf, but off the beaten track. Was Big Guy a scotch drinker? A vodka man? Were any preferences detectable, other than quality and obscurity? Yojimbo picked up a bottle of Burr McCracken, aged thirty-five years in the finest Scottish oak, and he had never even heard of such a whisky.

"You guys want a drink?" he called out.

Troxler and Baxter padded over immediately, like wide-eyed elves in Santa's workshop.

"Oh yeah. A *drink*."

"*God*. What is there?"

Their voices had a panting, ventriloquist quality, like they were drinking glasses of water as they spoke. Troxler's brow was deeply furrowed from the effort of speaking clearly. His voice modulation was decidedly unnerving.

"Yojimbo," said Baxter. "Mixer of drinks. I salute you."

"Say Bud, why don't you do the honors?" Troxler husked. "I gotta show my brother *around*."

"I'm just going to grab a beer," Yojimbo said.

"Scotch, rocks, lotta ice," said Troxler.

Yojimbo went with the import Budweiser, which tasted metallic and was sharp in the mouth. He followed his brother through the apartment, taking note of the generic framed poster art, the generic black and gray Conran's-style furniture, the floor-to-ceiling bookshelves stocked with a sprawling range of classic and commercial fiction, and finishing the tour beside Big Guy's impressively large CD collection.

"Okay, we'll start easy and work up to advanced," said Troxler. "Check out the stereo, tell me what you see."

"NAD amp. Rotel deck and speakers."

"Yuppie or vintage?"

"Sorry?"

"Would you say his system was yuppie or vintage? Is Big Guy a serious audiophile, or did he buy this shit from some upscale department store, put it on his card, and have the whole thing delivered in one piece?"

"I have no idea."

"Exactly. So let's move on. There'd be, what, five hundred CDs here? Quick perusal, then tell me, what kind of music is Big Guy into?"

"Uh, what? I'm going to be tested on this later?"

"No no. Just check it out."

"All right. Indie rock. Ooh, no, very mainstream here . . . lotta rap here too. Wow. *Hotel California* next to a Scorpions anthology. If I had to say anything, I'd say studiedly eclectic."

"Studiedly eclectic is the answer, but we're getting a little ahead of ourselves. Next question. Any idea what this photograph is?"

"For twenty points, I'd say it's the cover art of the . . . second Joy Division album."

"Or else it could be a straight repro of the Bernard Pierre Wolff photo the album cover was based on."

"And what? This isn't impressing me."

"It isn't supposed to. Big Guy's the main attraction. His apartment is merely a perfectly calibrated neutral environment for him to fill with his big personality."

"Ah. I see. Your friend's an *artist*. And here I was thinking he was just this rude arsehole who buys and sells content on the web."

"Did you actually say 'arsehole' just then?" Baxter cut in excitedly. "I *love it!* Do it again!"

"Sorry. It just slipped out. That would be arse*holes*. As in plural."

"Don't go there!"

"Who's an arsehole?" Big Guy demanded. He strode into the room wearing an impressive pair of linen pants, a crisp white T-shirt with a giant Chinese character flaming out across the chest, and a big-shouldered, lapel-less jacket that screamed advertising agency. Or record A&R. Or high-end merchant banking. Or anything cyber. It was kind of weird, actually. His clothes were totally striking, but it was the Burr McCracken all over again. Where the hell did this stuff come from? What the hell did it mean?

"Who's an arsehole?" Big Guy wanted to know.

Yojimbo threw Troxler an exasperated look, but his brother and Baxter were in the middle of a glee club routine, and the smoot or the DOA must have been really outstanding because they were harmonizing flawlessly, really hitting the notes:

> *I say Picasso and you say Picarso*
> *I call you an asshole, you call me an arsehole*
> *Picasso/Picarso, an asshole/an arsehole*
> *Let's call the whole thing off—de dum dum dum . . .*

One of the very few fringe benefits of growing up under the old man was that both Troxler boys could take care of themselves. As a teenage kid, shuffling from school to school with his little brother in tow, Yojimbo had survived his share of confrontations. The way he saw it, the majority of bullies and rednecks and skateboard-riding hooligans he encountered were an absolute picnic compared to his dad, and as long as they weren't packing Glock Nines or Mac Tens (like the boys out in Davey, but that's another story), they were all fair game as far as he was concerned. And Big Guy, standing there all tubular in his designer clothes, his buffed-up stomach and poochy little ass looking pretty ridiculous if you wanted to get down to it, well, it was probably time to have a word and shut the fucker down. Yojimbo ditched the sharp-tasting Bud and got himself up in Big Guy's face.

"I'm calling *you* an asshole, Big Guy. Do you mind?" he said pleasantly.

"Not in the slightest," Big Guy replied without hesitation. "You wrestle at school?"

"Nah. Track mostly."

"No shit? I spent my life in the computer science labs. Missed the whole varsity thing."

"Poor you. So what, you intend to stay on my case all evening?"

"Depends on you, dude. Your brother has you down as the family achiever, so I kind of figured you'd be calling the plays."

"Not me. I'm strictly here as an observer."

"I see. No bunny hunting for you."

"No bunny hunting."

"Well, see, that's too bad. We're at the point right now where club hopping has taken on a wearying predictability I can't say I like, and I was kind of hoping your addition to the party would pick things up a little. We could use a point man. A bunny wrangler, so to speak."

"You're talking to the wrong guy, Big Guy."

"Dude. What can I say?"

"Not a thing. You could direct me to the bathroom though."

"Down the hall. Second door on the left."

"Thanks."

First stop in the bathroom was the medicine cabinet. Yojimbo had hit that interesting stage of fatigue where the tiredness goes away but your eyelids fill up with sand, and the more he deliberated on the competitive rudeness of the evening, the more determined he was to see it through to the end. The night had obviously been set up to test his endurance, and endurance was something he had in spades. His brother had no idea what he was dealing with. Yojimbo pulled serious shiftwork in Melbourne, and he couldn't help smiling at the thought of his brother trying to haze him with sleep deprivation.

There was no harm in cheating, however. He took a quick look through Big Guy's medicine cabinet, hoping to luck out on some Vivarin or caffeine tablets, and exceeding his expectations by finding a prescription bottle of dextroamphetamine stashed away behind the miniature skyline of hair-care products and duty-free cologne. Dextroamphetamine. A major-league stimulant, prescribed for people with clapped-out metabolism. God knows what Big Guy was up to, running loose with a supply of pharmaceutical speed in his bathroom, but the orange pill bottle leveled the playing field in a way that one-eightied Yojimbo's dread of the oncoming hours.

> *You say Picasso and I say Picarso*
> *You call me an asshole, I call you an arsehole . . .*

He took two capsules and swallowed them, pocketing the bottle just in case. Aside from the dextroamphetamine (and the Prozac), there was a startling array of mail-order drugs in the content salesman's cabinet. Five bottles of Viagra, for instance. In Australia, Viagra was the party aid of choice in the pink belt of Sydney. Yojimbo had read feverish reports of the gay hordes terrorizing the populace with huge boners visible within the tightness of their leatherwear. "Viagra makes you horny" was what it came down to, and Big Guy had enough Viagra to keep himself horny for months on end. The thought of Big Guy hopped up on speed and in a state of permanent arousal was particularly disturbing, and Yojimbo shut the cabinet and studied his face in the mirror. For some reason he was reminded of the scene from *Grease* where the greaser with the furious skin lays the hardline on John Travolta as they prepare to race up and down the Daytona Beach canal. "The rules are . . . there ain't no rules!" the greaser declares, snapping gum and grinning like a weasel, and there was something wonderfully American about that moment of clarification. Like anarchy and mayhem were things you needed to define. Not so in Australia. Gauntlets were rarely thrown, challenges rarely issued. Australians tended to rush in and hit you at the slightest provocation. Most of the time without warning.

Yojimbo stared at his reflection, at the lines burnt and etched around his eyes from the ozone-depleted harshness of the Australian sun. He was thirty-six, but he looked and felt older. His hair was turning gray and his face had filled out, and the boyish enthusiasm that was once so visible in his features had hardened into something else, some other quality that made him seem wistful. Now that the playing field had been leveled, he found himself looking forward to a night out with his brother in a way that surprised him. How long had it been since he really cut loose? Five years? Six years?

I've been away for a long time, he thought. *Funny how nothing much has changed.*

"Yo bro," said Troxler by the liquor tray.

"Yojimbo," said Baxter. "Ever had an Irish car bomb?"

"What's an Irish car bomb?"

"You drop a shot glass of whiskey into a pint of beer and chug the fucker down."

"I'm good."

"Aw c'mon. Marty tells me you can drink."

"I can. And I will, probably. But not right now."

"You pussy."

"Don't you pussy me, you big girl's blouse."

"Big girl's blouse? Is that like rhyming slang from down under?"

"No, it's just an expression. My personal favorite is 'Get a dog up ya.'"

"That's *funny*."

"Your mood seems to have improved, bro." Troxler grinned.

"Yeah, well. So what are we doing?"

"Waiting for Big Guy to change."

"Big Guy hasn't changed?"

"Big Guy is changing. Listen, one scotch. For old times' sake. For the old man, may he rest in peace."

"Getting a little ahead of ourselves there, Marty. But sure. For the old man. Give me a shot of that Burr McCracken."

"Ah, yesh. The Burr McCracken. At your shervish, shir."

"On her majesty's *shecret* shervish."

"Not too much. That's good."

"You pussy."

"Watch your mouth you goddamn nancy boy."

Big Guy had been standing beside his CD towers in a kind of zen state. He had dimmed the apartment's lighting and was playing the Dust Brothers "fat 'n stinky" mix of the 2001 Theme, his shoulders pulsing in time with the kick drum. His expression was distant and his mouth was set in concentration. He looked like someone torn between several courses of action. Troxler and Baxter were deep in the pop culture zone, riffing on this lame-ass TV series and that ugly Condé Nast masthead battle, and Yojimbo sipped his scotch and kept his eye on Big Guy, watching him warm up to the music, an ominous bulge shifting around in his trousers. Big Guy had rhythm, Yojimbo noticed. His body was as wrong for the dancefloor as it was for all that gym work, but he used what he had effectively, and the distant expression fell away from his face and he was suddenly engrossed in the music, working up all those arm-pumping rave moves that look suspiciously like they've been copped from the studio audience of every TV evangelist not yet busted from the airwaves.

The dextroamphetamine was starting to take effect, and a gust of good cheer caught Yojimbo by surprise. Pharmaceutical speed provided a smooth high with none of the jaw grinding and nasal unpleasantness you associate with the street-dealt, truck-driving variety, and he found himself grinning across the room for no particular reason.

And then the strangest thing happened. Big Guy came out of his zen state, and he was suddenly all business. He bustled through the apartment with a completely different energy to anything he had previously displayed, telling the group to finish their drinks and prepare for departure with a new intensity that verged on upbeat charisma. The dancing appeared to have jolted loose a new personality. He slapped a meaty hand on Yojimbo's shoulder and steered him through the hallway, and as the group paused at the front door and relaced their Kenneth Coles, Yojimbo caught his first fleeting whiff of transformation. In the twenty-odd seconds it took him to step into his Blundstones, he felt the apartment shift ambience. The place seemed friendly in a way he was positive it hadn't been when he arrived. Big Guy's hand on his shoulder seemed solid and dependable, and there was this moment by the door where he had the impression the hallway was shifting focus like the Hitchcock zoom in *Vertigo*. Troxler, Baxter, and Big Guy crowded around him, feeding hungrily off the positive energy slewing end to end from bedroom to lounge, and the next thing he knew he was out on the street, watching his brother win a cab-hailing contest by whistling through two fingers, like in the movies.

Standing against the Uzi chain-link fence, looking out across a thick crowd of filmically incorrect punks and bikers while the hardcore band thrashed and gyrated like Sea Monkeys rocking the house in a big silent fishtank, Yojimbo tried to process that moment in the hallway. It had to be the dextroamphetamine—although a speed rush didn't explain his brother's Q&A by the stereo. Didn't explain the innuendo-loaded way Big Guy kept insisting that he go home and *change* . . .

"What's the story with Big Guy?" he called out to his brother. "Does Big Guy have a name?"

"Yeah. Emmett. But I'd advise you to stick with Big Guy. He was in this lawsuit and is kind of keeping a low profile. He trades as Big Guy. Has this whole corporate identity and everything."

"So what was the deal with his stereo? What exactly were you trying to point out?"

"Long story. Big Guy took some damage from this girl, and it sent him off the deep end. He was pulling long hours and she eighty-sixed him because she couldn't stand the lifestyle. Fucked his career as far as I can tell. So he's in revenge mode. Has this thing where he can work up personality types to fit whatever scene we're crashing. He's a shameless sport-fucker, basically. Hits on girls. Has different characters for uptown and downtown. Does this classic Park Avenue Master of the Universe routine . . ."

"And the stereo?"

"We usually wind up back at Big Guy's apartment with a couple of bunnies at the end of the night. Big Guy tends to stay in character, at least until morning, so the apartment and the furniture and the CD collection have to be generic enough to keep his character alive."

"Wow. So forgive me for asking, but is Big Guy a seriously depressive type? I couldn't help noticing that he keeps a lot of Prozac in his bathroom."

"Nah. Prozac floats his boat. Big Guy's program is to burn sick amounts of cash until his shareholders force him into liquidation.

Lotta booze, lotta drugs. I get the impression he's having a whale of a time."

"Is he in your book?"

"Yeah. Guys like Big Guy are everywhere right now. Huge content traffic. Lotta action in the trade shows, where sex is a big part of networking."

"Bunny hunting."

"Bunny hunting works both ways. There are high-level bunnies out there who hunt with a vengeance. Don't be surprised if you're hit on this evening."

"Can't wait."

"Gotta say, bro. You've really perked up."

Troxler's book jacket smile revealed itself briefly, lighting his face with the slightest hint of uncertainty.

ROGUE MALES

The term "bunny hunting" was coined by *Rogue* magazine in the summer of 2000, the year that it exploded in the States.

Like *Maxim, Rogue* was a UK import modeled on the WWF Smackdown of magazines, the groundbreaking *Loaded,* which hit London newsstands in '94 and pushed the envelope of lowbrow to levels that astonished even the extremely trashy British tabloid press. *Loaded* was a lad magazine. It defined and championed lad culture, a city-based, young male demographic fueled by a high disposable income and an insatiable hunger for tits, beer, and football in no particular order. It was *Loaded* that trademarked the best-selling combination of cleavage-baring fashion model and hoo-hah! coverline, and within a year, the majority of quality English men's magazines like British *Esquire* and *GQ* would be baring flesh on their own covers in a frantic bid to keep their readership from shifting down to first.

Around the time British *GQ* threw in the towel and went

tabloid with a lad-style fashion spread and the most desperate-sounding coverline on record – Sixteen Pages of Hot Chicks in Pants! – the big debate in publishing was whether the high-class low-brow formula would translate to the American magazine market. Three and a half years of focus groups and market research would elapse between the through-the-roof success of *Loaded* and the through-the-roof success of U.S. *Maxim,* which blitzkrieged the metropolitan newsstands after a shaky start in '97. Lad culture begat badboy culture, which had been sitting around, fermenting noisily in the millions of frat houses and sports bars and pool halls of America, and you really have to wonder what the focus groups were thinking. Within six months of the first *Maxim* coverbabe, the honor roll of tuxedo-wearing Brosnans and Gibsons and Jordans and Clooneys had been shunted from a seasonal half of *GQ* and *Esquire* covers, to be replaced by the now-regulation supermodel hot shot. Hollywood starlets wearing no clothes to speak of. S. Faludi wringing her hands in the bleachers as the backlash tide rolled in and stayed in.

Rogue's place in the badboy demographic was more specialized than that of its newsstand competition, as it was originally conceived as an in-house webzine to service the Hotel Regis casino chain in the UK and Europe. The Regis franchise was the brainchild of English advertising magnate Markson Stahl, whose genius for lowbrow defined the British lad phenomenon, and his formula for *Rogue* was simplicity itself. Email, online gambling, and netporn. A snow-balling roster of B-list starlets and models who you could not only ogle, but (depending on the amount of money you were losing at the tables) actually meet in the Regis VIP rooms. ISP software was free of charge to anyone who walked through the hotel doors, and the franchise had wrestled market share in six of the big U.S. gambling cities. "Bringing Vegas to the People!" was Stahl's corporate slogan, and he ran his hotels on the premise that if you were old enough to gamble, you were old enough to do pretty much anything you wanted within the sanctity of his privately policed casino walls.

Our man C. C. Baxter was ahead of the curve, switching ISPs to Stahl in the early days of *Rogue* and quickly developing what he would call an "ironic fixation" on the actress Kari Wuhrer, formerly of the TV series *Sliders,* and a breast-baring veteran of many B- and mainstream movies such as *Anaconda* and *The Crossing Guard* (where she gets to spend quality screen time with the old and fat Jack Nicholson). This was in the days when Baxter still had excellent hair and could flaunt his family's wealth with brutal aplomb. There's no easy way of saying this, but the motivational key to Preston Gregory Baxter is that he's losing his hair fast, and when it's gone, he's going to end up with a penis-shaped head. He has a competition swimmer's overdeveloped neck and shoulders, coupled with very smooth skin and an almost feminine brow. Right now, he's in the *Hudson Hawk* phase of the Bruce Willis hair cycle, which means he still has a few years before he's going to have to make the call and start shaving his head like every hipster downtown, and the terrible thing about the bald hipster option is what happens when he laughs. His face turns purple.

The pre-millennial Baxter was more hirsute and less in-your-face than the post-crash, war-profiteering version, and was thus a regular and welcome fixture in the Footlights Bar of the Atlantic City Regis, where his ironic fixations were nurtured and indulged. Gambling enthusiasts will no doubt remember the Atlantic City Regis as being the first of Stahl's casinos to stage a big budget musical based on a John Grisham novel, and the lavishly cross-marketed production of *John Grisham's The Firm* (featuring the sultry Ms. Wuhrer in the Jeanne Tripplehorn role) had Baxter flying down every second weekend and chewing through his trust fund like a man possessed. Long before he hooked up with Troxler and Big Guy, Baxter had been a binge gambler in St. Louis, alternating marathon hours of MBA study with marathon hours at the blackjack tables of many riverboat casinos, where he was convinced he could beat the odds and multiply his substantial monthly allowance. This never happened, of course, but he was one of those guys who always finish the evening recouping losses at the bar, and it was only a matter of time before he alienated entire pit crews with his furious drinking and parenthetical wit, and wound up being expelled from the Mississippi with that particular lack of delicacy the gambling industry does so well.

Like so many people who work in the pop culture realm, Baxter had an enormous appetite for trivia. He was all over *Loaded* when it first appeared in London, and watched the transatlantic dumbing down of content with the amusement and cynicism of someone who has never performed to his full ability and knows it. *Maxim* was a hoot, the same way Hooters was a hoot, and Baxter's intellect was such that he could slum just about anywhere and pull off the kind of wry detachment in the face of oblivion that carried the Kerouacs and Bukowskis through the twilight of their work.

But *Rogue* . . . *Rogue* had a different integrity that was frighteningly sincere. You had the sense that the *Maxim* and *Details* crew came from quality and stooped to lowbrow because the market demanded it. There was always that hint of Harvard condescension; that "we-could-be-writing-for-*The-Simpsons*-but-instead-here's-a-hot-babe-go-knock-yourself-out"-ness that playfully cuffed readers about the head. Starlets were interviewed faux-fawningly. The article headers could be chillingly erudite. *Rogue,* by contrast, could be likened to the dumb, good-natured smile on Eddie Van Halen's face as he cranks out that too-fast-to-be-humanly-possible guitar solo in the music video for "Jump." It had a disarming, meathead quality you couldn't fuck with. It was lowbrow for the people, by the people, and it took a dim view of editorial smugness. And, unlike the *Enquirer* or the *Star,* it didn't presume to judge, because its bedrock was the high-gloss misery of gambling. You didn't judge when you were pissing away your mortgage payments; you just got down to the business of the dream and left when it was over, without complaint.

Standing now in the big-haired throng of Uzi patrons, waiting for a sliver of bar space to appear before him, Baxter was your classic *Rogue* male. His objective for the evening was to get laid, and he viewed the prospect of getting laid to be a basic human right, reinforced by hundreds of thousands of web page pictorials of men and women in various stages of undress who seemed only too happy to cheer the concept along.

Just as "Two pints of lager and a packet of crisps" had nailed the everyman Zeitgeist in pre-millennium Britain, "Fire in the hole!" was the rallying cry of the new Bush economy. And as the recession loomed and scrip millions turned to vapor, the tenet of bunny hunting as put out there by *Rogue* somehow legitimized the practice of going out, getting seriously drunk, and hitting on members of the opposite sex until some form of liaison was achieved that night. No phone numbers on napkins. No callbacks. Dinner and a movie was for wimps. It was straight-up, competitive sport-fucking, and it was best done in a pack of like-minded young professionals. Preferably with money on the line.

Baxter's hair was receding, so he was up against the clock, and he adhered to the bedpost-notching promise of bunny hunting with the same tenacity that had him returning to the Regis for that one-shot mythic takedown of the house. Anyone who has ever gambled seriously knows that what they are doing is venal and stupid, but there is a reckless energy in gambling that can bring you as close to a natural high as you can get without exercise, and Baxter lived for this feeling. He loved the dignity flatline that comes with staking your rent money or children's college fund on a handful of cards in some sleazy casino—and the dignity flatline was a big part of the

Manhattan club scene, providing him with a shifting pit floor of opportunity. The chance to wager his ego on a bit of risky play.

"Oh, you're an *angel!*" was his opening gambit. "Come over and talk to me and my friends."

"Gentlemen. This is Sophie, Marissa, and what was your name again?"

"Claire."

"And Claire. And you appear to have a bit of a Murphy Brown thing going on. Do you work in broadcast news?"

"No. Sophie's at Barnes and Noble dot com, and Marissa and I are in real estate uptown."

"Not interesting. Could you *pretend* to work in broadcast news?"

"Sure. Would we be talking a major network, or public access?"

"I'm thinking major. You're very well turned out. Legend?"

"I'd concur with you there, Greg. The young ladies are, as you say, very well turned out. A lot of polish on display. Obviously from good homes, although there does seem to be a variance in height and heavy reliance on platform soles that could rule out the possibility of fieldwork."

"You don't like the boots?"

"Sure, if you're the bass player from Kiss."

"Don't listen to him. He's a short man trapped in a tall man's body."

"He's in *pain.*"

"So you guys are what? Some kind of comedy team?"

"Backup singers."

"*Really?* Who for?"

"Uh, that would be—"

"—Garth Brooks. We work with Garth."

"Are you serious?"

"Oh yeah."

"Yeah, he's a . . . great man. A *spiritual* man."

"We get to wear those checkered outfits."

"Oh my god! I saw him play in Central Park."

"That was a terrific gig. Really low-key."

"When was that? Four, five years ago?"

"Couldn't tell you. I was in my Keith Richards period."

"Right. We all were. Garth especially."

"Five years of my life . . . a complete blank."

"You look familiar. Do I know you from somewhere?"

"Maybe." Troxler smiled modestly. "I'm sort of a journalist."

"*Sort* of a journalist."

"Yeah, I write books and comment on things. I was on *Letterman* last year. You might have seen me there."

"You were on *Letterman*? No kidding. So is Dave, you know, as cranky as everyone says?"

"Dave just walked off during the ad break. Left me sitting on the couch with the guy who does the voice for *Welcome to Moviefone!* And it's like, he talks like that in real life."

"Who does?"

"The Moviefone guy. I had to make smalltalk with the Moviefone guy while Dave stalked around the back of the studio like Martin Sheen in *Badlands,* gesticulating angrily at some kind of unseen enemy. It was really weird."

"Sounds like it."

"How are we for drinks? Ladies?"

"I'm good."

"I'm good, thanks."

"You look like you could use a huge fluffy cocktail."

"Well . . . I'll settle for a vodka tonic."

"What was your name again?"

"Marissa. This is Sophie."

"I'm Greg. This is Martin. Who are you this evening, Big Guy?"

"Nick. The party promoter."

"This is Nick. He's a party promoter."

"Cool. What kind of parties?"

"Event parties. In Miami."

"He doesn't like to talk about it."

"I just want to chill out, you know? Have a few drinks, a few laughs—"

"God! I love Miami!"

"We were at South Beach three months ago. South Beach is great!"

"We went to the VH1 summer fashion awards!"

"That was one of yours, wasn't it, Big Guy?"

"Yeah, Nick. One of yours?"

"Hey. I just came here to chill, okay?"

"He's burnt out from all that celebrity access. All that VIP powder roomery and glam . . ."

"You girls coming to the boat party?"

"What's the deal with that? It starts at midnight, right?"

"Yeah. The DJ's a friend of ours. You should come along."

"What are we doing?"

"We were going to meet Tony and Leo—"

"You have a friend called *Leo*?" Troxler laughed. "Is he, like, guzzling brandy snifters in his own booth at the Oak Room? Is he a wheezy millionaire, by any chance?"

"No, he works in the DA's office."

"Well fuck him."

"Fuck him and the horse he rode in on." Baxter sighed. "Guys like that are responsible."

"Responsible for what?"

"Just . . . responsible. I hate those responsible guys."

"So what are *you* guys doing?"

"Having a few drinks here, moving on to Lotus . . ."

"Have you been to Lotus yet?"

"No. It's just opened, right?"

"Yeah. You should come. The DJ's a friend of ours."

"I don't know . . ."

"Could you get our friends in as well?"

"That would depend on whether they're cool or not."

"Yeah, see, we're the kind of people your friend Leo the assistant DA has been sworn to destroy."

"Stick with us and you might get into trouble."

"I feel a lot of trouble coming on as we speak."

"Trouble. Yesh. Shome unsheemly behavior. Perhapsh you ladiesh would care to join ush?"

"Sure."

"Okay."

"Why not?"

The dextroamphetamine had knocked the edge off his fatigue, and Yojimbo was cruising comfortably in fifth, nursing another Amstel and sampling the bar chat. Advanced blowhardery was hardly his forte, but he had to concede a certain respect for the directional flow of conversation – directional in the sense that it wasted no time in steering the girls toward the first base of hookup, the bathroom stalls – and the fact that no one directly asked each other what they did.

Apart from feeling marginalized by his noninclusion in the party-within-the-party (and would he have gone if he was asked? he wonders), Yojimbo's primary objective for the evening was to avoid getting sucked into the slipstream of bullshit the other guys were putting out. Certain patterns were emerging in the group dynamic. Baxter appeared to be the designated spruiker, supplying the group with a constant flow of punchline-friendly dialogue that kept the conversational energy up, while giving his friends enough room to score points and show off. His brother was trading on his neophyte celebrity – no surprises there – and Big Guy had morphed into Nick the party promoter, which was cheap and bizarre and really fucking weird. To make matters worse, Big Guy appeared to have assigned himself some kind of sports-pro competitive handicap, and was doing an aloof slowburn in sharp contrast to Baxter's funnyman routine. He looked like a party promoter, too. The lapel-less suit and tight fitting T-shirt not only reeked of veteran club life, but also recalled the casual attire of Don Johnson in *Miami Vice,* and Yojimbo's second whiff of transformation came with the startling realization that Big Guy hadn't planned this persona. Nick the party promoter had been created on the spot. Everything about him was one big cynical ad-lib, right through to the evening roundup back at Big Guy's apartment, where there were enough props to keep Nick alive until the bunny hunt was over.

Why does Martin want me to see this? he wondered.

A bit more background on the Troxlers. Part of the reason the old man had been able to get away with so much choleric behavior in his time was that he was damn good-looking as a young man. His resemblance to B-movie actor Tab Hunter was uncanny, and he had parlayed these looks into a kind of weatherbeaten Sam Peckinpah maturity that works well on the big screen in two-hour increments, but is seriously hard to pull off in real life. His wife, Dottie Troxler, was still turning heads in a Sunset Boulevard aging bombshell kind of way, and the kids had benefited from the gene pool (even now, Martin is looking forward to his own "lion in winter" years, because he can imagine himself roaring like a bear on the Upper East Side literary circuit and pulling it off with the old man's panache).

A good deal of Yojimbo's quiet authority comes from the fact that he looks like his dad, and he's the kind of guy women tend to seek out at parties. Even at Uzi, where he was underdressed, he seemed more self-contained and accessible than the majority of Valley Girl punks with their Adam Ant quiffs and chunky jewelry, and the disappearance of his brother's posse opened up a space for introduction that was quickly capitalized upon by a couple of well-dressed Asian women in their mid- to late twenties.

"—you look like you've been abandoned."

"—are your friends doing what I think they're doing?"

"Well, that would depend on what you think they're doing."

"Drugs. Definitely drugs. This is that kind of hellhole."

"Oh really?"

"You're not from around here, are you?"

"I *love* your accent."

"You're not an undercover cop by any chance?"

"No," Yojimbo said, surprised. "Do I look like an undercover cop?"

"You're kind of dressed like one. Where are you from?"

"Florida. But I've just come back from Australia."

"That is *such* a cool accent."

"Australia? No kidding. Two of my really good friends are from Australia. You might know them? Brad and Becky West? From Sydney?"

"Ah . . . it's possible we may have cofounded some kind of avant-garde theater company in the early nineties."

"Are you *serious?*"

"No. Australia's really big. It's the same size as the States. The probability of me knowing someone you know is tiny, and yet you wouldn't believe the number of people I meet who have friends in Australia and seem to think there's a chance I might know them. Don't ask me why."

"Uh huh."

"I hear you."

". . . so, uh, what do you do?"

"Naoko is a recruiter, and I work in marketing and publishing for the WB. We just set up an office in Union Square."

"How is that?"

"Oh, it's great. We oversaw the Buffy books. We also do *The Handsome Devil,* which is coming along really well."

"There are Handsome Devil books? Already?"

"Oh, that show will be huge. It's going to take over where *Buffy* left off."

"It's only just started, though."

"Yeah, but the strategic planning is really sound. From a literary standpoint, we have the same team that did the *X-Files* novelizing episodes that haven't been aired yet. Television tie-ins will be the future of publishing. I'm serious."

"From a literary standpoint?"

"These guys can really write. These guys have won *Emmys.*"

"Yeah, but—"

"Do you have any idea how well the Buffy books did? The kind of numbers we're talking?"

"No."

"Put it this way, and this is confidential. The numbers are so good, we're looking at taking on the Patsy Cornwell/Sue Grafton public transportation demographic. Not so much with *Handsome Devil,* but something in an *X-Files* vein could definitely crack it."

"Wait a second. You're talking about, what? The *New York Times* bestseller list?"

"Sure, why not? *The X-Files* had mature, well-defined characters with a strong sexual chemistry between them, working for the FBI, solving a mystery every episode. That's the formula for any number of bestselling authors, except their franchise has only one writer. The WB has an *army* of writers, so who's to say you couldn't spin a literary brand off a television series and make it dominate the list?"

"Ah . . . well, I'd be inclined to—"

"It's just a matter of *perception*. On one hand you have Gillian Anderson as Special Agent Dana Scully in *The X-Files,* and it's perceived as low culture because it's television. Then you have Gillian Anderson touted for the role of Special Agent Clarice Starling in the new Hannibal Lecter movie, and it's suddenly high culture, even though the screenplay has nothing to do with the book. Both Federal Agents. Both Gillian Anderson. The only difference is hairstyle. Now—"

"Hang on a second. There's a huge difference between Scully and Starling. Starling is a literary creation. She was completely fleshed out in *The Silence of the Lambs,* which was a widely acclaimed novel that took the author something like nine years to write."

"Haven't read it."

"You're *kidding*. For you to make this particular case, you'd need to argue that the literary quality of an X-Files book is comparable to that of *The Silence of the Lambs,* which is an argument I can't see you winning. The fact that the same actress plays the lead is irrelevant."

"I'm not talking about quality. I'm talking about *perception* of quality."

"Okay . . . so?"

"So. Let's backtrack for a second here and suggest that instead of playing Clarice Starling – a role made great by Jodie Foster – Gillian Anderson signs on for the part of Kay Scarpetta in a series of films based on the Patricia Cornwell books. Patsy was a big Jodie Foster fan, by the way."

"Haven't read 'em."

"Ha!"

"Ha! yourself. She signs on. And then what?"

"And you have six bestselling titles to work with. Shoot a film a year, and in the six years it takes you to make them, Patsy's banged out another six books. Six potential *bestsellers*."

"Yeah, and what does this have to do with quality?"

"Everything if we're talking mass market. If you're talking capital L lit. you can go back to your garret and mooch around in your turtleneck and beret. People read books for entertainment. People watch television for entertainment. The only difference between films based on books and books based on films is that the book books have the cachet of coming first."

"So what are you saying? If you could somehow get a whole lot of Handsome Devil books out into the marketplace before the show aired the episodes the books were based on . . ."

"Not Handsome Devil. Something more mature, like, say, a series based on similar characters to the George Clooney/Juliana Margulies characters in *ER*. With big issues at stake."

"You'd get these books on the market and turn them into best-sellers ahead of the actual TV series?"

"Don't sound so shocked."

"Forgive me for saying this, but that just sounds . . . wrong."

"Forgive me for saying this, but you sound like a snob. We have extremely talented writers in our stable. Some of the best writers in the world work in TV, creating the kind of quality storylines which really translate to the mass market genres—"

"The mass market genres?"

"Medical. Legal. Law enforcement . . . Romance is a big one."

"And you have the means to do this? Have people write the books before the series is out? What happens if the series bombs?"

"A big part of the publishing strategy is to make sure the series doesn't bomb. And no, we don't have the means to do this yet. It's the future. But it's coming soon to a cineplex near you, believe me."

"Wow. I can hardly wait."

"Yeah, sure."

Naoko the recruiter had drifted away from the conversation, and was staring into the middle distance, paying no attention to Yojimbo and her friend from television marketing. Her dialogue contribution prior to the publishing discussion had consisted of "Drugs. Definitely drugs. This is that kind of hellhole," "I *love* your accent," and "That is *such* a cool accent," and it was thus a timely and pleasant surprise to see her eyes snap into focus, because the publishing discussion was going nowhere fast. Yojimbo threw a glance over his shoulder and was actually relieved to see Baxter approaching. Baxter in classic post-bathroom smoot mode. Sniffing and grinning and rubbing his nose.

"Yojimbo. Lone wolf. Catnip to the ladies."

"C. C. Baxter. This is . . . it's Naoko, right? And I'm sorry, I didn't catch your name."

"Lindy Minh. Very pleased to meet you."

"The pleasure is mine. The pleasure is ours, I should say, for we are a herd. A pack. A, uh . . . what do lions travel in?"

"A pride."

"Ah, yes. A pride is better than a pack. I'd take a pride over a pack any day."

"A pack of what?" Troxler cut in on approach.

"A pack of what*ever*. This is the lovely Lindy Minh, and her friend, the equally lovely . . ."

"Naoko."

"Naoko."

"God*damnit,* you're lovely!" Troxler blurted, his eyes as big as saucers. "Do you mosh? Will you do me the honor of having this mosh? In the pit? With the other moshers and associated moshers-on?"

"Sure," said Naoko without missing a beat. "You lead."

As Troxler and Naoko disappeared into the crowd, Yojimbo found himself on the periphery of a small party microcosm consisting of Baxter, Big Guy, the three girls they'd done smoot with, and Lindy Minh, who had seamlessly become part of the conversation. The three girls were a great deal more animated than they had been a little earlier in the evening, and there was no more talk of Tony and Leo. Tony and Leo had apparently been shitcanned. The prettiest girl in the group – not counting Lindy Minh, who was stunningly attractive in a corporate way – was working hard on Nick the party promoter, trying to draw him out of his sports-pro, competitive aloofness, and he was flashing her these aw-shucks-if-only-you-got-to-know-me smiles that made Yojimbo want to run over and blow his cover in the worst kind of way.

The depressing thing was that they made it look so easy. Talking to Lindy Minh just a minute ago, Yojimbo could feel himself hitting the wall of smalltalk, rebounding from it instead of crashing through. He was a smart guy who'd had plenty of girlfriends, and there was a time in his early twenties where he could shoot the breeze with pretty much anyone. So what had happened? Was it an age thing? Do you get to a point in life where things become so serious that you have no breeze left to shoot?

Obviously not, because his brother's crew was doing fine. Baxter especially had a knack for talking bullshit, and he had Marissa, Claire, and Lindy Minh riding along on some crazy train of thought as Troxler and Naoko reemerged from the dancefloor and made a beeline for the bathroom. Naoko was surreptitiously trying to signal her friend, but it was Troxler who aced it with a smile and a wink, and Lindy Minh peeled away from the group and followed them both to the back of the club.

Yojimbo watched them leave and had to fight the urge to follow. Not because he didn't approve, but because he couldn't bring himself to ask his brother to cut him in. The old family dynamic was turning out to be a pain in the ass. Troxler was setting him up to be the straight man, and it annoyed him to see Baxter playing along. The way they had jointly appropriated his conversation with the Asian women was a bit too slick and flaunted the drug angle a bit too auspiciously, and the irritating thing was that of all the people standing by the Uzi chain-link fence, it was a safe bet Yojimbo was the guy with the greatest clinical knowledge of drugs. He was a walking encyclopedia on the subject—not that anyone would ever know.

In truth, he *was* the straight man. The quiet guy. The older brother type. In Australia, he lived alone. Had job satisfaction. Called his own plays with a minimum of fuss. And the autonomy had spoiled him. He was efficient and calm, but rarely strayed outside his turf. His brother's ultimatum, while being a nuisance, held out the faint promise of variety, and part of the reason Yojimbo had agreed to come along was to check out something different. But not at cost to his dignity. Dignity was something he fiercely maintained. People were quick to use their fists in Australia, and Yojimbo, a black belt in three advanced schools of martial arts, was reminded of a passage in *The Sun Also Rises,* where Hemingway's narrator derides a Princeton boxer for waiting too long to square a beef. *He should have hit somebody the first time he was insulted, and then gone away,* the narrator muses, and this is a sentiment Yojimbo agrees with completely. The tacit understanding in the deal between brothers was that Troxler's role in the club trawl would be that of tour guide, not adversary. The late night, the weird friends, the smorgasbord of drugs notwithstanding, Yojimbo was prepared to see the night through as long as the basic code of respect was adhered to.

But he was starting to wonder.

And this was not a good thing.

THE UNCANNY X-MEN

Yojimbo's take on drugs and drug culture is reasonably sophisticated, and in order to do it justice, we are going to have to recount the story of the green sheep of Fitzroy, an amusing anecdote Yojimbo will occasionally trot out at parties, more for entertainment value than anything else.

The unsophisticated party version of the green sheep of Fitzroy story goes something like this:

When he first arrived in Melbourne, Yojimbo briefly shared a house in the hip inner-city district of Fitzroy. Grab any tourist guide and look up Fitzroy and you will find it referred to as "the cappuccino belt" of Melbourne on account of the high congestion of coffee shops and latté bars on Brunswick Street, the neighborhood's toned-down equivalent of the Vegas Strip. In its heyday, Fitzroy had been the bohemian hub of the city, and remnants of the legacy – the pool halls, dive bars, and secondhand bookstores – still lined the streets, catering to a more upscale crowd as is always the case when an artistic neighborhood is gentrified and tamed. In the eight months he lived there, Yojimbo fell in with a sprawling crew of creative out-of-towners; musicians and actors from Brisbane, Adelaide, and Perth, who viewed the upscale bohemia of Fitzroy as being an authentic vision of the beat generation decadence they had left home to wallow in.

Yojimbo roomed with a couple of guys in Argyle Street; a bass player and singer who took their decadence very seriously, throwing parties every other week, and they wasted no time in dubbing their new roommate "the workaholic boofhead in Davo's old room." Yojimbo was on a foreign exchange program at the University of Melbourne and had a monster workload to contend with, but the two musicians managed to drag him out of the house and put him on the guest list and set him up with girls who had a thing for Americans, and he had a pretty good time living there, all things considered.

The green sheep story takes place during a semester break on one of the rare occasions where Yojimbo had some downtime to play with. Gavan the singer had returned from tour with some killer acid he insisted the whole house drop that evening. A crew was assembled and Yojimbo found himself on one of Melbourne's charming old-world trams, traveling across town as the acid kicked in—and it was the strongest LSD he had ever come *near*. One minute he was listening to Brett the bass player talking shop with his girlfriend – a big-boned woman who was trying to market herself as some kind of avant-garde chanteuse – and the next thing he knew, he had managed to lose the entire group and was back in Fitzroy with no recollection of how the evening had come and gone. It was five in the morning. Nine hours had passed in what had seemed like nine minutes. And the acid was now producing an extremely pleasant chemical imbalance in his brain, altering his perception in such a way that it would ultimately shape his philosophy on drugs and drug use.

It was a warm November evening. Yojimbo was wide awake and in a state of mild euphoria, admiring the streetlights and the way they glowed so vigorously above the shifting brickwork of the Brunswick Street houses, and there was that flanged whooshing sound around him as though the buildings were somehow whispering secrets to each other, prompting him to stay outdoors and maybe check out the sunrise.

Laid-back as he likes to think he is, this was uncharacteristic behavior for Yojimbo, the workaholic boofhead in Davo's old room. As he strolled through Fitzroy, it occurred to him that what he was doing was taking the time to see the neighborhood in a way that he had never done before. He was focusing on things. Looking up at the houses and streetlights and sky, instead of staring at the sidewalk as he hurried along it, and there was that rare moment of synchronicity where he felt himself open up to the environment. Standing on the cross street of Brunswick and Elgin as the sky purpled slowly out of the blackness above him, he could feel the acid burning out of his system and felt a big pang of sadness that the trip was coming to an end. Despite the fact that it was hard to hold a straight thought, he had a strong sense of epiphany amidst the whooshing and shifting, and he threw a philosopher's gaze at the buildings around him and made this promise to Fitzroy:

"I will take the time to get to know you," he vowed.

And out of the darkness, a green sheep appeared.

Yojimbo had been hallucinating all night. The acid was industrial grade, the kind of thing you can imagine the CIA feeding to dissidents in the sixties, and despite the fact that he can recall almost nothing from the trip, his mind would occasionally kick back these chaotic flash-frame images from the evening as polaroid evidence that drugs can mess with your head. Even now, when he looked at things closely, he could see layers of density in objects as though the acid had endowed him with the ability to see the hidden skeletons of matter.

The sheep, however, was no hallucination.

It ambled across the cobblestones at sheep cruising speed, head down, flanks rolling from side to side, and Yojimbo must have been central on its radar because it walked right up to him and bumped its head against his knees, bleating hopefully like it was angling for a pat.

Fuck me. That sheep is green, Yojimbo thought.

As he reached down to verify the sheep's existence by running his hand through its fleece, he came to the disturbing conclusion that the sheep had been painted green with what looked like green spray paint. The job was very thorough, but you could see blast concentrations from where the paint had been trained in one place for too long.

The streets were completely deserted. There was no morning traffic. It was just Yojimbo and the sheep, sharing a quiet moment together as the sun broke above the terrace houses and flooded Fitzroy with the kind of lushly orange light you associate with films directed by Bernardo Bertolucci. There was something rather majestic about the greenness of the sheep; this particular shade of green being, without question, the color a sheep would be if sheep were green instead of beige, and whoever was responsible for the spray painting of the sheep – whoever had *art-directed* the sheep – had done an outstanding job, especially in the context of this splendid Fitzroy morning.

An unspecified amount of time rolled by.

And then the sheep resumed its slow tour of the neighborhood, meandering down Brunswick Street in no particular hurry, and then it turned a corner past the vegetable co-op, and that was it—

The sheep was gone.

Yojimbo walked home via the community park next to the housing projects. There was a park bench near the Town Hall with a rather pleasant outlook, and he sat down, pulled out his Ray-Bans, and watched the sun climb into the sky.

That was weird. That was out there, he thought.

The following day, he would learn that there was a children's playground across from the park, and that the playground featured the world's smallest petting zoo, consisting of a lone sheep which the tough kids from the housing projects loved to fuck with on a regular basis. The sheep had been spray-painted and defaced so often that the matter had been brought before the local council, along with the fact that the poor creature had developed an understandable exit strategy and was escaping the zoo via a series of rotting fence slats that needed to be fixed. The occasional appearance of a colorful if dazed-looking sheep was thus a commonplace and eccentric fringe benefit of Fitzroy's upscale bohemia, and of course the nouveau rich loved the folklorish barnyardery of the affair because it was quirky and edgy and posed no threat to their kids.

But still. A green sheep. At five in the morning. And then that mind-blowing sunrise? Pretty cool, huh?

This is the unsophisticated party version of the story. The advanced theory came later and was developed over a two-hour incubation period on the park bench, in which Yojimbo took permanent sunburn damage on account of the ozone hole directly over Melbourne. The acid was in repose, and the chemical effect it was producing filled him with an unparalleled sense of tranquility.

His immediate thoughts were as follows:

(a) *I would like nothing better than to maintain this exact level of tranquility for the rest of my life,*

and

(b) *The interesting thing about tripping is that the environment appears to actively deviate from the norm and send tangibly weird things like green sheep along to unsettle your grip on reality.*

As the unfiltered sun went grimly to work, Yojimbo lazily pondered the nature of chemically induced neurological imbalance – i.e., artificial euphoria – in terms of the window of time immediately before and after he had encountered the sheep.

The dilemma was this:

As great as his desire for enhanced perception/artificial euphoria might be, he didn't have the time or inclination to try and achieve it by chemical means. Achieving it by chemical means was a bad idea, in fact, because acid is particularly harsh on the brainpan. There was a girl he knew in Florida who had dropped something like three hundred tabs of ecstasy during the "Summer of Love" of '88 and '89, and she was a mess. She was right where Baxter would be in a couple of years if he didn't curb the drug use, and the thing with this girl was she talked bullshit *all the time*. She was a twenty-nine-year-old bag lady in the making, and no one had the slightest bit of sympathy for her. It was highly possible that she was having huge fun internally; that her party was black tie and French-catered and there were gifts for the guests and the love was omnipresent, but the simplest things outside the party – holding a job, maintaining relationships, doing the laundry, etc. – eluded her. She spent most of her time in tears.

And yet . . .

X-ray vision and whooshing aside, the perceptional high of the evening *had* to be innate. The state of mind that had Yojimbo vowing to get to know Fitzroy better must surely have been in his brain to begin with, and the drug had merely coaxed it out.

Ergo:

Brain + acid = hello Fitzroy.

The trick, then, for the judicious non-drug-taker, would be to try and achieve this state of mind without dropping acid. To coax the green sheep out of their petting zoos without the benefit of drugs. The equation Yojimbo was looking for was something like:

Brain + *brain power* = hello Fitzroy.

But this just sounds cheesy and New Age–ish, which is why it isn't included in the party version of the story.

Climbing to his feet, his skin ever so slightly hued an iridescent carrot color that would never go away, not ever, no matter how many years he spent indoors, Yojimbo walked home to Argyle Street, perusing the neighborhood as he went. He could hear the sound of partying three blocks from the house, and was unsurprised to find the kitchen full of strangers, most of them in reentry phase, smoking marijuana to cushion the blow of coming down. Brett and Gavan were pacing the kitchen in an excitable state, and had obviously decided to postpone their own reentry by dropping a second tab of acid. Their eyes were bloodshot and their facial muscles were rubbery, and they were wearing cute little cardboard-and-fabric hats, the kind favored by stewardesses on Asian airlines such as Cathay Pacific or Air Indonesia. In normal circumstances, Yojimbo would have retreated to his room, put the earplugs in (the ambience of the house being such that earplugs were a studying necessity), and tried to fall asleep, but instead he went to the fridge and pulled out a beer.

"Where did you get the hats?" he asked Gavan.

"Zintense!" Gavan barked. "Migod. Yah! Gnarly headfuck. Offamah *Jesus* sunbelievable! Ya seppo. Yah!"

"No kidding." Yojimbo sighed. "Sit down and tell me all about it."

And so it went. Yojimbo continued to study like a fiend, but the time spent outside study hours was slowed down and enjoyed, and he gave Fitzroy his best shot, applying his concentration to the fringes of perception the same way people work to improve their memory or learn a foreign language. And to some extent, the experiment was successful. Even at Uzi, watching his brother escort Lindy Minh and Naoko back from the bathroom, the I-will-take-the-time-to-get-to-know-you principle was humming away beneath his surface of annoyance. There was Baxter and Big Guy, and Big Guy *was* a green sheep. Nick the party promoter like Brando doing *Streetcar* at the Barrymore. Turning into Stanley Kowalski before your very eyes.

Lindy Minh and Troxler were talking shop.

"—I *loved* that book," Lindy Minh was saying. "I thought you nailed it. The marketing strategy of selling antiproduct to the anticonsumer (sniff)? And so many people bought it."

"Oh yeah. Bigtime."

"So what are you working on now?"

"I just finished a book for HarperCollins. *The Slum Lords*. Basically a look at the would-be dot-com millionaires who flourished under Clinton, and how they're flying to pieces in the new Bush economy."

"Cool title."

"Thanks. I wrote the guts of it before the market crashed, so I'm watching a lot of chickens coming home to roost."

"I'd love to read it."

"I have galley proofs at home. I'd be happy to float you a copy."

"Let me give you my cell."

Cellular phones were produced, creating a flurry of networking. Everyone in the group appeared to be packing, and numbers were punched into Nokias and Motorolas along with abbreviated descriptions of the people the numbers were attached to. The beauty of this system was that it now gave the phone owner latitude to ditch the group and move on to a new group, collecting numbers as he or she went (and this is where the Caller ID function of the new breed of cell phones comes into its own, allowing the user to collect an evening's worth of potential sex partners and then filter out the losers as one screens chaff from wheat. Not that Troxler/Baxter/Big Guy ever called back, but it was nice to know that the facility was there).

For Lindy Minh, Troxler keyed in a cryptic:

Ming Lindy. 917 ___ ____

bitch godess loved x-men ohyeah

For Troxler, Lindy Minh keyed in a surreptitious:

martin troxler 917 ___ ____

writer/cokehead

Nick the party promoter had unholstered his ultracompact Sony fliptop, and was entering the prettiest girl in the group's number with obvious reluctance.

"This just seems so . . . transient," he was sighing. "I've only just met you, and here we are, swapping numbers . . ."

"Don't worry about it. It's *fine*," the pretty girl was saying.

"I came up here to chill, y'know? The club scene in Miami, it's just so . . . *wrong*. I can't *begin* to tell you. . . ."

Hands in pockets, playing with himself at the Barrymore in full view of the public.

"Oh yeah. *Terrible*." The girl nodded energetically.

"I mainly spin trance, but there's that intensity, that charge, where the music's kicking in and you're hitting the k-hole . . . I couldn't handle it. I'm telling you. I had to step back and go 'whoa!' You know?"

"The k-hole," the girl breathed.

"Oh yeah."

Masturbating wildly to his first ovation.

Yojimbo had to go and get himself a drink.

In keeping with the irony, the Uzi bartenders were those annoying kind of guys who juggle their martini shakers and throw drinks together with an in-your-face verve, and if you tip them anything less then five bucks on an eleven-dollar cocktail, they just don't see you for the rest of the evening. Yojimbo's earlier request for a cheap imported beer had been met with much amusement, and now the guy simply wasn't coming over.

Some time passed. People were maneuvering around him, hitting the bar and being served immediately, and it had just occurred to him that the smart thing to do would be to intercept a big tipper and place his order with him, when a close rustle of hip-level activity preceded the arriving rush of Naoko, who vaulted a barstool and squeezed in beside him.

"Here. Let me," she said.

A cocktail artist was promptly summoned. Naoko waved away Yojimbo's money and tabbed an Amstel Light and a vodka gimlet. Yojimbo collected his beer and prepared to follow her back to the group, but Naoko pulled out her pack of Marlboro Lights, folded a matchbook around a match, and dexterously lit the cigarette she had speed-loaded between her lips.

"You want?" she asked, pushing the pack in his direction.

He shook his head. "No thanks."

Naoko was attractively corporate in a different way from Lindy Minh. Her chic was Asian badgirl, which, when done properly, can strike fear into the heart of every business class. She wore expensive clothes disdainfully, and trace evidence of her rebellious lineage was present in her hair. You could see the dynasties of color – the mid-nineties blonde; the late-nineties tealeaf brown; the early naughties electric blue/black – layered together with haughty indifference, and Yojimbo just knew she could wither you with boredom if you were unfortunate enough to lose her attention.

Right now, his brother's smoot had apparently lit her fire, and she was chatty to the point of being hyper, sipping her gimlet and snapping back the nicotine, and Yojimbo had to smile at her accent, which was classic Long Island. All those lengthened vowels, like cows mooing.

"So that guy is your brother, right? Younger or older?"

"Younger."

"He seems older. He's famous, right? Your brother?"

"Yeah. I guess he is. I've been away so I haven't seen it. But yeah. He's written a couple of books and he writes for *The New Yorker*. So I guess he's doing pretty well."

"That's an English accent, right? That I'm hearing?"

"Australian. But I'm from Florida, remember?"

"Cool accent," Naoko said. "You got a thing."

"A thing?"

"Yeah. That accent. It works. You should keep it."

"I should?"

"It works with who you are. You're what, six two, six three? One eighty-five tops? You ever do any acting?"

"Uh, no."

"Lucky you. It's *murder*. You gotta have a thing. Yours is good because it's natural. I could tell if you were putting it on. Everyone could tell. But yours is good. You're the kind of dream guy to place – I'm in human resources, did I tell you that? – and recruiting's just like casting. A résumé will get you in the door, but you gotta perform."

Yojimbo smiled. "I guess you do."

"You wanna dance?"

"Sure. Just let me finish my beer."

"It's okay. I don't wanna dance. I wanna do *something* though."

Cigarette two in lips preceding crush-out of cigarette one in ashtray. Naoko's fingers moving objects with precision, in spite of the impractical length of her nails.

"You're an actress? Outside recruiting?" Yojimbo asked.

Naoko brightened. "Yeah. I play a cop in a soap opera."

"You're kidding."

"It's a nonspeaking role, but it's like featured extra work. Every couple of weeks I get a call. There are a whole bunch of actors, and we play the behind-the-scenes cops in the stationhouse. I've been doing it for three years. I have my own desk and phone and everything. If there's a scene in the police station, we'll be there in the background, and you want to know what's really funny?"

"What?"

"It's the most twisted group of people you've ever seen."

"Really?"

"Big drug-taking crowd. Couple of heroin addicts. Everyone smokes pot off the set. You watch the show closely and you can tell the cops are wasted. The directors don't mind, though, because it keeps the energy level down."

"Wow. You do other stuff apart from that?"

"I go to auditions, but I haven't got my thing worked out yet."

"Right."

The conversation waned momentarily in a way that would have had Baxter smacking his forehead with exasperation. Wasted soap opera cops was top-shelf riffing material, and Naoko's boredom threshold was dangerously close to being breached.

I will take the time to get to know you, Yojimbo thought grimly.

"You ever watch *Miami Vice?*" he asked.

"God. How long ago was that?"

"Ages. I was at the University of Miami back in the days when they were shooting it, and it was like everyone I knew was an extra on that show."

"Really?" Naoko's eyes were glazing over.

"Yeah." *C'mon, riff with me, c'mon.*

"Who was in that again?"

"Don Johnson . . . and that other guy."

"Right."

"The extra situation was kind of the opposite way around from your police station. You had all these straight-arrow guys and girls from the drama department, fresh from a season of Shakespeare or Chekhov, playing pimps and hookers and dealers in the show, and of course they were all superfit and deeply tanned and healthy-looking. All these junkies with great skin and perfect teeth . . ."

"That's *funny*."

"There was this one time where they had Helena Bonham Carter on the show, and she was playing a . . . uh, oh—you're leaving?"

"There's someone I have to talk to," Naoko said briskly, the Marlboro Lights already in her pocket. "It's work-related."

"Oh. Sure."

"I'll be right back though. Don't go away."

"Okay." *Wow. A total crash and burn.*

"Having some trouble there, bro?" Troxler materialized at the bar, tamping a wad of cash into the space beside an ashtray and grinning with concern.

"Yeah. I just flamed out in conversation. With a girl who thinks you look older than me, incidentally."

"Oh bullshit." Troxler checked his three-quarter profile in the mirror behind the bar. "I don't think so."

"Hey. She said it, not me."

"Yeah, but you're the one who's graying prematurely. You're the one who's working round the clock."

"It's funny, Marty, but you do seem older. You've grown up a lot since I saw you last."

"Get out of here," said Troxler, obviously pleased. "You want a real drink, or are we still flying coach?"

"The Amstels are slapping me around as it is. You want to hear another bit of Australian trivia?"

"Sure."

"Light beer in Australia has low alcohol content, so you can drink all night and not get too hammered. Light beer here is low-calorie, so you can drink all night, get hammered, but not too fat. Subtle difference in priorities, don't you think?"

"No kidding."

"Yeah. My alcohol tolerance has turned to shit."

"Better fix that in a hurry. We're spending quality time with Dad."

"He's drinking? I thought they had him hooked up to the full ICU."

"Nah. He was chugging quarts of Four Roses, last thing I heard."

"Jesus."

"Yeah. He's not happy. It's going to be a shitfight."

"It's always a shitfight. The thing I'm wondering is whether driving down is such a good idea."

"You want to bag on the road trip? *Pourquoi?*"

"Too much suspense. I'd be more inclined to talk strategy up here, then fly down and get it over with."

"Think male bonding. Think adventure. We can eat in truck-stops, talk guy stuff—"

"Yeah, and the whole time, Dad's looming."

"You know Dad. He looms. Actually, they've got him on a wicked drug program. He's lost a ton of weight and wears this jaunty little hat—"

"Oh no." Yojimbo shuddered.

"Oh yes. On a one-to-ten scale of ugliness, it's ten. It's worse than Bartender Dad. I'd take Bartender Dad any day over this guy. This guy is *scary*."

"Well . . . he's dying, Martin."

"Yes he is. But he could at least make an effort and check out with class. Drinking Four fucking *Roses*. The old dudes from the Rotary sneak it over. He actually lets them in the house."

"Wow. That does sound frightening."

"Yeah, it's a freakshow. The house is *packed*. The house is full of sad local characters who come around to pay homage." Troxler closed his eyes and cleared his head by sniffing mightily. "I guess you've worked out that we're cruising off our decks?"

"I was all over that back at the sports bar."

"So you want to come in on a few lines, maybe? Help lubricate the flow of conversation?"

"What are you taking, straight cocaine or smoot?"

"Smoot."

"And what is that? Cocaine/heroin or cocaine/ecstasy?"

"You know, I've never gotten a straight answer to that. It's not like it comes with any packaging you can read."

"The name makes it sound like smack plus toot."

"Yeah, but it feels like perky E. The high is really lush."

"A lush high. Are you aware that your friend Nick the party promoter is taking Prozac *and* Viagra?"

"Oh god. Don't get me started."

"I'm at the point where I keep wanting to hit him."

"I'd advise against it. He has an ugly streak you do not want to fuck with. You want some smoot or what?"

Yojimbo unearthed the bottle of dextroamphetamine. "I'll pass. I took the liberty of loading up on some of Roger Ramjet's proton energy pills before we came here. Any idea how hard this stuff is to come by?"

"What is it?"

"Dextroamphetamine? They use it to stimulate the heart after a rhythm lull. It's a heavy-duty amphetamine concentrate."

"Wow. You swiped Big Guy's speed stash. You should probably give me some so we can share the blame if he finds out."

"I wouldn't advise it. My heart is beginning to pound like crazy."

"I'm kidding. So you're okay for drugs."

"I'm good. Love the idea of a lush high, but I'll settle for another Amstel if you're buying."

"No problem. *Garçon!*"

SIXTEEN PAGES
OF HOT CHICKS IN PANTS

The downstairs bar at Uzi was the size of a small motel room, and it was densely packed with the lush high crowd. The lights were out, and the atmosphere resembled that of a disabled subway car after the first hour in the tunnel, where the survivalists come out of the woodwork and the group dynamic is supercharged with fear, and it was uncanny how commuterlike the whole experience was. All that forced proximity and makebelieve upbeatness, made so much more vibrant by the smoot and DOA.

As far as Yojimbo could tell, the downstairs bar was an incubation chamber for the tactile phase of hookup. Body contact was unavoidable. You entered the room in a boxer's defensive stance – arms up, wrists protecting your face, a drink in one hand, a cigarette in the other – and it was only a matter of time before the lush high overpowered your judgment. And if you were a girl standing anywhere near Baxter, it was a matter of time before his hand was on your ass.

Baxter was king of the ass grab. He had a gentleman's knack for engineering close body contact without appearing sleazy. His ass hand was righteous. It landed with an enthusiastic slap. Reports vary, but women who have had their asses grabbed by Baxter invariably use words like "reassuring" and "supportive" to describe the experience. At the time of this writing, Baxter's hand was doing proximity work on the bodies of Claire and Marissa, keeping the ass in focus, but taking in the sights along the way, and Marissa in particular appeared to be warming to his touch. Naoko and Lindy Minh were jammed in close around Troxler, and Big Guy and the prettiest girl in the group were nowhere to be found.

The real estate women were talking.

"—no *way*! I do not believe you! Mary Kelly is selling?"

"She's been working Henry over since she married him. Those guys are out of there."

"I gotta make a call."

"Tell me about it."

"Wow. So who took it down?"

"Gina bitchface. Gina *teeth*."

"Gina *porcelain* teeth. Gina Cindy Crawford's dentist."

"How the fuck did that happen? I see Henry every summer."

"As if Henry's the key."

"Gina fucking here's my cleavage. Guess who's driving the red Porsche this weekend?"

"I guess we won't be drinking at Savannah's for a while."

"Hey, check it out! Zebra Hat Girl has arrived."

"Ooh. Zebra Hat Girl! In her fourth consecutive outing. Over the bridge, through the tunnel."

"From glamorous Bay Ridge. From Hollis Hills."

"The zebra hat look. The zebra hat look is her *invention*."

"Like the Fire Island straw hat look of ninety-seven."

"That was me! That was my look! Me me me me me!"

"Schiffer in *Vogue*. Stole my fucking look."

"Those goddamn supermodels. Whatever happened to them?"

"Phased out by the housewives. The Treenas and the Brandis."

"The Debbis. Zebra Hat Girl looks like she could be a Debbi."

"Oh totally. I could see her spreading for the camera."

"With an African theme. Our jungle covergirl this week is Bay Ridge Deb, *au naturel*."

"Animal attraction. An exotic girl."

"So can we pinpoint a time when the supermodels disappeared? It looked like there were going to be all these new supermodels, but then the market went housewife instead."

"There was a market glut of supermodels. The agencies put too many of them out there."

"So when did the housewives come in? When did we start putting them on billboards? It's completely out of control, you realize."

"The housewives go back to cheesy seventies porn."

"Not that I've actually seen a porn film."

"Not that I've actually seen a porn film, no. There was that Calvin Klein campaign with the underfed street kids, but they were street kids, not housewives."

"That streetkid period was weird."

"I kind of liked the streetkid period. There was an ambiguity about the models you don't get anymore. You know? Were they real street kids or were they the slumming rich? There was room for speculation. Whereas you look at the fashion spreads right now and the housewifey thing is just so boring because you can see their desperate, wannabe lives mapped out in front of you."

"Cheesy seventies porn. I'm telling you. The airbrushed *Penthouse* spread. The David Hamilton soft focus."

"Not that I've actually seen a porn film."

"Tell me I'm wrong."

"You're not wrong. Those Diesel ads are totally referencing the porn thing, but it's British cheesecake porn. The housewife thing is cheesecake. Spreading for the glamour, because, you know, getting your tits out is so glamorous?"

"Hey, it works for Gina Teeth."

"Gina Teeth is a work of art."

"So are Gina's teeth, apparently. I take your point about the cheesecake. There's cheesecake irony in Diesel, but that's Diesel. The majority of Times Square billboards right now are totally informed by airbrushed seventies *Penthouse*."

"Such as?"

"Kenneth Cole post–Albert Watson. The latest Gap ads. That whole Yohji Yamamoto sexy flight attendant thing."

"Oh my God! You are so right!"

"The clothes aren't seventies, but everything else is."

"You are *so* right. So what does that mean? The advertising companies are targeting fifty-year-old perverts?"

"No. Guys in their late thirties whose first taste of sex was glimpsed in the pages of *Penthouse* when they were, you know, twelve or thirteen."

"So it's a nostalgia thing."

"We're talking powerful imagery at an impressionable age."

"It's a gimme."

"It's a total gimme."

"Hey, I've just thought of a new young supermodel. That Czech girl. The one dating Yasmine Bleeth's ex."

"Housewife."

"She's been around. She did those Sandy Dalal ads."

"She's not pretty."

"Are you kidding? She's Linda Evangelista pretty."

"She's a housewife. You're not getting the housewife thing."

"What's there to get? You're talking housewife in terms of the Gap ads, and it's all about shooting some sultry bim in an ambiguous scenario where it looks like she might be on the floor taking it in the next ten seconds. Am I right? On the floor. Taking it. This is what you're talking?"

"Housewife is all about possibility. Seventies porn is all about possibility. The supermodels were all about impossibility. No way were you ever going to get in the sack with Claudia Christy Naomi Linda Kate. The Czech girl? I can see her in the sack."

"With Bleeth's ex."

"With Donald Trump. With Sean 'Puffy' Combs. I can see her in the limo on the way to the Royalton. Falling out of her little black dress."

"I still say she's pretty."

"You're smoking crack. Angelina Jolie is pretty. That Handsome Devil girl is pretty. *Bleeth* is prettier than Czech girl, for God's sake."

"Bleeth is so not prettier. Are you kidding?"

Baxter's ass and non-ass hands were kneading ass. A buttock in each hand. Claire (the more vocal of the real estate agents) was taking the kneading in her stride, whereas Marissa was clearly loving the attention. Earlier in the evening, she had slipped out of her heavily studded red leather jacket and was putting out a lot of cleavage in a spaghetti strap, low-cut Donna Karan. She had the after-hours party vibe of an Upper West Sider. Three and a half hours on the Hamptons jitney? I have this gym membership, but I never seem to go? Like so many real estate agents, Marissa was an art history major. She had worked at MOMA, overseen the mailing lists at a handful of Chelsea galleries, and somehow fallen into sales without ever imagining herself to be a saleswoman. The fact that she turned out to be a great saleswoman was no real surprise, because, unlike Claire, she never appeared to want the sale that badly. Real estate was like art in the sense that people bought for the right or wrong reasons, and if you could get good with that, you could pretty much sell anything. In the *Glengarry Glen Ross* model of sales, Marissa could be likened to absolutely none of the characters who appear in the play or film, whereas Claire was more of a lock for the Pacino type, with some of the Baldwin testosterone-fueled lunacy thrown in for good measure.

Claire was also an art history major, but she took her art very seriously. Her studio management gig at SoHo Tribe had been terminated abruptly when it was revealed that her take-charge personality was frightening the artists, and, if anything, her personality had become even more take-charge uptown. She brought a thinly veiled fury to the Hamptons sales force. There was no ease in her closure. She came at you with excessive eye contact and followed you from room to room, gallery-style, daring you to criticize the decor of houses she wouldn't live in if you paid her. Baxter's hand was on her ass, and that was okay because an ass/smoot transaction had been established in the bathroom (and there was something weirdly reassuring about his touch, she had to admit), but she was fully aware that a liberty was being taken, and if there was anyone downstairs at Uzi with the verbal firepower to put Baxter in his place, well, Claire would be that woman.

But let's not go there for the moment.

"—we're talking total Tom Ford without the gayness. The face. The hair."

"Sorry, I missed that. Who?"

"The new *Outer Limits* guy."

"Brad Matlock?" Troxler grinned. "I have a great story about Big Handsome Brad. When I first came to New York, I did the East Village thing and was living with a couple of actor/models off Tompkins Square Park. And Brad used to come around and spend forever in the bathroom."

"Doing drugs?"

"Doing his hair, as it turned out. Before he cut it short."

"It looks good short," said Lindy Minh.

"It does look good." Naoko sniffed.

"Yeah, well. This has no bearing on the story. This in no way relates to the story I am about to tell."

"Sorry. Keep going."

"Okay. I was writing from home and Brad would come around and he'd disappear into the bathroom for, you know, an hour. And then he'd leave. And it was like, 'Hi Brad, bye Brad.' And then I'd get up and go to the john, and Brad's *stools* would be floating in the toilet."

"I love that word, by the way. *Stools*."

"It is a good word."

"*Stools*. By Givenchy. *Stools*. By Clinique."

"So what was up with that?"

"Well here's the thing. He'd come over, crap in the john, and leave without flushing. Very strange, okay? This is back when I was reviewing hardware, and I used to get free shit from development companies. One of the best things they ever sent me was a prototype CUCMe camera, you know, the little cameras you perch on top of your computer so you can wave hello to your friends online?"

"Yeah yeah. The little round ones."

"I see where this is heading."

"Exactly. So we put it in the bathroom to monitor Brad's activity."

"On the can."

"Interestingly enough, he spent very little time on the can. We had extensive footage. I only wish I'd kept it. It would have been worth a fortune now."

"So what happened? What was he doing in there?"

"Well, the missing bit of information here is that there was a large mirror above the washbasin, and the bathroom was kind of small. If you stood up from your basic sitting position, you'd immediately see yourself in the mirror. Not an insurmountable problem for the average person, but for Brad, it triggered a total shift of priorities. He'd be on the toilet doing toilet stuff, and then he'd stand up and it would be like, 'You're a handsome devil, what's your name?'"

"Oh no!"

"Did you get butt shots? Did you get Brad's butt on camera?"

"There were butt shots, but the quality footage was of Brad interacting with himself in the mirror. Half a day would slip by. It was actually kind of charming in a 'just kill me now' kind of way."

"And look at him now."

"And look at him now. The new *Outer Limits* guy. That show will be around for, I don't know, another couple of weeks."

"Well he's got the hair right. I'll give him that."

"You know the problem with that show? They haven't marketed it properly. The marketing team is selling something completely different to what the writers have envisaged."

"Which is what? The old *Outer Limits* with a new cast?"

"No. You know. Edgy science fiction."

"Oh hardly. It's the 'guy with good hair' show. He could be doing anything. Riding police bikes in the remake of *CHiPs*. Lassoing horses. Playing the banjo in *Deliverance: The Series*. It's all about the hair."

"He has a thing. The hair is his thing."

"Yeah, but the show is going to tank, and it has nothing to do with mister good hair guy's hair. His hair will not save that show."

"You say it like it matters."

"It does matter. *Friends* is more than Jennifer Aniston's hair. *Friends* is excellently written and excellently marketed, with a great cast and great directors, but the important thing about *Friends* is that the product is seamless. The writing and marketing paths are aligned."

"Don't tell me, let me guess. You're in marketing, right?"

"I'm in the franchise arm of the WB."

"She does the Handsome Devil books. She did the entire Buffy series before that."

"Really? So I guess you know your TV."

"I know bad marketing when I see it. You want a really great example of bad marketing?"

"Sure."

"Last year, there were these enormous billboards around town promoting this cheesy *Deep Space Nine* knockoff sci-fi series. I'm trying to get the name here, which shows you how much of an impact the ad campaign made. You know the one. Fringe network. Loads of actors with dumb prosthetic facial enhancement."

"Yeah yeah. This is the one with the blue chick, right?"

"Right! That was the campaign! The blue chick was the sex interest! The blue chick was the Jeri Ryan of the series, and the marketing team went haywire trying to sell the show through her."

"Those billboards had a great tag line, I seem to recall."

"The hottest blue chick on television since Smurfette."

"That is a great tag line."

"Yes it is, but it's completely wrong for the show. The first principle of any show is that the audience has to believe the premise. You set up your premise and then you build your show within the framework of the premise. So. Our cheesy sci-fi show has a blue chick in it, and she's blue for a reason. She's from an alien colony where the people are blue. She has this backstory on how she hooked up with the rest of the cast. She has to be believable. God, I wish I could remember the character's name."

"Let's call her 'the blue chick.'"

"No no no! You *can't*. See, the second you do that, you're detracting from the premise."

"Which is?"

"That it's the future and a whole lot of bumpy-headed human-oids from other planets including earth – including a blue female alien who happens to be sexy – have gathered together to solve some cosmos-threatening problem."

"Oh okay. I see where you're coming from."

"Right. So the thing with this character—"

"Who, for the purposes of this conversation, we will call Lieu-tenant Smurfette."

"No no no! Oh sure—"

"The thing with Lieutenant Smurfette is the second you start marketing her outside the parameters of her existence – the blue planet, the backstory – you destroy the credibility of her character. She's no longer Lieutenant Smurfette. She's the chick with the great hooters and the blue bodypaint."

"Exactly! And the billboards did this."

"It was probably an easier sell. The focus groups came back with crucial data suggesting the show's core demographic was prepubescent youngsters with a thing for hooters and bodypaint."

"Yeah, but you're sacrificing the show's longevity by doing this. We never get to believe the premise. All we get to do is check out a fad. A blue chick with hooters! Shannen Doherty as a witch!"

"Lindy Minh, you interest me. I find you fascinating and attrac-tive. I see possibilities. For synergy between us."

"Have you ever thought about writing books based on television shows? I'm talking quality TV. But mass market. Crichton did it with *ER*. Crichton made a fortune off *ER*."

"Crichton *created ER*. And I have TV ideas, absolutely."

"We should talk about them."

"We should definitely talk about them. But perhaps we should adjourn to the powder room first. Ladies?"

"Sounds good to me."

"Sounds good to me too."

Across the room, Zebra Hat Girl moved toward the bar, the between-stripes whiteness of her hat glowing brightly in the dandruff-catching blacklight overhead. Baxter watched her with interest. His ass hand had massaged Marissa to submission, and she was snuggling against him in the familiar manner of an old sex partner whose interest has been rekindled. Claire was proving a more difficult reach, and he had contemplated switching hands, but there was something wearying about the Hamptons real estate thing, and, quite frankly, he was sick of their bitchiness. Uptown girls. There was something eerily generic about their appearance. They were never ugly or badly dressed. They never had quirks. They came from all over the place: the Midwest, the South, the Rust Belt, the Sun Belt, the eccentric leafy hamlets of John Irving's New England, and wham!—uptown Manhattan in a perfect ensemble with their hair and nails and datebooks. Hailing cabs like they'd been cabbing all their lives.

Zebra Hat Girl, on the other hand, presented something of a challenge. There was an intriguing cluelessness about Zebra Hat Girl. Baxter's pop culture search engine had already accessed the eighties/nineties bad film database, and had drawn a blank on **zebra hat/accessory/nightclub sequence,** so there was no clever irony behind Zebra Hat Girl's zebra hat. The zebra hat was her thing. It was a standard white Stetson in artificial fur, and the girl beneath the hat was curvaceous, if slightly overweight. Baxter withdrew his hands from the real estate women and pressed forward through the crowd, angling for a closer look at the girl in the hat. No polite withdrawal from the women he'd been fondling. He struck camp and moved on, Eastwood-style. Yojimbo watched him disengage, and noted the abrupt decompression process in which Marissa and Claire adjusted to his departure. The comfort zone had disappeared. The reassuring presence of Baxter's hands had gone the same way as the smoot, and like the smoot, it had an addictive quality that even Claire found hard to rudely dismiss. The man with the hands. The ass-grab king.

The music pounding through the hidden subwoofers could only be described as sweaty techno. The beats were muffled by the crush, but they impacted upon the heat of the room so you could feel the air mass pulsing against you at 480 bpm. The girls had stripped to their bra tops, and there was a wide-scale unbuttoning of shirts among the men, revealing a surprising (or unsurprising) amount of chainware. The men, by and large, looked harried and uncomfortable. The lights were out and they were theme-dressed and hip, but there was nowhere to hide in the downstairs bar, and their schtick was in-your-face. You could see them hustling. Opening their wallets and producing the Benjamins and maintaining the lush high through sheer force of will, and there was body contact and face time and bathroom time and cocktails, and then the dramatic exit and the journey into night. Everyone had some party to go to. The downstairs bar at Uzi was the coolest bar in town, and all the guys couldn't wait to leave.

The wretchedness of men, Yojimbo thought. The tactile phase of hookup in a sweatbox underground. Fourteen bucks an Amstel. Cigarette smoke filling the top third of the room. Big Guy and the prettiest girl in the group were standing nearby, and they were all hands-on, full-service. Big Guy with his shirt unbuttoned, doing the Miami thing with his weird buffed-up body, and if it wasn't for the dextroamphetamine and jetlag, Yojimbo would have shot through hours ago.

As it was, it was easier to cruise. The techno clanking through the speakers was in that French style of trip hop where it's basically a tricky dance rhythm over a slow reggae beat, and Yojimbo leaned against the wall and listened to the less frenetic jang of the guitar. An off-kilter conversation was taking place between instruments. The bass and guitar were fresh from the provinces and sounded slow and awkward in the city; the urban drums chattered intolerantly around them. The dialogue teetered on the brink of collapse. And yet the conversation held. Fast and slow rhythms connecting on the offbeat. A merging of cultures. At differing speeds.

"—so you must be Zebra Hat Girl."

"Oh, hi! I'm trying to get a drink, but no one's coming?"

"Well obviously you're intimidating the bar staff. They're frightened of you. They're afraid of the *hat*."

"They served me last week without any problem."

"That was last week. Word has obviously got around."

"What?"

"Oh come on. It was only the subject of one of those ultra-fawning Kevin Sessums blowjob actor profiles in *Vanity Fair*. You and Warren Donovan. Saving him from his latent homosexuality."

"Excuse me?"

"You and big queeny Warren. In Bel Air. Or was it Palm Beach? Hey Legend! Over here a second!"

"—excuse me for a moment. What?"

"We need some clarification here. The Warren Donovan/Zebra Hat Girl outing. Was that Bel Air or Palm Beach?"

"You're asking me? I would have thought the first port of call on that one would be Zebra Hat Girl herself. Martin Troxler, by the way. Love your work."

"That wasn't me!"

"I'm sorry?"

"That wasn't me! I don't know Warren Donovan! I don't even know who Warren Donovan *is*. You've got me mixed up with someone else."

"Yeah right."

"I don't think so. The hat is kind of a giveaway? You want inconspicuous, get rid of the hat."

"Not too many zebra hats in this town, young lady."

"And how is Warren? Keeping well?"

"I have no idea. I honest to god do not know Warren Donovan."

"I see."

"Have it your way."

"So . . . how about those Jets?"

". . . okay look. Obviously there's someone else with a hat just like mine, and she's going out with this Warren Donovan guy—"

"Excellent. We're making progress."

"Please. Continue."

"*It's not me!!* Let me take my hat off. See? *I'm not that girl!!*"

"By god, you're lovely though!"

"Zebra Hat Girl without the hat. I'm seeing an angle here."

"Bartender! A huge fluffy cocktail for this vision of beauty!"

"She's coming with us."

"Oh, no question. She's coming. So. Let's discuss your plans for the evening. Are there places you have to be? People you have to meet?"

"Well, I'm here with friends—"

"Can we assimilate them? Make them one with the Borg?"

"Can you *what*?"

"Let's cut to the chase. You're a great-looking gal with big New Jersey hair, and we were wondering whether you'd accompany us to an exclusive party. . . ."

"Where's the party?"

"On a boat. We're friends with the DJ."

"Does it, like, cost to get in?"

"For you, no. For your friends . . . well, that depends on your friends."

"It's my sister and her boyfriend. They're giving me a ride home—"

"And where's home?"

"Jersey City. How did you know I was from New Jersey?"

"Good question. *How did we know?*"

"Over the bridge. Through the tunnel."

"We'll burn that bridge when we get to it. In the meantime, I'm late for an appointment in the powder room, so you'll have to excuse me. I'm sure a ride can be arranged."

"So you're a Jersey girl?" Baxter said, leaning forward and raising an eyebrow. "I'm in brand management myself, and I have a couple of Jersey-related questions I'd like to ask you. We have the bartender's attention. Let me buy you a drink on the company tab."

"A Tom Collins would be great. Can I put my hat back on?"

"A Tom Collins, a Black Label on ice. And yes, absolutely. You put that hat back on."

"So who is this Warren guy? Is he an actor?"

"He is, but he is not the reason we are here this evening. The reason we are here is to discuss New Jersey. *New Jersey*. The home of Springsteen and Bon Jovi. The birthplace of Sinatra. So much to offer, and yet, from a New York perspective, a cultural disappointment. A missed opportunity."

"Have you ever been there?"

"Never. I've been to Atlantic City, which is gambling heaven, but I think the Mob can take credit for that. What I'm talking about is the perceptional hurdle New Jersey has to jump in order to be taken seriously by the rest of America. Harsh words, I know, but they need to be addressed."

"New Jersey's great. I *grew up* there."

"Yes you did, and no one can take that away from you. But let's be honest here—I'm sorry, what is your name?"

"Kirsten."

"But let's be honest here, Kirsten. You're partying on our turf. We're not partying on yours. Why is that?"

"There are plenty of places to go out in New Jersey. There's Hunka Bunka. There's Foxes—"

"Yeah, and the Devils are a great hockey team. But a state must be more than the sum of its parts, which is why we're devising a series of marketing protocols to help ramp you guys up into the twenty-first century."

"What? You're doing what?"

"We're looking at rebranding New Jersey."

"Oh no! You're *joking.*"

"I never joke." Baxter frowned. "Right now, we're approaching phase three of development. We've replaced the common violet. We're awaiting sign off on 'The "Can-Do" State.' And we have a killer short list of alternative names. You want to hear my favorite?"

"Sure."

"Alphaville."

"Alphaville."

"See? It's working! 'Hi, I'm Kirsten from Alphaville.' Say it."

"I'm not going to say that. It's stupid."

"Maybe so, but it sure as hell is going to get me across the Hudson and shakin' ass at Hunka Bunka. There's a party downtown and everyone's invited, but are we talking downtown here or down-town Alphaville? Over the bridge, through the tunnel. You know what I'm saying?"

"I have no idea what you're saying. You're saying you want to change the name of New Jersey to Alphaville, but you've never been to New Jersey. That blows. I'm sorry."

"Don't be sorry."

"It's condescending. I'm proud to be from New Jersey."

"Alphaville. Alpha-*ville.*"

"No. That just sounds dumb."

"Yojimbo! Help me out! I'm taking heat from the demographic!"

"I wouldn't live in New York! New York is *crazy!*"

"—were you calling me just then?"

"Yes I was. Yojimbo, Zebra Hat Girl. Zebra Hat Girl, Yojimbo. We're discussing Alphaville."

"The movie?"

"The state. Kirsten here is from downtown Jersey City. What does that say to you?"

"Not a lot. I seem to recall a reference to the New Jersey Turnpike in a Simon and Garfunkel song, but I was more interested in the turnpike angle. You know, why exactly is it called turnpike? How did that name come about? That sort of thing."

"New Yorkers are *way* too arrogant."

"My point is, if we change the name of New Jersey to Alphaville, we can shake some of the stigma associated with—"

"—who's 'we'? Who's the 'we' we're talking about? We, the people?"

"We, the people."

"Well there you go." Yojimbo smiled. "I've always had a problem with the notion of instigating change in the name of 'the people,' because the people doing the instigating invariably have no connection with the people they're doing the instigating for."

"Oh, come *on*. Lighten up, for god's sake."

"He has a point."

"Oh, kill me now! You guys!"

A couple of feet behind Baxter, Claire and Marissa were gridlocked in dense bathroom traffic, trying to merge within invitation distance of Troxler and the two Asian women without appearing pushy. An interesting dynamic had been set in motion by Baxter's departure. Claire and Marissa had registered the Zebra Hat Girl approach and were intrigued yet offended by the shift in interest. The fact that Troxler had been called in to say a few words and that Zebra Hat Girl had taken her hat off in the wake of his pronouncements seemed to suggest that: (a) Zebra Hat Girl was a somebody (because Troxler was talking to her, and Troxler had been on *Letterman*), and (b) Troxler and Zebra Hat Girl were close (she had, albeit briefly, removed the zebra hat). An hour had passed at Uzi and it was time to move on, and in terms of traffic and available action, Martin Troxler and his mysterious cachet of unexpected celebrities and shy party promoters was definitely the team to move on with. The problem, apart from the perceptional upgrading of Zebra Hat Girl, was that Lindy Minh and Naoko were killing them for access, and this is a new trend in clubbing (and beach-going) that Claire has been kvetching about since she rejoined the singles scene and started scouting around for a more successful husband: *Asian women are stealing our men.*

The exact scale of thievery remains unclear. We can put a lot of it down to multiculturalism and the fact that a growing percentage of Asian best friends have been turning up to bar mitzvahs from a very early age, but the floodgates are open now and the Jewish community has been facing an onslaught of super-attractive Asian women who have been competing with and outperforming the Park Ave. Japocracy on their own turf and terms. Who knew? Who saw it coming? One minute the paper's jammed in the copier and only Lindy Minh can fix it; the next thing you know, she's running the company! She's at the beach! She's wearing a power outfit and clubbing with a vengeance and making more money than the Hamptons team combined, and it drives Claire crazy to see Lindy Minh and Naoko a few steps farther up the bathroom line.

Nick the party promoter and the prettiest girl in the group had returned from an extended bathroom session by the look of things, and they were deep into the tactile phase of hookup. Their faces were shiny and they were fondling each other's clothes, and Claire found it hard to suppress the thick clot of envy that had lodged in her throat. Sophie always got the good break on guys. The thing with guys was that supply was stacked against you. It was a seller's market, which meant you didn't have much time to shop around. Outside the usual parameters of attractiveness and charm, the thing you had to look for when speculating on the guy market was the hidden worth of the career path—emphasis on hidden.

If there was one thing Claire had learned in the fast-lane, high-stakes Manhattan hostess circuit, it was that nothing was a straight shot. The research, the tennis lessons, the travel money she'd blown tracking down her first husband turned out to be a complete waste of resources because the future was in computer geeks, not Ivy League lawyers, and how the hell were you expected to see that one coming? All these girls from college with their easygoing geek millionaire husbands, and the bitter irony was that they were the exact type of guy she had been trained to turn away.

Right now, the guy market was like the real estate market in the sense that emotion played a large role in acquisition. Women were lowering their expectations or taking on a property with the intention of gutting and rebuilding it from the ground up, and a lot of the emotional chicanery and flat-out competitive bitchiness in the uptown singles circuit was attributable to the fact that men had figured out that their commodity was scarce, and were playing the market accordingly. Claire had met a million Troxlers and Baxters in bars like Uzi, and their asking price was way too high. They came in hard and they expected you to bend. Manhattan was full of glad-and ass handers to the point where discerning speculators were looking farther afield, and Miami-based entertainment professionals were the kind of men you wanted to talk to. Of all the coded information in the downstairs bar, only Nick's five-digit zip was worth the flirt. Sophie was making serious headway with the party promoter, but she was a dilettante when it came to the negotiation process in which a "try before you buy" encounter is taken further than the following week, and Claire really hated to watch someone else squander the opportunity to close. Sophie and Nick would have their moment, and then what? A trip down to South Beach if she was lucky. Relationships like this had to be nurtured and managed, and Sophie had no idea what she was dealing with here. To her, this party promoter guy was just a guy. Unlike Claire, she wouldn't have picked up on the faint trace of Boston in Nick's accent. She wouldn't have noticed the MIT signet, and she definitely wouldn't have asked herself how a shy, self-effacing intellectual from Massachusetts could wind up running event parties to the scale of VH1 Fashion. You don't walk into South Beach and say "Here I am, let's throw a party!" You have to be connected. Either by old money or by the Mob, and Nick seemed far too shy to be a mobster. He was in great shape, which triggered the usual gay suspicions, but he was all over Sophie so he was obviously not, so what you were looking at in the first round of appraisal was a well-educated guy with some family lineage and entrepreneurial drive, with the confidence to think outside the cube in terms of career. And obviously available.

The bathroom line was moving slowly, overseen by a large Italian bouncer with the regulation black T-shirt, headset, and heavy chainware of bouncerdom, who appeared to be taking kickbacks in exchange for multi-person occupancy of the disabled-access stall. The disabled-access stall was big enough to take a wheelchair, but there were no wheelchairs in the downstairs bar (which is probably just as well, as getting a wheelchair down the stairs would have been a major operation), so the oversized cubicle had been turned into a kind of Japanese love hotel for smoot and cocaine enthusiasts, in which a flat-rate twenty bucks would buy you ten minutes of quality hoovering, with the amenities thrown in as part of the service. Naoko and Lindy Minh were chatting discreetly as Troxler slipped the bouncer a couple of bills, and then the three of them did that annoying "remember me" routine, where you relate to the bouncer as a person, not a gatekeeper, so that farther on down the track if there's a problem at the door, you can use his muscle to lever-age your way past the doorbitch. The fact that Troxler was a master of this goes without saying, but Lindy Minh and Naoko had impres-sive Asian form, and Claire could feel the evening slipping away from her. First Zebra Hat Girl, now this.

Marissa was sipping her gimlet and gazing thoughtfully at Baxter, while Sophie and Nick struggled through the complex blocking of a Richard Gere sex scene in which expensive clothes are manhandled with passion, but no actual sex appears to take place, and it was obvious Claire's bathroom merge strategy was going nowhere fast. The only mitigating factor in what was shaping up to be a dismal evening all around was the dark-horse presence of Troxler's brother. No introductions had been made, but the family resemblance was striking. He was deeply tanned (a plus) but a bit too casually dressed (a minus), and he appeared to be irritating Bax-ter with a lot of earnest smalltalk. A convergence was taking place, brought on by the usual grass-is-greener-elsewhere constraints of club hopping, and Claire allowed the tidal pull to bring her back within range of Baxter's hands. Marissa, Nick, and Sophie followed suit. Contact had been made. The tactile phase of hookup had been floated with success. The unspoken next step was to regroup and move on. The now-pounding techno had added an uneasy spin to the lush high, and you could tell by the way it made the conversa-tion choppy.

"—you drive around Manhattan in your . . . El Do*rado,* while your faces turn the color of . . . avo*cado.* You can drive around all night, but you cannot resist our stare—"

"—I can *so* resist your stare—"

"—and yet you're partying on our turf. *And* you went to NYU. Can't you see we're trying to help you out here?"

"Help who out?"

"Our less fortunate friends from The 'Can-Do' State."

"The 'Can-Do' State?"

"That would be New Jersey—"

"—Alphaville. Alpha-*ville*. The point I'm trying to make here is that there is no film school in Joisey—"

"—that's not true!"

"—Frank switched allegiance the second his balls dropped—"

"—that's not true! You fucking liar!"

"What are we doing?"

"Boat party sounds good to me."

"Soph, you coming?"

"I'm coming."

"—flush with cash. Let me say that again with extra crispness. Flush with Cash. We can put you in a cab and have you back across the Hudson—"

"So what are we thinking? Two cabs?"

"You *wish*."

"—so what do you think of Nick? He's nice, right?"

"I'm a Mediterranean girl myself. I love Corsica, the Riviera—"

"—was thinking the Continental for some continentals, but I know there'll be a line—"

"—going now, no question. Three-cab spread."

"—see, I told you. Three cabs."

"—well, do the math. Two Suzie Wongs, one housewife. At least with Tony and Leo—"

"Gentlemen, ladies. The night is young."

"Zebra Hat Girl! Love your work! You coming?"

"Get over it Marissa. I'm going."

"Three cabs. Jesus."

"Is that your final answer?"

"—and away!"

TOTALLY WIRED

The three-cab spread had been broken down efficiently, and Yo-jimbo got to briefly watch his brother's crew in action. No discussion took place. The second the six-girl/four-guy party was out on the street, a well-oiled shepherding machine conveyed three groups of girls from sidewalk to cab door with an almost filmic intensity. Men in suits hailing cabs. A pomo audience of faux punks looking on. And Zebra Hat Girl: leather pants, one of those Halston knock-off off-the-shoulder numbers you see in fashion magazines from time to time but can actually only buy in suburban malls—and the hat. Which was causing quite a stir. The star presence of Trox-ler, combined with the Billy Wilder stylishness of the group exit, made the sight of Zebra Hat Girl stepping into a cab a bit of a high-light for the door line, and there was that wonderful moment of reappraisal where a fake fur stetson was suddenly the coolest thing in town.

Equally impressive was the way the cabs had materialized. One after the other. Hurtling up to the curb. As he sat in the back of cab three (with Claire and Zebra Hat Girl, Baxter up front giving directions), it slowly dawned on Yojimbo that the three-cab spread had been road-tested to perfection. That Troxler, Baxter, and Big Guy had done this before. The key was a combination of momentum and faith. The second the first cab had pulled up, Troxler had climbed inside without a backward glance, leaving the door open for Lindy Minh and Naoko, who followed without prompting. Big Guy had jumped in cab two, leading the way as though it was very possible he might just take off and disappear into the night, and it had been Baxter who had hustled Marissa and Sophie in after him. And cab three was a done deal the moment cab two drove away. Zebra Hat Girl had blown her ride to New Jersey, and Claire was in the bag because her friends had gone first.

Apart from the obvious question of what would have happened if, say, Lindy Minh and Naoko had politely but nonnegotiably refused to climb into the cab (And what *would* have happened? Would the wheels have fallen off the bus? Was there some kind of prerehearsed contingency strategy worked out for these very situations, or was it simply a matter of factoring drugs into the equation and letting the serious pull of more drugs make these questions redundant?), the thing that struck Yojimbo as being thoroughly remarkable about the three-cab spread was that it happened so naturally. No curbside milling. No smalltalk. Once the call had been made, the group had moved on.

And now the party vibe. Like distant conga drums.

Zebra Hat Girl is squeaking in her pants, clearly turned on by the speed and efficiency of what to her is an entry-level celebrity club hop, the kind of thing the paparazzi risk life and limb trying to capture on film, and her struggle to contain the excitement is almost charming. There is tension between Claire and Zebra Hat Girl, a tension not lost on Yojimbo, who has overheard a few snatches of

Zebra Hat Girl—directed upscale bitchiness from Marissa and Claire, and has figured (correctly) that old C. C. Baxter, old Bud, has brought Zebra Hat Girl along for polemic entertainment. I.e., a cat-fight. The heat is the faintest simmering blue, melting zero ice from Claire's smile as she says she *loves* the hat, and Yojimbo makes a mental note to watch out for Zebra Hat Girl and make sure that she gets back to Jersey City unscathed. The dextroamphetamine is motoring through his bloodstream and he smiles with good cheer at the sudden realization that he now has a mission for the evening. A raison d'être. A chance to foil Baxter's nefarious plans.

An interesting cab jam has formed up at the intersection of far East Thirty-fourth Street and the depressing stretch of road beneath the FDR Drive. The cabbies are at it, working their horns as a dense collection of high-glam partygoers staggers out into the traffic, only to be confronted by a daunting line to the wharf where the party boat is harbored. A major-league line. A real Noah's Ark scenario, in fact, because there is no possible way you're going to fit all these people on a standard Circle Line–type cruiser, which means the door scene will be brutal and humiliating with all kinds of low-level nightclubbing currency exchanged and names dropped and Benjamins produced and tenuous party- and drug-based relationships falling apart with the usual spectacular bitterness, etc., and of course Baxter's energetic line of patter about being friends with the DJ is a lot of motivational hooey. The party details were gleaned via an internet bulk mailer. There once was a time where the club lords of Manhattan had taken a personal interest in one-off events like boat and warehouse parties, making them truly exclusive by screening the invitation list at invitation-list level instead of having you turn up and then telling you to go home again because the place is wall to wall with a better cut of jacket, but those days are sadly over. Synergy between publicists is a mainstay of the naughties, with email lists being collected and traded like last year's

Pokémon cards, and the end result is invitational spam. Give me your poor, your tired, your huddled masses, every Saturday at Thrush. Three floors of UK trance w/ Brit DJ w/ accent. $25. First drink on the house.

Big Guy, staring out from the quiet visage of Nick the party promoter, studied the block-long line from the window of his cab and felt not the slightest bit alarmed. Why this is, we can't tell you. Big Guy has always been a difficult read (and this without factoring in the apparently infinite number of on-the-spot personality changes he can aggregate in the pursuit of first-encounter sex), to the point where even Troxler, who has spent many a long night drinking *mano a mano* with Big Guy in the Stuyvesant Street apartment and who has always been fascinated by, and though he'll never admit this to anyone, secretly envious of Big Guy's strike rate with women, has never managed to punch through the fourth wall of Big Guy's method technique and find out whether the man is driving the character or the character is driving the man. Like Brando, Big Guy hates to talk shop, and this drives Troxler crazy.

The cab ride from Uzi to the wharf had been relatively quiet. Directions had been given. A smoot-filled amyl nitrate bottle had been produced, and a lot of hoovering had taken place in the backseat. Smoot tends to knock you around at the outset of consumption, and Sophie had nuzzled territorially while Marissa pointed out the occasional East Side architectural highlight, complete with broker names and floor-by-floor pricings, and Nick had nodded and said "cool" and asked the hard-looking cabbie if he could smoke a cigarette out the window of the cab. The cabbie had gone, "No problem, mon," with the amused inflection of men who make their own rules, and Nick had stripped the plastic off a pristine pack of Silk Cut Executive 30s: unavailable in the USA, but a big fave among the upscale lager/crisps crowd in London. Bad for the lungs, but nicely packaged. Studying the zoo of party hopefuls as the cab pulled over to the curb.

Manhattan by night. Fierce steam pluming through the subway grates and orange-taped workholes, alluding to the promise of godawful weather, but not delivering. Very industrial in its feel, this part of the city. Authentic chain-link fences. Crunchy gravel underfoot. Marissa in her fetish heels and red leather jacket, staggering from the cab and regaining her composure on the sidewalk, flushed and lushly high and loving the passivity of being smoot-smacked but wanting to get proactive on the guy thing and being too lushed-out to get proactive and worrying about not worrying enough about getting proactive to the point of a total zone-out in the style of an Asimov robot, shut down by conflicting directives. Claire as usual displaying some restraint, but staying close to the casually dressed elder statesman guy who was like the Letterman guy's brother or something. Wearing those brown workboots that somehow purple with age. The eight-year age difference between Marissa and Claire is an interesting study, because you can see the twenty-nine-year-old Claire in a studded leather jacket and low-cut top and glossy cigarette pants with wicked heels, whereas the Marissa-as-Claire-in-second-husband-mode is more of a stretch, visually speaking. The post-thirty, zip-code-hustling Claire has mellowed back to a black woolen dress that hugs her gym-honed, Vargas girl body right down to the knees, and she's wearing knee-high black leather boots you just want to get down and check out in more detail. The nod to maturity comes in the form of a Chanel silk scarf she has thrown over her shoulders, and the scarf has weathered the transition from Uzi to party wharf with exceptional dignity. Claire, as Baxter has observed, is an uptown girl. Blemish-free. Hair cut in a grown-out blond bob that complements what we can only assume is a Mediterranean tan. And those boots. Real action-in-the-bedroom boots. The kind of boots that caused Baxter to exclaim, "Oh, you're an angel!" in the first place. Claire, flirting casually with Yojimbo while roving the line for a familiar face, and she has a big ripe horsey smile with perfect teeth and a slightly oversized tongue, the kind of tongue that seems to be standard issue in a certain type of American women and is the subject of many a polarizing *mano a mano* conversation between men. Some guys just love a big tongue. Can't get enough of them. Tend to fixate on various properties and capabilities of a big tongue in the speculative manner of guys *mano a manoing* in late-night environs with enough obscurely labeled top-shelf booze inside them to keep the conversation honest.

Yojimbo can tell that Claire's gaze is drifting past him, but he doesn't really mind. An old girlfriend in Melbourne had crowd-scanned compulsively, and described the practice as "camera two–ing." The girlfriend had worked in broadcast news and had this thing where she mentally perceived any conversation-driven moment as being an ideal opportunity for multi-camera coverage, the idea being that you secured a quality audio and visual feed from whoever you were interfacing with and then stationed a battery of imaginary cameras around the conversation's periphery in order to catch enough cutaway material to save the interaction if the primary feed was boring. Yojimbo had found this explanation novel and jolly at the outset of the relationship, but it quickly transpired that the girl was something of a perfectionist in terms of camera-two coverage, and the second her primary feed was up and rolling, her attention span collapsed. Claire was hanging in there, working with the available material, but the available material seemed to consist of lists of travel destinations, the majority of which were beach- or ski-based.

In a funny kind of way, Yojimbo can empathize with Claire. She's partying with a younger crowd and holding her own competitively, but there's something in her face that reminds him of his earlier reflection in Big Guy's bathroom mirror. A wistfulness, maybe. She's out on Friday night with a couple of work friends and has hoovered a few lines in the Uzi bathroom, and she's now pulling footage for an imaginary travel show while camera-two-scanning a long line of club kids, and it's like, why? Half the kids have loamy, metal-infected faces where you can see the holes where their piercings have been, and in the half-light these blackened holes resemble the *Gray's Anatomy* textbook illustration of buboes so graphically that Yojimbo feels a creepy Nosferatu chill as though the plague has taken hold and they are standing in exodus while the city burns behind them.

Baxter marshals the group into a VIP line while Troxler and Big Guy call the play.

"Take point, I'll close it," Troxler murmurs.

"Thirty seconds, Bud, from the time we start talking."

Again: momentum and faith. Troxler and Big Guy close ranks and lead a fast-paced procession up the side of the line. A VIP procession. Some head-turning, some commentary, no complaints from the crowd. When we refer to Troxler's star presence, we are really only referring to the star presence of a guy whose face is recognizable to the kind of people who make it their life's work to catalog and identify the faces and names of, say, the entire second-unit cast of all ten seasons of *ER,* but you would not believe how many of these people are out there. Troxler's done *Letterman* once, appeared on a couple of TV panels and chat shows, and milked the interactive circuit for all it was worth, and yet he frequently gets that thing where people mumble his name whenever he walks through a crowd. He's not at the point where thick-necked strangers in baseball caps have started yelling, "Yo Marty! S'up?" whenever they see him in the street, but he can imagine it happening and has worked up a number of noncondescending, blue-collar responses to keep it real when they start, and these imaginary interchanges are an odd source of comfort to him, especially when he's coming down from a big night on smoot.

Yojimbo can feel the energy of the line jump, and smiles distractedly at the cowboy/finance battlespeak deployed by his brother. "Take point, I'll close it." Like he's Michael Douglas playing his dad in an Oliver Stone western. The VIP procession has a jittery will-we-won't-we vibe: Claire beside him, striding along in her magnificent boots, no stranger to closure but probably keenly aware that the boat party demographic falls outside the usual parameters of what she likes to call "The Circuit," and she's either buying the hype and steeling herself for some glamorous slumming, or else she's dreading the whole affair. The headstrong presence of Nick the party promoter somehow legitimizes the youthful landscape around them, to the point where Yojimbo has to remind himself that Big Guy is a content salesman, not a nightclub impresario. Personal embarrassment aside, he'd like nothing more than to watch the fleet of doorbitches take his brother's crew apart, but he can tell, this far in advance, that it's not going to happen.

They've crossed the road and followed the line to the wharf, and the wharf is going off in a roiling carnival of entry. The survival-of-the-fittest paradigms of Noah's Ark–style survival – i.e., "climb on board this boat or perish" – are violently in play, and the fleet of doorbitches – fleet in the sense that there are many of them and they're all wearing crisply white nautical dress uniforms with epaulets and braiding – are having a hard time containing the disruptive behavior of the B-list. Three inconsolable groups of refused party-goers are disputing the call with security, and it's first-glance apparent that there aren't enough bouncers to deal with such a motivated rush on the party vessel. It's like *Titanic* in reverse. The boat is a large three-deck ferry, modified for private cruises, with a loading capacity of six hundred people, and incredibly enough (or maybe not: Troxler and Baxter have been on DOA for hours), the majority of partygoers are visibly blasted. Just left of starboard, a group of young men with Scot or Irish accents dressed in what appear to be mint-condition Sgt. Pepper's Lonely Hearts Club Band costumes are trying the patience of the house muscle, huge black guys in nautical white who are wearing brightly colored leis around their necks for some reason, and the guys in the Beatle uniforms are actually pushing the black guys in the chest and crowding them back toward the water. *"C'mere ya devil! Ah wantae kiss ya onna mooth!"* one of the skinny guys calls out, and it's a green sheep moment on the wharf at thirty-four. The Hearts Club Band are just kids, but there's that foreign thing to contend with, and Yojimbo recalls a Samuel L. Jackson anecdote, delivered in chatshow or magazine format, in which Samuel L. and one of his tough bloods from the 'hood clear out an entire London underground carriage full of white soccer hooligans by bellowing, "We ain't niggers, we *American* niggers!" at the first sign of trouble, thus queering the expected deal of conflict by adding a foreign element into the mix. Skinny kids in Sgt. Pepper costumes should be more absurd than dangerous, but who can tell? Let security handle it. More security over here!

Baxter stalls the procession thirty feet from the water while Troxler and Big Guy move in on the gate, and Yojimbo can't help but marvel at their timing. The head of the wharf and gangway are blockaded by authentic seafaring types in Moonlite Cruise uniforms, obviously the crew and last line of defense, who seem on the verge of drastic action, like calling the party off, and the two girls and one huge black guy who appear to be running the show are very much in conciliation mode. The girls are blonde and dressed to resemble luxury cruise stewardesses. Stewardess one is working a cashbox, stewardess two is dispensing the same brightly colored plastic leis as worn by security. Both girls and the huge black guy are running simultaneous interference with the Moonlite Cruise staff and a bunch of noisy line frontrunners who are clearly not taking no for an answer. The girl with the leis seems close to tears. As far as Yojimbo can tell, the plastic leis are the key to admission. A cheerful touch. The boat's lower deck is packed with partygoers, all wearing leis, and the *doof doof doof* of techno is already at headache-inducing volume. The head Moonlite Cruise guy looks like Charlton Heston playing Moses or an outraged astronaut on the Planet of the Apes. He has the bristly beard of an old seadog, and clearly doesn't like the way the evening is shaping up. The huge black guy is trying to placate him, and this is crucial to the timing of Big Guy and Troxler's successful gate crash.

Here's how it works:

The girl with the cashbox is stonewalling a couple of unlikely dudes in Austin Powers velvet. They know the DJ, apparently. The huge black guy has told them to fuck off, but they're hanging in there, trying to get some minor celeb already on the boat to come back out and vouch for them. Cashbox stewardess is visibly oldskool and has a very low tolerance for pushy second-raters, and in normal circumstances – at a normal nightclub with tight security and an operating staff who understand the intricacies of quality door control – she would have set the bouncers on them in no short order. But she's fighting a battle on two fronts here. The Moonlite Cruise crew is on the verge of mutiny, and her hired muscle is nowhere in sight. The boat is three quarters full. She has a mental punch list of invited VIPs who are fashionably late and have not yet boarded. What she wants to do is clear her quota, shut the gate, and get on the phone to a couple of dealers (interesting dealers; the kind who carry enough product to light up entire nightclubs; the kind who turn up with henchmen and live the life and pick and choose the events they attend, and they're always late and they're always charming on the phone and they said they'd be here and they're not here!), and she's really pissed off at her friend with the leis, who is out of her depth and sinking fast. A whiny group of Elizabeth Wurtzel trust-fund victims has sensed weakness at the gate, and is pressing the advantage, demanding to be let on the boat for whatever fucking reason. It's going to kill her professionally to let these idiots on board, but what can she do? The cashbox is full to overflowing and there will be no party if the dealers aren't found, so she decides to make the call and fill her quota with numbers. *Okay,* she signals the Austin Powers crew. *Give me your money and get on.*

The lead dude moves forward with gusto. He's wearing burgundy pinstripe bellbottom flares and has the ticket money ready, a billfold of twenties. He jerks his head at the boat. *We're on.* Two girls and three guys surge in behind him, wearing vintage secondhand from Lafayette or St. Marks, and you can tell they've been partying since the early afternoon. Happy folk. East Village new arrivals. Absolutely no match for a quality line jump, and Troxler and Big Guy walk right through them.

The guy with the money is counting out the door charge, and Big Guy does this fluid standover maneuver where he grabs the guy's shoulder and hustles the poor bewildered hipster away from the cashbox. Big Guy as Nick the party promoter, but none of this shy, self-effacing nonsense. He's pulling the full Palm Beach Mafia routine. Miami via Staten Island. Faux goombah. His touch is gentle but firm and he's smiling a creepy Mickey Rourke/Steven Seagal "please don't make me break out the rough stuff" smile where his lips are moist and kind of disgusting, and it obviously does the job because the lead dude backs up fast. Big Guy leans in and whispers something to the dude. It could be anything. B-movie dialogue, a benediction in Latin. Whatever it is, it ties up the attention of the East Village crew, who are wide-eyed and dysfunctional in crisis. There seems to be a problem. Someone is having a word to their man. It's a beautiful layup. The East Village kids think the buffed-up fellow in the charcoal suit is high-level security, whereas cashbox stewardess assumes he's part of their crew, only better dressed, and the next thing she knows, she's taking money from Troxler. Crisp hundred dollar bills.

"I only have Benjamins," Troxler confides. "Three for the boat and two for your discretion."

He delivers this in three-quarter profile, holding the pose as though he's waiting for the flash, and then he fans three bills into the cashbox, smiling easily at both stewardesses as he slips them each a folded C-note. Oldskool girl first, then the girl with the leis. Cliché as this sounds, this is actually a supremely difficult thing to pull off. Troxler has walked in cold and made them take his money, and the timing is critical because it's a white guy on white girl situation. As a rule, the practice of slipping cash to strangers is not a cultural maxim of white America. Tipping, sure. But not in-your-face machinery greasing. To pull off a Sinatra or Puff Daddy–style palm grease, you're going to need an ostentatious community infrastructure – i.e., a Rat Pack or posse – to legitimize the arrogance of peeling banknotes from a roll and pressing them into the hands of non-hotel staff, and this kind of infrastructure does not exist in old or nouveau white Manhattan. Hollywood, sure, but not here. The Wall Street crowd does not do this, and white gangsta rappers really shouldn't. Troxler does it because it's a high-pressure moment (failure to board at this point is unthinkable) and because he has a clear shot at the two stewardesses, who he knows could use the money. Would he attempt this if they were black, or if the huge black guy wasn't talking to the captain? Probably not. Interracial palm-greasing comes with a fat manual of cultural idiosyncrasies, and the last thing you want to do is get it publicly wrong. Besides, he's hedging his bets by using the D-word as he greases. "Discretion" is industry code for "celebrity on board." What Troxler is doing, despite previous assurances that this never happens in Manhattan, is alluding to being part of an ostentatious celebrity infrastructure, like a fleet of security guards surrounding Bruce Willis, and he's slipping the stewardesses a couple of C-notes to make things easy for his boss. It's sucky, but it works. The oldskool stewardess gives him the nod, and the girl with the leis says, "How many?"

Farther up the wharf, Baxter's counting down from thirty. It's his job to walk the evening's club trawl through the gate. Neither he, Big Guy, or Troxler has discussed this, but they're all a bit worried about the way Yojimbo's dressed. Yojimbo's wearing an amiable dark gray sweater, classic-cut black Levi's with a lot of wear in the crotch, and Australian Blundstone workboots, a favorite among backpackers globally. He looks like he's just flown in from Nepal. Baxter has VIP-crashed enough nightclubs with Troxler to know that Troxler will evoke some kind of celebrity alert in the course of securing a passage onto the boat, and of course the big problem with celebrity alerts is that people tend to scrutinize you closely. Yojimbo's casual attire is a liability, and Baxter feels disappointed (and slightly cheated) because Troxler, in his low-key, super-ironic way, has hyped his older brother as being the legitimate star of the family. Feed the guy enough obscure top-shelf booze, and he has all these stories from pre–Sun Belt Fort Lauderdale in which Yojimbo *was* the neighborhood samurai.

The real estate bunny with the great boots has apparently run out of beaches to namecheck tanwise, but she's still hanging close with Troxler's brother, probably more for protection than anything else. The Sgt. Pepper crew is rucking security with the practiced mob scrum of soccer hooliganism. They're drinking beer from those oversized cans you can find only in import liquor stores, which is bad news because the beer is like 12-percent alcohol content per volume and tends to facilitate Arsenal- or Millwall-style rucking. The black security guys are healthy and sharp (as opposed to crack-addled and skeevy), which means they're nightclub pedigree and not project-trained, and their stylish blackspeak and threats to bust caps in asses is having absolutely no effect on the rampaging Beatle fans.

And Zebra Hat Girl is loving it. Zebra Hat Girl is totally down with the Diesel billboard scenic mayhem of the wharf, which is odd because she's the only person in the group who's not off her head on drugs. Her excitement, like Yojimbo's sweater and jeans, is unlikely to weather the distaff scrutiny of a celebrity alert, and Baxter goes "fuck this," and ends the countdown early. Baxter, god bless him, is a true nightclub veteran. The netporn, the gambling, the drugs and drinking aside, he's the one member of the group who comes from old money and feels genuine entitlement. In the distance, he can see the girl with the leis handing Troxler an armful, and he revises his play and leads his party toward the gate, arranging the frontline so that Yojimbo is wedged between himself and Zebra Hat Girl. The Asian girls and real estate women know the drill and fall in behind the frontline with haughty boredom and glam, and Baxter's attention is totally fixed on Yojimbo. Yojimbo in his sweater looking slightly perplexed. They reach the gate, and Troxler almost falls over himself planting a lei around his brother's neck and shoulders.

"Complications?" he asks Baxter.

Baxter shakes his head. "No complications," he says.

Zebra Hat Girl removes her hat in a splendid display of big New Jersey hair, and Troxler gets up close and places a lei around her mane.

"Help my brother on the boat," he whispers in her ear.

Big Guy has joined Claire at the rear of the group, and is his shy, self-effacing self once again. The East Village kids are keeping their distance, craning their necks and rubbernecking shamelessly, and the consensus of opinion is that the guy in the sweater is who the fuss is all about. The lead dude is glaring daggers at Yojimbo, shaking his head at the groupies and hired goons while being secretly thrilled by the celebrity encounter. Three days in New York and this is the business. Showbiz folk behaving rudely. Famous people in sweaters and jeans. The Wurtzel girls are checking out Yojimbo, and they're making a show of being unimpressed. Some boring rich guy in black 501s. How very nineties. Hello?

The huge black guy finally returns to the gate, and waves Zebra Hat Girl and Yojimbo up the gangway. Zebra Hat Girl takes Yojimbo's arm and walks him up the ramp onto the deck.

"Are you okay?" she whispers earnestly.

"Sure," Yojimbo says. "Why do you ask?"

Naoko and Lindy Minh are presented with leis, and Baxter escorts them quickly up the gangway. Marissa, Claire, and Sophie trade "isn't this kitsch?" smiles with the cashbox stewardess, and then they board the boat with Nick the party promoter, and walk across the dancefloor to the bar. Troxler follows at a distance, pausing briefly on deck to watch the scuffle on the wharf, where it looks like the black security guys are waging a losing battle against the Lonely Hearts Club Band. The boat party obviously has some kind of sixties theme. The deck is crowded with zoot suits and cocktail frocks; girls with Doris Day perky uplift bumming cigarettes off guys dressed like the young Michael Caine, and it takes him a while to realize that the clothes are all new. Thin lapels. Tight-fitting sweaters. Stylish retro for the new millennium, and he winces at Marissa in her Terminator leather, weaving toward the bar on six-inch fetish heels.

A blonde stewardess appears at the prow and stands beside him as the water slaps the boat. "Who was that guy?" she asks. "The guy in the sweater. Who is he exactly?"

Troxler shoots her a look of feigned innocence, followed by a medley of smiles from his various book jackets.

"Just some guy," he says cryptically. "Nobody you'd know."

THE POETRY OF WAR

By the time the party is out in the river, Baxter has ponied up cash for not one but two rounds of drinks and had the pleasure of hearing the lower-deck DJ spin the Vasquez mix of "Creep." There are two DJs on the main and lower decks, but the main attraction appears to be some kind of live act on deck one. There's a drum kit on a porta-stage, flanked by two Russian Sovtek Marshall stack–style amplifiers draped in glittery tinsel, the size of which suggests that the live act will be significantly louder than the already loud techno blasting across the East River from two floors of boat.

Vasquez's "Creep" deploys the big distorted E chord from the Radiohead breakout single, plus bizarre cuts of Monica Lewinsky chattering away to Baxter's answering machine. Baxter is gallantly low-key on the subject of Lewinsky, but the truth of the matter is that the whole affair was handled badly. You (and he) didn't have to be a rocket scientist to see that Monica had sought out fame by association and got the real thing by mistake, and that this real-thing fame was the American Dream as Ancient Mariner's albatross: 100-percent smiling deference from the highest order of Manhattan social life, except you couldn't chitchat to Monica about her work as you tend to do with celebrities, because Monica's work was off the public record. Monica's work had been done. Monica had no chitchat-worthy work to speak of. All she had was this albatross, which you weren't allowed to look at or mention, and it was equal parts fascinating and heartbreaking to watch her circulate at parties, trying to pass herself off as a regular celebrity. Baxter had posted the very MP3 files now sampled by Vasquez in the fascination stage of their brief liaison. Lewinsky had apparently been charmed by Baxter's ability to see "the real Monica" within the morass of skewed perception and smiling uptown deference, and rewarded him with heartbreaking candor in the form of many answering machine messages (playing right now, in fact) in which it becomes quickly evident that she's having a rough time in Manhattan and could use a friend real bad.

Unlike Big Guy, who has taken his shirt off and gone native and is wowing the ladies with dancefloor verve, Baxter plays the game with large amounts of self-loathing. "Oh, you're an angel!" is symptomatic of this. Baxter will go to a party and use this exact same line on every woman present, just to see what happens. It's like he's courting rejection. Lewinsky withstanding, he's used "Oh, you're an angel!" on an Easton Ellis list of supermodels and actresses, engaging them all in conversation with the withering exception of Mira Sorvino. His original take on Lewinsky was that she got what she deserved, and, along with the fact that they were too good not to post, the MP3 files have a kind of Smithsonian virtue in that they provide an oral history of an oral history, so to speak. He registered the domain name via a hard-to-find and expensive porn rerouter, coded the site in self-taught Dreamweaver and Flash, and then leaked the address to *Suck* and *The Onion*. It was a classic new-media prank, and it paid huge personal dividends. And now the big Radiohead E chord. All these fucked-up club kids squealing their ecstasy squeals and waving their arms in time with Lewinsky, and ten months down the track he still can't purge himself of the bitter tang of betrayal. Cool mix though. Nice sampling. Clean loops. He can't bring himself to dance, but does this ironic cocktail saunter from dancefloor to bar, and Nick the party promoter cocks his fingers into a pistol of homage and uses his thumb to mime hammer striking pin.

Yojimbo knows nothing of the Lewinsky/Vasquez backstory. He's alone at the bar, watching Claire, Marissa, and Sophie pointedly exclude Zebra Hat Girl from their upscale zone of dancefloor, while a dealer named Simon stands next to him, transacting. Pills in one hand, bills in the other. Despite the fact that the boat is a narc's paradise, stingwise, Simon adheres to basic maxims of transaction. He likes you to hold your money low when you pay him, and he nods furtively and says "good work" and "well done" when money and product change hands. The market is bullish around the lower-deck bar. Half the clientele know Simon by name, and the other half go, "You're Simon, right?" Simon has obviously been briefed on the evening's sixties theme. He's wearing gray linen slacks and a *Dr. No* Bond–era terry toweling deckshirt in a slightly darker, almost charcoal gray. The products he's dispensing are "mercs" and "scorpions," and the more experienced partygoers are making a run on the slightly stronger mercs, which have a little Mercedes-Benz logo stamped into the tablet. A sizable crowd has converged around the bar, and Yojimbo sees a couple of sallow kids in Sgt. Pepperwear lingering around the periphery. They must have overwhelmed security and stormed the boat like pirates. A European trend that has yet to take root in the States is the combination of highly caffeinated energy drinks, such as Red Bull or Black Stallion, with hard liquor, primarily boutique vodka, the idea being that you can chug down hundreds of these babies and continue to chug because you're wired to the eyeballs on caffeine. The Hearts Club Band team leader, a sprightly fellow in McCartney blue, has a cooler full of vodka in penis-shaped bottles, and he's passing out the Red Bull like there's no tomorrow.

"Arr matey," Baxter says on approach. "Tharr's a likely storm a-brewin'."

"You're telling me." Yojimbo frowns. "I can't believe they let those idiots on board."

"Perhaps they swam."

"Perhaps they did. Best left the fuck alone if you ask me."

"Yesh . . ." Baxter sighs, already bored. "Any sign of your brother?"

"Upper deck. Upper upper deck. Bathroom?"

"Bathroom for ten points. I notice you're not dancing."

"No talent for it. Prefer to mooch and barprop."

"A moocher. A propper upperer of bars."

"Unlike Nick from Miami who *thrives* on the dancefloor. Unlike Nick who's a disco king."

"I believe the term is 'goosing.' My hip friends tell me you goose to this music. There's loose goosing and heavy goosing. See those kids over there? They're goosing loosely. Disco is dead, you understand."

"I thought disco was back. I thought disco was back with a vengeance."

"Nope. Although Kirsten is breaking out some wicked steps, I notice."

"Kirsten?"

"As opposed to Claire. Who I'm sensing interest from, Yojimbo speaking."

"So this is what you do. Pull groups of women together and take them on the road."

"Beats mooching. Beats propping up bars."

"Yeah well."

"Yeah well exactly! So what, you're going to stand around and sip Amstels and have a lousy time as a matter of principle? Lighten up for chrissakes! You're on a frickin' *boat*. Here, I'll even spot you some cash to purchase some timely mood enhancement from Mr. Drug Dealer next to you. Hey dude! Hey ecstasy man!"

"His name is Simon."

"Hey Simon! Yo!"

Baxter is boisterously drunk in a way that could be endearing if you're as fucked up as he is, but if you've been sipping Amstels or dealing ecstasy at a semiprofessional (i.e., sober) level, the sudden rush of Baxter is problematically rude. Simon deals his mercs and scorpions out of cute plastic boxes the size of your thumb, and there's a concentration level required in taking money and dispensing not just quantities but different makes of product, not to mention saying "well done" and "good work" and feigning recognition of people who come up and act like they're old buddies from way back even though he's never set eyes on them before in his life, and the way he sees it, people like Baxter are an occupational hazard.

"Yo S-man!" Baxter exclaims. "X-man! Over here! Yo!"

To which Simon grunts: "Take a number. Get in line."

Which in turn kickstarts a torrent of dudespeak – yo dude, no dude, dude yo, said no – into which the verb "fuck" is introduced, transforming the patois into a brisk fuck-you-speak which wallpapers Simon's transactive flow without impeding business one iota. Baxter carries on excitedly, thinking he's found a worthy sparring partner and grinning at Simon throughout the exchange, and Simon is grinning back with the kind of ferocious zeal a boisterously drunk person might construe as "hail fellow, well met" argumentative respect, but which a certain Amstel-sipping bystander can tell is motivated more by good old-fashioned contempt.

Two whiny girls from the earlier door scene want to know what the problem is. Valuable trust-fund time is being utilized poorly, and it goes without saying that they're being vocally supportive of Simon even though they (a) do not know Simon and (b) will not remember, recognize, or even say hi to Simon later on in the night. They want their drugs and so what's the problem?

The problem, Yojimbo quickly realizes, is that Baxter is a hundred times better at whaling on a bunch of privileged white girls than he is at verbally sparring with a street-smart drug dealer, and he cheerfully abandons the dudefight (and says "good work," by way of dismissal), and it's no-holds-barred fur and claws from there on in.

Yojimbo stretches his arms and decides to take a little air on deck. Unlike the majority of clubgoers, he's dressed warmly enough to enjoy the view outdoors, and he braces himself against a railing and watches the Williamsburg, Manhattan, and Brooklyn bridges sail by. He's fatigued to a place beyond boredom, a pleasant state of mind in which the ride is quite enjoyable, and he has to admit, the view of Manhattan is spectacular from the Battery. The night sky is the color of smoke, and the World Trade Center looms high above the landmass. He can hear the water as he looks up at the twin towers, but the brightness of the city has fogged out the stars. Incredible, really. To build a city so huge as to put the heavens in perspective. He does that thing where he mentally subtracts the modern architecture from the skyline, busting it down to the bedrock of metropolis, and the canyons of stone and steel have a human element about them that the massive glass towers somehow don't. The Empire State when we were building an Empire. The Empire State when we *believed*.

Snippets of Baxter pitch and yaw through the window—

"Like that English accent's *real* . . ."

"Don't think so darlin' . . ."

"Bad news rhinoplasty . . . should *sue* the motherfucker! . . ."

—but the water's smooth and the wind is calm, and Yojimbo's amiable gray sweater is made from real fleece from real Australian sheep, and was purchased from an old-style department store that was genuinely old-style and sold camping apparatus and Cornish Blue kitchenware and was secretly an outpost of childhood memories, and the dextroamphetamine is leveling out gently. A couple of hours too soon.

"I *knew* you were fucked up!" Marissa exclaims, tottering out onto the deck. She's huddled in her jacket, trying to light a cigarette with her purse, drink, and lighter in both hands. "You were so quiet! You're having a good time, right?"

"Sure," Yojimbo admits.

"So what are you on? What's in the bottle?"

Yojimbo blushes slightly, because she's busted him studying the label of Big Guy's dextroamphetamine supply.

"I guess you could call this the Rolls-Royce of speed," he says.

"Cool," Marissa says, snapping away at her lighter. "How many do you take?"

"I had two. I probably wouldn't advise any more than that. Anyway, they're not mine. They're Nick's."

"Nick's great," Marissa says.

"Nick's the best," Yojimbo agrees. "Why don't you give me your handbag and light that thing in the doorway?"

"Thank you," Marissa says with a kind of stunned gratitude. She smiles and disappears inside the cabin. Seconds later, she's back.

"You don't want to go in there," she says. "Sophie and Claire are fighting."

"Really? What about?"

"I'm not sure. They're not saying anything, but it's probably got something to do with your friend. Anyway, it doesn't matter. They fight all the time."

"You're kidding. They're not fighting over Nick?"

"It's like ancient history, you know?"

"Nick's a deeply troubled person. You have no idea."

"They're best friends, but they have these fights."

"Last thing you want to do is get involved with Nick."

"Sophie dated Claire's husband. After they broke up or something. They're good friends, but they have this all stuff to work out."

"Sophie dated Claire's husband?"

"Oh god. Last summer?"

"You're *kidding*."

"It was awful. We were in separate houses and had to go to the beach at different times? Heavy shit, man."

"Wow."

"So yeah. I'm giving them some space. And what's the deal with the girl in the hat? Is she like a friend of yours?"

"I think Martin knows her."

"Martin's your brother, right? He has something to do with that Handsome Devil show?"

"No. He writes books."

"No kidding. That show is *great*. And what's up with your other friend? Greg? He's nice one minute and standoffish the next."

"Greg is a mystery. I have no idea what Greg's story is."

"He's cute though."

"In a deranged kind of way."

"He is cute. He should chill out a bit more, but he's okay. So. Are we going to take some of Nick's speed?"

"I guess we are. Here's your handbag and drink. Let's see what we have here."

"The Rolls-Royce of speed. How strong are we talking?"

"Plenty strong. Feel-my-racing-pulse kind of strong."

Now that Yojimbo's drug-taking credentials have been established – he's split a tab with Marissa and given her a whole one for later – the conversation fleets along. They talk about art, specifically Hopper v. Rockwell. Marissa considers Rockwell to be an illustrator, not an artist, and has disparaging things to say about his wholesome vision of America. Yojimbo is alarmed by such an easy dismissal, and rears up on his hind legs, T-Rex style, contending that Rockwell was the real deal for reasons of "emotional authenticity."

"The thing with Rockwell is that he paints these sly kids and rueful sailors and conspiratorial policemen," he says. "And you can use words like 'sly' and 'rueful' and 'conspiratorial' to describe them. Everyone looks bored in a Hopper painting."

"Oh please."

"If emotions are colors, Hopper's palette is gray."

"If emotions are colors, your guy is red, white, and blue."

"That's such a cheap shot."

"You're so cute! You love Norman Rockwell! You sleep in pajamas, right?"

"Getting a bit personal there—"

"And you're a Bacharach fan, I can tell. So what else are you into? Big fluffy towels from Bed Bath and Beyond?"

"I just hate the fact that the art establishment somehow has this idea that Rockwell wasn't an artist."

"Dogs named Rover? Kissing on the second date?"

"Yeah yeah. So what are you saying?"

"I'm not saying anything. I'm saying you're cute. Your jeans look crisply ironed is all I'm saying."

"I've literally just stepped off a plane from the other side of the planet."

"I mean that in a good way."

"I'm so glad to hear it."

Inside the cabin, a wormhole of tension has opened up between Sophie and Claire. The dancing stopped being fun pretty much after the first set of beats morphed into the second, and there's that smoot imbalance where Sophie is up while Claire is coming down fast. It doesn't help that the dancefloor is crowded with pocket-sized Asian girls, or that Zebra Hat Girl is trading disco moves with Nick. Claire feels old and pissed-off and unadaptable. She thrives in the plushness of The Circuit, specifically the Velvet Lounge or the Spy Bar or Nell's, but she also has friends who do their hunting in the offworld colonies, and return from safari with unbelievable men. She's written off Troxler and Baxter completely, has seen through Nick's self-effacing routine, and she had something going with Troxler's brother for a few minutes before the conversation fizzled. Nice guy. Good-looking, but no spark. Claire perceives him as a traveler type. A man of few possessions. The sort of fellow who values experiences over material wealth, and is permanently in transit. But not a beach or ski-slope type of guy. This in itself is no reason for tension, but Claire has been fuming over a comment Sophie made while they were waiting for Baxter to buy them drinks. It was obvious to Claire that Sophie and Marissa had hoovered smoot with Nick during the cab ride to the boat, because both girls were exuding respective sheens of contentment, and as they were standing at the bar, waiting for the drinks to appear, Claire noticed that Sophie had undone the top two buttons of her blouse to reveal the exact same swell of rose-colored bra she had unbuttoned to reveal the entire fucking summer she was romping in bed with Claire's ex-husband. For Claire, the unbuttoned blouse and Victoria's Secret strap and cup is a key to a past she'd rather forget, and then Sophie leans in, exposing yet more cleavage and red bra fabric – signature red, *Marnie* red – and whispers with smoot-lush approval in her voice:

"Go for it. He's your type."

Which is completely the wrong thing to say to a person

experiencing the subtext-rich paranoia of smoot withdrawal. Claire understands that Sophie means Yojimbo. Yojimbo is her type, Sophie's saying. And apart from the "excuse me, how dare you" presumptuousness of such a remark, the blouse and bra have triggered a flashback where Claire is now 100-percent sure that Sophie and her tennis-playing ex have discussed her in lurid, postcoital detail, making disparaging remarks about her preferences in men to the point where Sophie, her unbuttoned blouse signifying the very same sexual availability that had her bastard ex-husband chasing her from beach house to beach house in full view of The Circuit, is saying she thinks Claire has a thing for casually dressed backpacker types. Oh really?

The ridiculous hat-wearing girl has monopolized too much of the party promoter's time, and Sophie, who is extraordinarily attractive and doesn't need to show cleavage and muss her hair while dancing, is fighting a turf war, Claire can tell. And this "go for it, he's your type" business is infuriating because, as she's suspected all along, there's no solidarity uptown. It's every girl for herself in this godforsaken city.

Claire takes a break and wanders over to the bar, where Baxter's systematic haranguing of the trust-fund girls has been so successful that Simon and associated drug traffic have taken their business upstairs, and for a few seconds, she sees Baxter unplugged. Baxter has a drink in his hand and he's staring across the bar with a perfectly slack face, his eyes dull, his expression inanimate. He's not musing, reminiscing, or deep in thought. Nor is he bored. He's just unplugged. Recharging. And the truth is, there's something profoundly sad about the sight of him sitting there.

"Hey," she says, settling into place beside him. "Wake up."

And he does. He literally comes to life. He turns in her direction, his eyes focus, and a light comes on behind them. Musculature firms up in his face, and he smiles his killer smile.

"The Poetry of War," he says.

"Excuse me?"

"I used to work down there" – he sweeps an unsteady hand at the financial district – "when the place was going *off*. Good men under me. Advertising men. Soldiers. We were making America great, you understand."

"So what happened?"

"Supply lines were cut by the enemy." He shrugs. "Our boys were left to twist in the wind. No homecoming parade. An Oliver Stone film if we're lucky. What the public doesn't understand is that a war was fought on American soil. It was a war and it was . . . *beautiful*."

"Wow. You've lost me."

"Well exactly. You're an uptown girl. A *Sex and the City* fan. The kind of person whose lifestyle we were fighting to upgrade, and we're ghosts to you now. The Repossessed. But see, the thing you're missing here is that we were truly touched by the hand of god back then. For three glorious years we lived in danger, and danger completed us. War completed us. Nothing quite like war to make you leap out of bed and eat your cornflakes every morning."

"Are you *serious*?" Claire shudders.

"Oh god yes." Baxter sighs. "But it's the poetry that kills me. Dot com was as epic and as stupid as Nam, but the thing with Nam is that it has a really cool narrative language. The language of Nam was crafted by poets, whereas all we got was the nine-to-fivers from *The Wall Street Journal*. So, you know. No magic. We don't get to put a weed up Charlie's ass or anything. All that work and we didn't rate so much as a frickin' voice-over."

"You're still in Saigon. No final missions for your sins."

An appreciative smile lights Baxter's face. "You're an angel!" he exclaims. "Let me buy you a huge fluffy cocktail!"

"Let me buy *you* a cocktail," Claire says coolly. "And while we're at it, maybe we should adjourn to the bathroom and do a few brisk lines of whatever it is we're snorting."

"Don't *go* there!"

Baxter could use a smoot break right now, but he's not carrying. He only has the DOA he's promised Troxler. Which is mad fat, admittedly, and would do him and Claire right through the night. The question, then, is one of commitment. Does he want to sign on for the full Claire experience, or continue to play the field? He has options, and hasn't even switched on his bunny-hunting engine. There are club girls all over the boat. Whacked out of their minds and highly tactile. And him with his specialist hands. He likes the fact that Claire is slightly older and somewhat out of place at this party, because there's nothing better than teaming up with a caustic outsider and pushing the envelope of dope-fueled commentary. The girl has wicked boots and dry wit (and an oversized tongue, he can't help noticing), so what to do?

"A vodka tonic, straight up," Claire tells the bartender.

"Johnnie Black on ice, lotta ice," Baxter says. "My man Nick is the smoot connection. Why don't we take our drinks and drag him off the dancefloor?"

"Sure. Sounds good." Claire smiles thinly.

Because it's not what she's angling for. The smoot is silver lining. What she really wants is a break from Sophie. A break from Sophie, a break from Marissa, a serious break from the chick in the hat, and her heart sinks when she hears that Nick is the smoot connection, because it means he *is* the party. And if he's the party, then everyone's invited. Which means literal facetime in a bathroom stall with Sophie, Marissa, Zebra Hat Girl, et al.

An interesting plateshift in the party dynamic: Baxter's disclosure that he's not carrying prompts Claire to lose interest in him. One hundred percent. It's as though he's turned to ash in front of her, she's that not interested. Which is a pity, because the DOA Baxter's carrying is a zillion times more powerful than any smoot she could hoover, and Baxter has merely been stalling commitment. Claire smiles thinly at Baxter, and Baxter senses the interest loss and smiles his riverboat casino full-house smile right back at her. Senator, thanks for playing. He takes his scotch and throws it back, his eyes never leaving Claire's face as he drinks, and then he slaps the glass on the bar and grins with good cheer. Lewinsky is off the air. The hunt is *on*.

Upstairs on the main deck, the hunt has been in full swing for the best part of an hour. Despite cramped and unpleasant bathroom conditions, Troxler, Lindy Minh, and Naoko have managed to hoover their way through a gram of smoot plus the glassine of low-grade coke Naoko was carrying. The high is as lush as a vindaloo curry in an Indian restaurant with carpeted walls. Troxler feels heat behind his eyeballs. He's sweating like a pig. Naoko has already shown him the green and red snake tattoo that starts on her buttock and winds its way around her breast, and her skin is slippery and shiny with sweat. The snake tattoo is her thing, apparently. She plays a cop in a soap opera, but has higher aspirations. A hitman or like a rogue cop's sultry girlfriend, for example. She has no problem with nudity. Nudity's *cool,* she sniffs and gasps. More tantalizingly, she's made Lindy Minh blush and make shushing noises about some girl-on-girl-on-guy experience they apparently had on vacation up the Cape, the end result being that Troxler is now seriously interested in scoring three tabs of DOA off Baxter.

"Aah, Jesus." He swallows and pants. "We should get out of here. We should *dance!*"

"Fuck yeah!" exclaims Naoko.

"Been here forever. Gotta see the skyline. Gotta get out," husks Lindy Minh.

"Red hot and wired!"
"Red hot and ready to rock!"
"Fuck yeah!"
"Outcoming! . . . outgoing, I mean!"
"Fire in the hole!"

And so they're out in the main cabin, buffeted by techno, staggering around under adverse conditions because the main cabin is solidly packed in the manner of indie rock clubs worldwide, and it's obvious the evening's sixties theme has some promotional connection with the band about to play. The dancefloor is standing room only. The bass player and drummer can be heard beneath the music, fine-tuning their instruments. The drummer's kick sound is huge. Lindy Minh and Naoko are chest-high in the crowd, but Troxler's tall enough to see the stage from the back of the cabin, and the bass player and drummer are these classic rock bitches. Rail thin. Fantastic racks. Heart-stoppingly beautiful. The bass player is wearing a silver-gray Emma Peel bodysuit with many zippers and buckles, and Troxler can tell, even from this distance, that her bone-white road-battered Fender Precision bass is vintage. And through a Sovtek Marshall. The rhythm section from hell.

The bar is overcrowded and impossible to breach, and Naoko and Lindy Minh have fought their way to the stairwell. They're heading downstairs to take a little air on deck. Troxler follows at a distance, torn between a smoot-fueled directive to find Baxter and transact some DOA, and his old Fort Lauderdale instincts to stick around and check out the band. He chooses the drug imperative, but indulges lushly in the thickness of crowd long enough to see the singer walk onstage.

And of course the evening now makes sense.

The singer is Demonica, a brief alumna of the Joss Wheedon vampire-slaying franchise, whose spinoff TV series was staked through the heart by the WB after six months of development. Which was a damn shame, as far as Troxler is concerned. Demonica was the goods, apparently. There was a retro premise behind her character (killed in the sixties, brought back to life, etc.), and she fronted this high-camp Barbarella-style girl act with loads of double-edged irony on account of it being monster rock performed by actual monsters, the point being that, according to the trades, she had talent to burn. Troxler seems to recall a music video in which Demonica and band pull off a note-for-note and frame-by-frame re-creation of the Bananarama music video of the Motown hit "Venus," and being impressed and aroused by the sight of Demonica in a tight red latex She Devil costume, tormenting souls in a Bosch- and Alighieri-inspired cavernous hellscape while hitting the high notes and working the stage like she'd been there all her life. Which she had, it turned out. And which is why her show was canceled.

Troxler can't remember the details, but it had something to do with that show *Felicity,* and the thirty-two-year-old production assistant who passed herself off as eighteen and scored some kind of development deal because of her "unique take on teenage life." The girl was ultimately busted, but not after unleashing the focus-grouping hordes on youth programming, the net result being the imposition of a kind of *Logan's Run* ceiling on female leads. Once you turned thirty, you were dead in youth television. And thus poor old Demonica had her show canceled and her contract paid out for the simple reason that she had been around the block a few times too many.

And here she is right now. In the red latex She Devil outfit. Which does and does not fit right in with the evening's sixties theme. Troxler's search engine is fully engaged, trawling for She Devil references in sixties pop culture (British sixties, if the guys in the Sgt. Pepper costumes provide a visual clue), but he's smoot- and coke-whacked and is having a hard time keeping his thoughts in order. He has to find Baxter. He has to keep the Asian girls engaged. His brother is downstairs, probably having a righteously boring and high-minded time, and Troxler is torn by equal-part desires to impress and unimpress his older sibling. And here's the meat. Here's the narrative engine. What Troxler wants, more than any pleasure on offer this evening, is to connect with Yojimbo in the way of their childhood. To make connection. To establish the heavy trenchfire, "cover me, I'm going in," solid, dependable line of communication they had when they were kids in Fort Lauderdale growing up under the old man. Troxler wants trust. He wants approval. And the thing with the slum lords and Baxter and Big Guy (and the drugs and the bunnies and the party on this boat); the terrible thing about this whole fucking evening is that he's 100-percent sure he's not going to get it. Three books, a byline, an Audi, a loft, and it's still not enough to win his family's approval. What do they want from him? What more could they possibly want? He sends money. He's paying for the old man's treatment and funeral. He set his mom up for life via an investment portfolio he pretty much had to insider-trade, so why is he the failure of the family? Can someone explain this to him? Could somebody possibly spare a moment and come up and maybe tell him why this is, because he's fucked if he can work it out himself.

Troxler's eyes are watering, and he sucks back a headful of smoot-bitter air. "So on to Babylon," he thinks. A club bunny has been giving him the eye, so he chisels his face into three-quarter profile and smiles wolfishly across the crowd. You work hard, you play hard. You take your baggage and dig the deepest hole. This city can be the business, or this city can be the loneliest place in the world: it's your call and you make it and you get on with it, okay? So spare him the trenches. Spare him the solid communication lines. Don't bother covering him because he's not going in.

Troxler hates smoking but loves bumming cigarettes off women, and he scores a Lucky Strike off the club bunny before heading downstairs. He's going to find Baxter, buy some drugs, and take a little air on deck. He loves his brother, but it's a speculative love. It peaks and troughs according to demand. And there's a shitload of activity in the marketplace this year, what with the old man tanking and his brother flying in, and the way that he sees it, there's a big fat premium on Troxler Love right now.

Which is the perfect time to sell up and get out.

A LITTLE AIR ON DECK

The weird thing about Zebra Hat Girl is that she's really hitting it off with the party promoter. It's all about dancing and she has shameless disco moves, the best one being this gratuitously sexy *Saturday Night Fever* maneuver in which she flails her arms either side of Nick's torso while swiveling down into a squat, and then back up again. Every now and then she puts her hands above her head, and twinkles her fingers like the ceiling's filled with stars.

And Nick is into it. Nick has gone the way of Kurtz in the Congo. Nick is a bona fide dancefloor king with Zebra Hat Girl as his partner, and he's pulling off the kind of synchronized hip- and groinwork you'd need to spend serious time at a dance academy to master. A crowd of teenage tranceheads, mostly guys, are crowding the floorshow, obviously turned on, and they're pumping their arms and whooing as Nick and Kirsten bump and grind. Baxter can't help but grin and shake his head at Big Guy's latest transformation. Apart from a memorable black-tie evening in the Plaza ballroom, where "Kurt," the Tulsan oil heir, had pulled off a brief but perfect waltz with a Budweiser heiress, he has no recollection of having seen Big Guy dance. In fact, he's pretty sure he recalls a late-night Burr McCracken conversation in which Big Guy had come out of his usual depressed funk to declare that "dancing was a venal practice for fags and desperate men with no self-respect." But hey. That was months ago. This is now. Claire signals Sophie, who leaves the dancefloor immediately, and they have to wait until the end of a frustratingly long drum-and-bass track before Nick and Kirsten disengage.

This does nothing to improve Claire's mood, and she stalks off to find Marissa, who has taken her second tab of dextroamphetamine and settled into a pleasant groove with Yojimbo out on deck.

"Smoot break," Claire announces. "Aren't you guys cold?"

"It is a little chilly," Yojimbo admits. "You want to go in?"

"We're checking out Battery Park City." Marissa giggles. "As in 'an exciting new concept in community living.' You know? Like, there's an entire community of city dwellers down in Battery Park—"

"—and we'll never, ever meet them. Smoot break," Claire says brightly. She's not messing around. "You coming?" she asks Yojimbo.

"I'll pass," he says easily. "It's been a while since I've seen a city this big. Go ahead. I'll catch you later."

"You want a drink?" Marissa asks. "What are you drinking? Amstel? You want another Amstel? I'll bring you an Amstel when I get back."

"That would be great." Yojimbo smiles.

And so he's on the lower deck by himself, enjoying his half tab, watching the city drift by. The band on the main level has monopolized the crowd, and he hears hoots of excitement as they launch into the opening bars of what sounds suspiciously like an old

Supremes song. No slouch on the perceptional front, he's already worked out that the evening's sixties theme is tied to some kind of band-related promotion, but he figures it's probably in tandem with a clothing label or film. The Sgt. Pepper uniforms are particularly bewildering. They're cheaply made and have the look of costume store about them, but the Scottish and/or Irish guys are wearing them with a grim sense of purpose, like they're expecting a rival party boat to appear on the Hudson so they can throw a few punches and kick a few heads. His thoughts drift across the water and are easily distracted by the appearance of his brother, who careens through the cabin doors, a cocktail in each hand and many plastic leis around his neck.

"So you're having a shitty time." Troxler grins and sniffs and winces. "Well gee whiz! Who would have thought?"

"Sorry?"

"I said to myself, 'Well fuck me, my older, wiser brother is in town. Five years since I last saw him, at what? Two phone calls a year? Thanksgiving thrown in if we're lucky?' And this is my fault too, I admit. Could have dropped a dime, but didn't. Because we're not close. My brother and I. Not close. Is the final analysis. Have a fucking cocktail."

"I have an Amstel on the way."

"*Have* a *fucking* cocktail!"

Naoko's low-grade coke has muscled in behind the wheel, and Troxler is driving with reckless abandon. He *wants* this conversation. He's keyed-up enough to floor the pedal of his thoughts.

"So I guess it's time we had the idealism/pragmatism debate," he says. "Get the old idealism/pragmatism debate out of the way so you can assume the moral high ground and maybe get yourself laid."

"The idealism/pragmatism debate?"

"I'll even let you start first. Does that sound fair?"

"I take it I'm playing the white side of the board." Yojimbo frowns. "I'm the idealist, right?"

"Oh certainly."

"And how come I get to be the idealist? I'm on record as throwing long for idealism? I don't think so. And what does the moral high ground have to do with me getting laid?"

"The moral high ground?"

"Yeah. You said the moral high ground would get me laid."

"I never said that."

"Yes you did."

"No no no. Oh. Yeah yeah yeah. I remember. You get the moral high ground by winning the . . . argument. And then you've won. I'll even let you win right now if you like. Okay? You've *won*. You've kicked my *ass*."

"Cool. So now I can get myself laid."

"Exactly! You've kicked my ass, so you can go fuck any bunny on the boat. Lighten up is what I'm trying to say."

"Lighten up is what Baxter said. I'm light. I'm fine."

"Hardly. I'm sensing bigtime disapproval here."

"Oh bullshit. What you're sensing here is twenty hours of transpacific plane flight. What you're sensing here is jetlag. Twenty hours from Sydney to New York, and they even made me sit through *Pearl Harbor*."

"Didn't see it. Any good?"

"No idea. I spent the whole time listening to this woman going on and on about the horror of alcoholism."

"Could have been worse. She could have gone on about the horror of cancer. Or the medical profession. Doctors are the enemy in Fern Grove right now."

"So I gather."

"But anyway."

"But anyway. The point is, Marty, I'm fine. I could have used a good night's sleep, but then I'd be sleeping. I'd be missing the nightlife, the disco, the boogie ah-ha."

"A certain grimness in your voice there."

"The younger generation at play."

"See, here's the thing that really pisses me off. You come in and it's like, my god, you're all grown-up like Doug Ross in the third season of *ER*. The Caesar cut, the gray hair overnight. And I'm not believing it. Time has not done this to you. This is the industry at work."

"I'm sorry?"

"This is Harvey Weinstein on the phone, dialing up a stylist."

"Of course. This is the *Love Boat* and I'm the featured guest."

"And here you are."

"And here I am."

"So let me ask you something. Quick question. Have you actually bothered to read any of my books?"

"I've read all your books, Marty. Mom even gets you to sign them before she sends them to me, remember?"

"No kidding. She sends them along."

"Uh, *yeah?* I get clippings, columns, all kinds of stuff."

"And you read them."

"Of course. What are you looking for here exactly?"

Troxler nails his cocktail and pitches the glass into the river. "What makes you think I'm looking for something?" he demands. "I'm not looking for anything. I-am-King-of-the-World!"

"Call it a hunch. An educated guess."

"King of the world, I tell you!"

"Oh, for god's sake. Come on. You're sensing bigtime disapproval. There is no disapproval. I'm sensing a shitload of anger, but maybe I'm overreacting. The point is, this evening has the weirdest vibe and all I'm saying is that we can talk it through if you want. You want to clear the air? Fine by me."

"Clear the air."

"Sure."

"You want to clear the air?"

"Well I sure as hell don't want to spend the next couple of months tiptoeing around you. I just got back. I'm happy to be back. We're both ripped to the gills. Let's chat."

"You're hardly ripped to the gills."

"Yeah, and you're doing this passive/aggressive routine and it's starting to piss me off. You got a beef? Come out and fucking square it."

"A beef, you say."

"I'm not going to ask you again."

Some kind of equestrian event is taking place in the remodeled Chelsea Piers, and the stadium lights are kitchen-white and blinding. For a few seconds the boat explodes in a spectacular halogen frieze, which the Troxler brothers respond to in different ways. Yojimbo leans into the light, looking up at the gray-on-black skyline, and in his dextroamphetamine-pleasant state of good cheer, it's like the Fourth of July. The sky is firework-lit in gentle celebration. Whereas Troxler's in the grip of a Nam strike. *Targeting flares above the DMZ! Incoming! Incoming!* The naked light means vulnerability, his platoon under fire, and he sweats through the attack, jarred by the heavy guitar- and basswork upstairs to the point where he actually collapses against the rail as the boat passes through the light and settles back into darkness.

"Was that great or what?" Yojimbo says.

Troxler is breathing heavily. He has contained the horror and no longer wants to chat. The casebook is closed. He's scored DOA off Baxter in front of Naoko, and floated the idea of some after-party partying, and Naoko is into it. Lindy Minh could be convinced. His brother is a lost cause. His brother is too fucking jolly to be believed. Ho ho ho. His fucking brother. Was that great or what?

"I have a beef," he says peevishly.

"Uh huh?"

"It's not particularly interesting, and I don't really care if we square it or not. But I'm at a bit of a loss as to what you're doing in New York."

"How do you mean?"

"Well it's obvious you don't want to go on any roadtrip."

"I didn't say that."

"Oh please. 'I'm not sure a roadtrip is such a good idea'? A lazy hundred, right now, says you're holding airplane tickets for both of us."

"I'll take that hundred. May I point out that it's four in the morning and we're sailing around Manhattan on a boat? It's not like I'm not playing along—"

"—and so you should. You've been gone for five years. Put a bit of distance between yourself and the old man, which is fine, except I'm the guy who gets to watch him do chemo. Mom's great, but she's usually potted by three, and it's got to the point where I just can't stand it. It's like a retirement village down there. All these fuckers from the Rotary moving slowly through the house. It's the saddest thing you've ever seen."

"And the old man is doing . . . what?"

"Chugging quarts of Four Roses and playing rubbers of bridge. Jaunty hat. Dressing gown. Chuckling over his cards."

"Right. So he's mellowed. The thing with this is—"

"—it's a *retirement village*! A home for *old insurance salesmen*! And here *you* are. Back in the picture. Jetting into town to escort me home like you're head of the fucking household or something. And it pisses me off. I don't need your fucking escort."

"Who said anything about escorting you?"

"This is Mom's idea, isn't it? She's worried I'm not going to show."

"Mom has nothing to do with it."

"Oh yeah? So how come you flew to New York? You don't want a roadtrip. Why didn't you blow me off and fly straight to Fort Lauderdale?"

"I flew to New York because I wanted to see *you*. Dumbass. Of all the people back home, you're the guy I wanted to see. Okay? So is there anything else you'd like to tell me?"

"Like what?"

"Like why you're all paranoid and passive/aggressive. Like what we're doing on the boat cruise from hell."

"Ha! You said you were enjoying yourself."

"Oh, I am. But seriously, what's up? We're not out here because of Dad, right? There's more going on than just Dad."

"In the sense of what? You and me?"

"You're the one with the beef. Dad playing bridge sounds very disturbing, but okay. We go down, we play some bridge with mellow Dad. You're mad at me because I haven't been around, but you haven't been around much either. Last time you were down was when?"

"Hectic publishing career. You do not get to guilt me on this."

"I'm not trying to."

"Of course not. You're the quiet achiever. The family's off the rails and here you are. So what if I say I'm not flying down with you? What if I say I still intend to drive?"

"Then drive."

"Yeah, but see it's *you* who's reneging. This is the thing I can't stand. You just can't do it my way, can you?"

"I *am* doing it your way. Cut to the chase, Marty. What's bugging you? Is there some trouble up here I should know about?"

"Nah. I'm just sick of knocking myself out, doing all this stuff, and it's never good enough, you know? I'm honest-to-god *making* it here, and it's not like anyone gives a shit."

"You're kidding me. All I ever hear is how well you're doing."

"Oh hardly."

"You're doing well, right? You're doing okay?"

"Shit yeah. It's not that. It's just . . . you know."

"What?

As Troxler wrestles this question, the black hole of conflict between Sophie and Claire has just turned supernova. They're in the lower-deck bathroom, attacking the smoot, and Claire is acutely aware that the whole thing is a farce. Six people jammed in a bathroom stall, with Zebra Hat Girl having a seizure of excitement? She's over it. With the noisy exception of Zebra Hat Girl, everyone is hoovering aggressively. Even Marissa is getting stuck in. So Claire demurely keeps her distance and makes smalltalk with the party promoter while she waits her turn. Nick has spread a generous amount of powder across the paper dispenser, so the hoovering is vigorous and time-consuming, and right out of the blue, right out of *nowhere,* the party promoter clears his throat and says—

"So. Sophie tells me you used to put out for cash."

And the blood drains from Claire's face because she doesn't know that Big Guy is joking. She has no idea that this, to Big Guy, is a wryly arch conversational gambit. She has absolutely no way of knowing that the required response here is a sleek, ironic head toss, some devilish eye sparkle, and, "why yes, I used to fuck guys for money all the time." How could she know? This simply doesn't happen in Claire's discerning circles. She's completely unaware that Big Guy is joking. All she knows is that the party promoter has just disclosed some unspeakably rude intelligence about her – rude intelligence attributed to, and no doubt from, that unscrupulous, husband-stealing Hamptons bitch Sophie – and the Mediterranean brown drains from Claire's face because not only does this rude intelligence have some basis in fact, but she's also misheard what

Nick has said. It's noisy in the bathroom. The tiles amplify the piglike sound of snuffling from the stall. And as far as she can tell, the party promoter has cleared his throat and said—

"So. Sophie tells me you used to put out for Cach*et.*"

—which is the deepest-hidden fear of Claire's existence. To even hear that word spoken aloud. Cachet. *Cachet Cachet Cachet!* For less than twelve months in the early eighties, Claire worked three nights a week for Sydney Biddle Barrows, the Mayflower Madam of tabloid fame, while putting herself through the Institute of Fine Arts, and it's a résumé glitch she's worked hard to eradicate. *Cachet!* A finishing school for uptown new arrivals. For nine or ten months in 1983, she consorted and partied with the Upper East Side circuit, and then she bade the agency farewell and went legit with a vengeance. Hence the gallery work. The tennis lessons. Hence husband number one.

But the whole time since, she's lived in fear of being busted. She looks nothing like the eighteen-year-old agency girl she was in '83, and most of the old crowd she consorted with has moved out of New York, but there was one time in Southampton . . . Jesus, she doesn't even want to *think* about it. Her husband somehow found out. And got all excited. Went on and on about "revitalizing their sex life," and "exploring this new development"—which was pretty much the end of husband number one. And now it's out. Her ex has dished postcoitally to Sophie, which means it's only a matter of time before The Circuit's crawling with the news. After all these years. My *god.*

Claire's thin smile tightens beyond breaking point. She stammers some kind of response to the party promoter, and Nick's eyes gleam with a sudden understanding. Well well well. Who would have guessed? Big Guy's interest in Claire has suddenly exploded through the ceiling. All kinds of lurid thoughts are flooding through his mind.

Except that Claire has just given herself over to the old *Glengarry Glen Ross* model of closure, and she briskly changes the topic of conversation and informs the party promoter that she's going to the bar. Would he like a drink? she inquires. Sure, Nick grins. Scotch, rocks. And Sophie? Another vodka tonic? Another vodka tonic, Soph? That would be great, be right with you, Sophie calls out from the stall.

And so Claire exits the bathroom, shaking with anger and blinking away the tears, acutely aware that the wealthy party guy from Florida now thinks less of her because of something she did nearly twenty years ago, for chrissakes, and the way she sees it, if they're going to treat her like a hooker, she may as well give them the full treatment. She crosses the dancefloor, straddles a barstool, and hits the bartender up for a scotch, two vodka tonics, and a spare cigarette if he has one. She hasn't smoked in years. The bartender is a young guy in a Moonlite Cruise uniform, slightly older than the boat-party crowd, but old enough to affect a "here's looking at you, kid" air of worldweary nonchalance as he lights Claire's cigarette and throws some liquor over ice, and as he takes her money and starts to make her change, his *Casablanca* routine gives way to youthful amazement as he watches Claire open her handbag, pull out a bottle of eyedrops, and squirt a liberal jet of fluid into two of the three drinks.

This, in fact, is an old agency trick. Unsanctioned by Cachet, but an easy way of dealing with unreasonable johns. In Claire's experience (which, it should be noted, was high-end and nonseedy and took place a long, long time ago when she was a completely different person), a liberal squirt of eyedrop solution in a cocktail is an effective way of taking an unreasonable john out of play— especially if the reason the john is unreasonable in the first place is because he's been bingeing heavily on powder drugs while working up the nerve to invite you to his party. Smoot is a relatively new thing, but back when cocaine was the upscale drug of preference, you could have a john in the bathroom within fifteen minutes of spiking his drink. It's a particularly vengeful form of retribution, because whatever they put in eyedrops plays such fantastic havoc with the internal plumbing of your average snowman that he will more than likely throw up and soil (Claire says "soil" instead of "shit") his pants simultaneously. She's only done it twice, but it was ugly both times. She pauses only to reapply lipstick and mark her vodka tonic with a kiss on the rim, and then she's off across the dancefloor with her cigarette and drinks, leaving a wide-eyed kid tending bar behind her.

Five minutes later, the kid's still shaking his head as he cracks an Amstel and pours some scotch over ice.

"So what do you think was in that bottle?" he asks.

"Could be anything." Troxler shrugs. "Liquid acid. Mescaline. You're the expert, what do you think?"

"Hard to say." Yojimbo frowns. "You said she squirted a full eyedropper into the glass. Whatever she's taking, it can't be all that strong. My guess would be some kind of liquid 'drine."

"And how come she only spiked two of the drinks? What's up with that?" the bartender wants to know.

"Process of natural selection." Troxler grunts. "You want to go back on deck or stay here?"

"Here's good," Yojimbo says.

"She was real pretty, too . . ." the bartender starts, but there's a brightness in Troxler's eyes that makes him stop. After a few uncomfortable seconds, he takes his damp cloth and scurries over to the far side of the bar.

"Okay, so back up," Yojimbo says. "You seem to think I'm attacking your work, but I'm not. The stuff Mom sent me seemed just fine."

"Oh please."

"You're reading too much into this, Marty. I have no clue about your work, because I have no clue what your work entails."

"But you think I'm slumming."

"No, you think you're slumming. This has nothing to do with me."

"So run this by me again? I'm writing NFL for *The Miami Sun Herald,* and this is honorable, tradesmanly work—"

"No. All I said was that I liked your sportswriting. I admired the craft."

"Whereas everything else is bullshit. Whereas everything else I've written is schtick."

"See, this isn't coming from me. I'm not saying schtick or bullshit."

"So what are you saying?"

"Aw Marty. C'mon. One minute you're telling me how you made a smart call and got a book contract, the next minute you're telling me that I don't take your work seriously. This is a weird conversation."

"All right." Troxler pauses to grind his teeth audibly. "We're going to play a game. I'm going to tell you what you think of my work, and you get to tell me whether I'm right or wrong. Does this sound fair?"

"Not really. But okay."

"Okay. Here's what you think. You think I'm slumming. You think that, with the exception of *Totally Wired* and a couple of *Esquire* articles, everything I've written is postmodern schtick wherein I undermine the integrity of my project by announcing to the reader that I have a thesis, but couldn't be bothered to follow it through—"

"I think this?"

"—and in doing so, I'm deftly killing expectation so that I

don't have to face the pressure of delivering Big Thought. Which is, you know, my job. Big Thought is my job, I'm syndicated out the wazoo, so the pressure of delivering Big Thought should be frightening. Which it is. But, see, here I am, deftly killing expectation by affecting this hip slacker pose wherein I say to the reader straight out: 'Big Thought? On this subject? A greater man would step up to the plate and hit this out of the ballpark for you, but me, I've just got out of bed. I'm too hungover to bother. But hey. Here's a tired and hungover guy's take on a Big Thought issue. Now get out of my life and leave me the hell alone.'"

"Wow."

"Wow indeed. And here's the thing. What you think, all the way from the other side of the planet with zero exposure to my pressure and deadlines, is that I should manfully shoulder the responsibility and read many newspapers and stoke the Big Thought fireplace so many Big Thought flames burn bright on the page. Am I right?"

"You're way ahead of me."

"It galls you to think that I have a perfectly good opportunity to pontificate, and I'm wasting it. That's what this is about, isn't it? It really pisses you off that I don't give a shit about doing a good job."

"But you do give a shit."

"No I don't."

"Yes you do. This conversation is rooted in the fact that you care so deeply, you've developed a whole rationale and philosophy to justify the fact that not doing a good job is okay by you."

"*Slumming,* I believe, is the word you're looking for here."

"I don't think you're slumming."

"Oh, but I am. Slumming with a vengeance."

"So slum quietly, Martin. Slum in righteous triumph. Do not feel the need, on my behalf, to articulate the deftness of your hip slacker pose. Just live the life. And be nice to Dad when we're down in Fort Lauderdale."

" . . . wait a second. You said you *don't* think I'm slumming?"

"As far as my understanding of what slumming means. Slumming is where you work below your ability. Like a surgeon patching bodies in a casualty ward. Or a concert pianist playing show tunes in a lobby. You're there in mitigating circumstances. You're broke and you need the work, or you're on holiday and are just sitting in for a couple of weeks because it's a good thing to do. There's invariably a transience in slumming—"

"Unless, of course, you're a trust-fund king."

"—which you're not. In my experience, people slum temporarily. You slum because you're trapped, or you slum out of altruism. Either way, what you're looking to do, in some cases quite desperately, is move on."

"I've moved on. I'm *there*."

"Right. So what you're doing is something else. You've built a career on the foundations of slumming, which means your infrastructure is weak. Your opinions are quick and easy. You threw some shit together and it took off and here you are, deftly killing expectation. Rolling out of bed and yawning at Big Thought."

"Yeah yeah. Punchline."

Yojimbo smiles and takes a swig of his Amstel. His brother's short attention span is nothing new.

"Try this on," he says. "Big Thought is heavy. Your slum foundations are weak. Your construction can't take the weight of Big Thought, because you've jerry-built the basement. If you attempt to build upward using Big Thought bricks and mortar, the weight is going to crush your foundations and kill you. So what do you do?"

"I have no idea."

"You build *light*. You build light because you can't build heavy. You'd like to build heavy, but you can't. You want the punchline? There's your punchline, Marty."

"That's it?"

"That's it."

"Senator, thanks for playing. So what, this is an original idea? No cribbing? No paraphrasing?"

"No. The thing that really gets me is that if you check out the big irony crowd, the people who make slumming an art form, what you see is people who fiercely believe that, if push came to shove, they could actually do the work. If they bothered to stop yawning, they could take Big Thought down."

"But this is not the case."

"Not if you haven't done the work. The fact that you're in some hotel lobby playing 'Memories' with an amused look on your face does not automatically mean you could front a philharmonic at Carnegie Hall. Slumming is a downward process, which is the thing nobody seems to realize. A concert pianist will spend hundreds of thousands of hours mastering the piano. 'Memories' in a Hyatt lobby is a picnic by comparison."

"It's 'Memory.' Not 'Memories.'"

"Oh, is it?"

"Yeah. Everyone makes that mistake. I hear what you're saying, though. It's like Baxter with his ironic dancing."

"Right. Baxter probably thinks that, if the stakes were high enough, he could dance like Michael Jackson. But you just know he never went to discos as a kid. Never sweated the moves out. Never got down. So what he does now is a deliberately shitty pisstake of dancing with this look on his face that says 'I could dance like Jackson, but why the hell would I?' You know what I mean?"

"Yeah yeah. This is good. So why can't I build heavy?"

"Because you'd have to do the work."

"And why don't I want to do the work?"

"Because you're lazy."

"Of course! That's it! You've cured me!"

"Go in peace, young man."

Smoot-whacked as he is, Troxler is aware that his brother is on to something. For all of its pop philosophy and neat turns of phrase, Troxler's forthcoming book is a tad Hunter Thompsonesque in the thesis department, in the sense that there is no thesis to speak of. There's a lot of histrionic writing on the nature of greed, as well as many colorful anecdotes charting the folly of wealth too easily earned, but, as is so often the case with Thompsonesque gonzo, the book's about the sizzle, not the sausage. Troxler's closing summation in *The Slum Lords* slinks away from any probing analysis of the New Cynicism, choosing instead to offer up a personal account of the research process, with much eye rolling and journalistic cliché. Heavy tunes were playing on Wall Street. The going got wired, so the wired turned pro.

Hunched over the bar, sucking scotch through his ice, the thing that bothers Troxler most about his brother's "rotten slum foundation" analogy is that it pretty much nails the essence of the New Cynicism, right down to the spectacular range of doomed second projects taken on by dot-com players in the months before the crash. Prior to April 2000, the way to get rich in e-business was to float your company on the Nasdaq and then pay someone else to make it work. Revenue projections were beside the point. Hysteria bankrolled the Silicon Alley gold rush, and when reality and share prices finally came back to earth, what you were looking at was a lot of fledgling companies with flimsy infrastructures and flawed business plans, many of which had acquired bricks and mortar holdings they were in no position to maintain. They built heavy and crumbled, crushing shareholders and trustees, and, in many cases, solvent blue chip companies with experienced management that should never have been acquired in the first place.

The connection between slumming and slum is obvious, of course, but the slum foundation metaphor has a visual appeal that fits Troxler's time-honored obvious/incredulous criteria. And the only reason he hasn't come out of his defensive crouch and taken his brother's head off in argument is that he knows he should have come up with this concept himself.

"Just out of interest, what do you think of 'the naughties'?" he asks carefully. "As a term for the decade. You know, eighties, nineties, naughties."

"It's okay." Yojimbo shrugs. "Why? Did you invent it?"

"Not really. I actually read it on a wall."

"As graffiti?"

"Yeah. In Tribeca. 'Welcome to the naughties.' Just down the block from where I live."

"Sounds kind of cutesy."

"Yeah, but it works. Naught equals zero. Naughty is wicked in a playful kind of way. Clinton was naughty. Whereas Bush is plain old-fashioned *bad*."

"Right."

"The dot-com thing was spectacularly naughty. And, like Clinton, it went largely unpunished. The guys in my book are still out there. A few of them have just scored these unbelievably huge consulting contracts, so the stage seems set for a full decade of naughtiness."

"You think Clinton went unpunished?"

"In the sense that he wasn't impeached. You don't?"

"God no. You get one shot at the presidency. The thing with Clinton is that he could do the work. He was a smart guy. He put his thousands of hours in. And he's ruined. You can blame the media all you like, but at the end of the day, he left the building under a big cloud of scandal, and he doesn't get to redeem. Your dot-com guys in consulting? Are in consulting. It's not quite like running a successful business, is it?"

"Yeah well. Money can't buy you love, sure, but it lets you park your yacht right up next to it. My guys are still driving Porsches. Eating out every night."

"And?"

"And what? If only we'd tried harder? If only Bill had kept it in his pants? Look, I'm just a guy who writes *about* stuff, okay? My paychecks aren't governed by whether we're on the right track or not. Shit happens. I cover it. The sillier. The better. I'm not in the business of supplying the answers. That's someone else's job."

"Some other Big Thought writing guy."

"All I'm asking is what you think of 'the naughties.' We're talking pop culture, here, not moral rationalism. This is a two-box multiple-choice question, and while I'm deeply impressed by your Ayn Rand/Alan Greenspan analysis of the ethical threat to the American workplace, all I'm asking you for is a fucking tick in a box."

"Regarding a piece of graffiti you read in Tribeca."

"A piece of graffiti is correct."

"Okay. So are there copyright issues where graffiti is concerned?"

"Good question. My people have done research, and apparently not. It's in the public domain. It's just one of those things where it needs a product to push it, which is why I'm sweating so hard on publication of *The Slum Lords*. If I can claim 'the naughties' and make it part of the vernacular, then it's hookers and blow from there on in."

"Wasn't your first book about the guys who did that?"

"Yes it was."

"And didn't you spend a lot of time ridiculing those guys in print?"

"Yes I did. May I ply you with alcohol? Buy you another drink?"

"I'll get it. You want a scotch?"

"I'll take a beer. Hey listen. I take your point on Clinton. And I really like your 'slum foundation' thing. For a man of science, you're pretty handy with the language."

"Take it. Make it your own."

"Ha!" Troxler emits a rueful bleat of laughter. "I *wish*. Too late for that, bro. We rushed the book through production. Too much of a hurry to get 'the naughties' into print."

"Oh really?"

"Yeah. Too much of a hurry to trademark the decade."

"That's too bad."

"Oh hardly. I'd take a trademark or catchphrase over Big Thought any day. More money in broad, populist catchphrases by a factor of, oh I don't know, several hundred percent—"

"In which case," Yojimbo says, "this round's on you."

SHAGPILE

Demonica's band is called Shagpile, and this makes perfect sense to Baxter. He's right at the front of the stage, manic on smoot, having such a good time that people are keeping their distance. Zebra Hat Girl is up there as well. She's taken her hat off and is waving it around, and Claire and Marissa are taunting her cruelly from the back of the cabin. Sophie has disappeared and Nick the party promoter is strangely subdued.

Shagpile's repertoire appears to consist of classic hits from the sixties, played with seventies zeal. It's loud on the main deck, and the girls can really shred. The guitarist in particular has this Johnny Thunders thing going where she splays her legs and coaxes masturbatory riffs from her low-slung Les Paul with requisite facial mugging: a dead ringer for Thunders in the hair department, but little else as Thunders was a short, ugly guy, whereas the Shagpile guitarist is tall and quite stunning. All the band members are quite stunning in fact, which is why Baxter's up front and grinning like a fiend.

By the time Yojimbo and Troxler turn up, Shagpile are halfway through their set. The chemistry between band and crowd is special. The room, the acoustics, the energy, the occasion—the whole thing has come together in one of those rare gigs where the band performs its songs instead of playing them. Right now, they've shifted decades and are powering through an unabashedly sexual version of Thin Lizzy's "Boys Are Back in Town." Yojimbo checks out the throng of gangly dance boys competing for Demonica's attention by yelling "boys are back in town" in the chorus as though they might, in fact, be the boys in question, and he can't help wondering whether any of these guys were alive when this song was first released. The answer would be not, he suspects.

Marissa sees him and gives him an enthusiastic wave, cheerily oblivious to her earlier offer of a beer. She's pinned her hair up in a messy bun, and is grooving unselfconsciously to the music without any of the irony his brother and Baxter are laying thick on the dancefloor. Now that he's bummed his first smoke, Troxler continues to hit women up for cigarettes, and he's perfected the Tab Hunter sleazy beefcake approach right down to the old man's technique with the lighter. (He bum-puffs the cigarettes when he gets them, however. A childhood bout of asthma has instilled a fear of deep inhalation, so he tends to draw lightly and exhale clouds of smoke. It's a sore point. Big Guy once accused him of "smoking like a girl," and they nearly came to blows.) Claire is also smoking, but with zero irony or unselfconscious charm. She looks distressed and a little bit queasy, so Yojimbo leaves his brother and makes his way to the back of the cabin.

"Are you okay?" he asks her.

"Uh huh." Claire shrugs. "Why?"

"No reason. Let me check your pulse for a second."

He takes Claire's hand and runs his fingers across her wrist, and Claire's thinking, *yeah yeah, stupid hit on me routine,* as he finds her pulse and determines that it's steady. The liquid 'drine she squirted in her drink was obviously of the mild variety. Or vitamins. Probably a B-shot. He releases her arm and smiles sheepishly.

"You okay there?" Claire asks him.

"Just checking. Where's your friend?"

"Soph? I think she went to the bathroom."

"Right."

Once again, the wall of smalltalk. Insurmountable. Yojimbo drinks his Amstel and watches the band while Claire keeps her eye on the party promoter. Mr. Big Shot from Miami. He's standing next to the Letterman guy in the middle of the dancefloor, and it's been what, half an hour since she spiked his scotch? He should have lost his shit (literally) long before now. She appropriates another cigarette from Marissa's pack and glares daggers at Big Guy for forcing her to smoke. The bastard. The band is too loud and the guy scene is way too little league, and the significance of the chick in the She Devil suit with rubber pitchfork has not been lost on her, as this is definitely hell.

"Hey everybody, look outside!" Demonica purrs. "The Statue of Liberty! The greatest gift-shop souvenir on god's great earth! And we're gonna play a song—a New York song for *New York Fucking City*!"

The guitarist rips into the dinosaur metal chords of "No Sleep Till Brooklyn" while the drummer lays down a Zeppelin beat, but it's all a clever ruse. The song they actually play is the old Kiss crowd-pleaser "Rock and Roll All Nite (and Party Every Day)," which sets the audience off in a frenzy of moshing. There's beer all over the floor, and the mosh-induced heavy rocking of the boat has taken its toll on the weak of stomach. The deck is lined with club kids throwing up into the water. It's a hot and funky nausea fest, and the thing Claire doesn't understand is how the party promoter can still be out there on the dancefloor.

Big Guy's not sure either. He feels sick, which is unusual. The vigorous gym work, combined with his astronaut-like constitution, tends to factor sickness out of the day-to-day equation. Sickness is for wimps. And yet these awful flushes of queasy liquid in his bowels have a subversive quality he just can't shake, and he's finding it hard to maintain focus on Nick. This is going to sound weird, but Big Guy's engine for Nick is built around the musculature of Nick's pelvis and ass. Nick is all about the body. The self-effacing routine is nothing more than window dressing for the real motivation, which is dancefloor-based. The core of Nick's being (Big Guy has discovered) revolves around a signature ass-driven rhythm – kind of like stamping – in which a trancelike thought plateau is achieved through the repetition beats of techno. It's a spiritual thing. Big Guy has been channeling enlightenment via Nick's ass-driven rhythm, and even now on the dancefloor, watching the band, he's wanting to experience higher consciousness through this physical mantra. Except he can't, because he's on the verge of shitting his pants. He wants to stamp, but he can't stamp. His bowels are full of liquid and his sphincter muscles are aching horribly, and he's in the middle of a fucking mosh pit for chrissakes! With all these dead-eyed trance kids crashing into or around him. The fabric of Nick starts to slowly unravel.

Troxler can tell that something is wrong – the sweat is standing out on Big Guy's forehead as he swats away the club kids who stumble into range – but his usual fascination with his friend's transformation technique has been completely blown out of the water by the band.

Shagpile are fantastic.

Shagpile are sex on mag wheels. He can't believe the WB let these girls out the door. Everything about them is perfect. Demonica is perfect. The bass player is perfect and can slap. The guitarist is a serious babe who plays searing lead like Stevie Ray Vaughan. The drummer is hot and hits as hard as Dave Grohl. It's a total package. And it's a shame Big Guy's behaving so strangely, because this would be the perfect time to have him value-add his dance persona and morph into a music producer or A&R dude.

Outside, the Statue of Liberty glows and pulses. The ferry has turned at the Chelsea Piers and trawled back down the Hudson, and is presently circling Liberty Island, where the statue is like this huge visual effect. It looks like a monster Hollywood prop made of cardboard and papier-mâché. Neon green and cobalt blue. Shipped in especially for the party.

Troxler feels young and nostalgic for youth, while Zebra Hat Girl, who is seventeen and lives at home with her parents in Fort Lee, feels grown-up and overwhelmed by the crowd. The smoot she's hoovered is her first real taste of the lush high lifestyle, and, as is always the case, the first taste is the strongest. She's in sensory heaven. She thinks Nick is cute and she thinks Troxler is cute and she thinks Baxter is cute and *funny*. Some of the stuff Baxter was saying? *Fun-ny*. Her body is warm with sweat and her leather pants feel heavy and stiff, and the band lighting is a vibrant mix of deep reds and deep purples. She's out of her depth in every direction. Her big priority is to not blow her cover and let slip that she lives in Fort Lee instead of Jersey City. Jersey City has a tougher cachet than Fort Lee, and she's desperate for Baxter and crowd to perceive her as one of those savvy Jersey City chicks who, you know, do it with guys. The real estate women frighten her, as do the severely corporate Asian girls, and she wants to talk. The smoot has made her chatty and she has all these things she wants to say, but it's probably safer to keep on dancing. So dance she does. And as she dances, she makes flirty/funny/sexy body contact with Baxter, brushing up against him and stroking his cheek with her fingertips, and she'd like nothing more than to call a time-out and tell him *everything*. Her hopes, her dreams, her teenage life in Fort Lee.

And it's heartbreaking to watch, because Baxter's bunny-hunting engine is fully engaged. His predator engine. He's sized up the boat and assessed the level of play, and come to the conclusion that the only black chip game worth talking about is right in front of him. He wants Shagpile. He's crackling with form and wants a high-stakes challenge, and it doesn't get any better than this. The girls are dressed like fetish superheroes and are flaunting sex shamelessly, and the name of the band is invitation enough. Like waving a red flag at a bull. He's blissfully unaware of the Demonica/Buffy connection. All he knows, in his booze-and-DOA-fueled state, is that the bunny in the devil suit is putting out like she wants it, and C. C. Baxter is the man for the job.

And then there's Zebra Hat Girl. Getting all proprietorial and bumping up against him on the dancefloor, and it's too fucking sad to be imagined. Off her tits on smoot. Waving her stupid hat around. He's pretty sure no serious damage has been done so far, but she's cramping his style and he needs to lose her in a hurry, so he moves in close and shuts her down.

"Hey, Kristen. Kirsten. Whatever your name is," he bellows.

"It's Kirsten. And you're Greg, right?"

"Yeah yeah. Listen. This isn't a barn dance. We're not in the country."

"Sorry? What?"

"You're dancing like a cowgirl. Not a good look."

"Like a cowgirl?"

"Yeah, you dumb bitch. You're fucking line-dancing. You want to line-dance, go find yourself a fucking barn. You're embarrassing me."

"Oh." Zebra Hat Girl stops dancing.

Baxter continues with random abuse, piling on the sarcasm about her big hair and squeaky pants and how Uzi's the kind of zoo where bridge-and-tunnel girls are allowed in only to enhance the irony of the theme, but it's like he's mouthing words at her. All she can see is the meanness on his face. His cheerful mask has slipped away, and he just looks evil. Cold-eyed and sweat-drenched and thin-lipped and evil, and then he snaps out of it and goes back to whooping it up in front of the band.

And it's devastating.

Zebra Hat Girl goes to pieces. She's outside, sobbing into her cell phone, trying to get her sister on the line. She's leaving messages and paging and leaving messages and paging, and of course her sister's not answering because they've had this huge argument in the downstairs bar at Uzi. The terrifying thing for Kirsten is that she's really gone out on a limb by following Baxter to this party. She's not even sure why she went. Independence, maybe. An adjunct to the newfound confidence she feels whenever a nightclub bouncer cards her on her sister's ID and lets her in because she might be twenty-two. She still has puppy fat and is curvaceous in the Halston knock-off, and the funny thing is that she's a far better demographic fit on the boat than Troxler's crowd could ever be. It's a young person's party. If she had been dancing farther back, she would have heard the Wurtzel girls pouring scorn on Baxter's hairline, on the fact that his salon tan defies the range of human fleshtones.

As it is, she leaves messages and pages until she's all paged out, and then she needs a drink because the phonework and sobbing has been so intense. Where was she? Oh yeah. *Wow*. There are these cute guys on deck in completely wack clothing, like marching band clothing? Pouring vodka into these strange little cans?

"What are you drinking?" she asks the cutest guy.

"So here's the deal," Baxter's saying. "We kill Nick. Love the guy. No offense. But what we need right now" – he sweeps his hand stage-ward – "is a new guy with serious music biz connections—"

"I feel sick." Big Guy grunts.

"—unless Nick is connected, which I'm sure you are, but what I'm thinking is that you're the wrong *type* of connected. We need a rock god, not a dance god. Am I right? Legend?"

"A rock god would be handy." Troxler sniffs.

"I'm actually thinking we should all be rock gods. We should be like scouts from Sony Music or something. And you know what I can't believe? I can't believe you gave me shit about that business-card idea. That was a good idea."

"That was a stupid idea," Troxler says.

"Oh yeah? If we had Sony cards right now, we'd be set."

"Dudes. I don't think you understand." Big Guy groans. "I'm sick. I'm a minute away from shitting my pants kind of sick."

"I didn't think you got sick."

"No way can you get sick." Baxter shakes his head emphatically. "This is *not* the time to get sick. This is a once-in-a-lifetime opportunity, I'm telling you."

"I've always wanted to say that. *A once-in-a-lifetime opportunity*."

"Hey. Fuck you."

"Feel really fucking awful."

"You check out those girls? You want to come up the front for a second?"

"Buddy boy." Troxler smiles.

"Oh, come *on*. I can't believe we're having this conversation."

"No offense Bud, but the Handsome Devil chick is doing it for me. I could use a TV connection right now."

"You're killing me."

"Nothing's stopping you from having a rock fest. Have a rock fest. Knock yourself out."

"It's the *setup*, you asshole. The setup is beautiful. Four girls, four guys—"

"—you're really not paying attention, are you?"

"Read my lips," Big Guy says. "Not playing. Count me out."

"You heard the man. Not playing."

"Are you guys shitting me or what?"

Baxter takes a furious breath. When he's like this, there's no stopping him. He pulls his keyring out of his pocket and hefts the heavy Porsche medallion so it jingles in his hand.

"Okay," he says. "My Boxster's back on the table. Same deal as last time. But you gotta be in it . . . to win it."

"Oh, you suck!" moans Big Guy. "You suck a yard of Satan's cock, you evil motherfucker!"

"Gotta say, Preston. You pick your moments." Troxler grins.

Baxter owns an olive-green Porsche Boxster, which he garages in SoHo and hardly ever drives. A couple of months ago, after a big night of black-tie partying, he wagered it in a kamikaze bet that the three Whitney sisters were fair game for an approach. The fact that they were either underage, engaged, or had a serious, family-approved boyfriend didn't even make the preliminary discussion. "Kurt" from Tulsa had pulled off his perfect waltz; Imogen, Tiffany, and Chloé Whitney were the logical next progression. Adjusting his cufflinks while Troxler passed out the cigars, Baxter outlined the terms of competition. Winning would be determined by the level of liaison achieved. Gentleman's honor, etc. etc. In the event of Troxler or Big Guy taking out the gold, he'd exchange his Boxster for the trade-in cash value of Troxler's Audi or Big Guy's Jeep Cherokee.

"So what happens if you win?" Troxler had asked.

"I have the shatishfaction of winning," Baxter replied.

It goes without saying that a lot of smoot had been snorted in various Plaza bathrooms, and that the whole affair was an unparalleled disaster. The evening was so embarrassing, in fact, that Troxler and Big Guy secretly agree that Baxter deserves to lose his Porsche, and they've vowed that if he's stupid enough to ever bet the thing again, they're going to take it from him as a matter of principle. He can afford a new one. It's no big deal.

"Same terms as last time?" Troxler arches his eyebrows.

"Uh huh."

"The shatishfaction of winning."

"Yesh."

"Okay, this time you're giving me your keys in advance. I swear, Greg. We do this and I win, I will take your fucking Porsche."

"Son of a bitch," moans Big Guy.

"So what, you want to award some kind of point system across the hierarchy of the band? What happens if we all score?"

"Negative on the hierarchy. We'll just wind up hitting on the chick in the devil suit. Go with the flow. See what happens."

"Gimme your keys."

"Manners."

"Gimme your fucking keys."

"Guys." Big Guy growls. "I'm in, but I gotta go to the bathroom. My shit is melting. I gotta regroup."

"No problemo. How are we for party food?"

"Three tabs of DOA. Big Guy?"

"A quarter of smoot if we're lucky. Hey Baxter. Love you like a brother."

"And?"

"I'm taking your Porsche. You know that."

Baxter claps a hand on Big Guy's massive shoulder.

"Of course I do, Emmett. Of course I do." He smiles.

Downstairs in the lower-deck bathroom, Sophie has been throwing up for the best part of an hour. She's hysterical with sickness. It came on so suddenly, and it's all she can do to sit on the can without shaking. Her makeup is ruined and she wants to go home, but of course she can't go home because she's on this boat with these hustling drug dealer types, and she's not at all sure how she got here in the first place. Like Zebra Hat Girl, Sophie's never tried smoot before, and she was rushed off her feet by the whole experience. *Never again,* she vows. She's sick of going to these meat market nightclubs and staying out all night while Claire truffles for husbands, and she can't wait for Claire to shack up with some guy so she can get back to her own life, which is quiet and bookish and sensibly organized. She's a strategic planner at Barnes and Noble dot com, and has been fighting to retain her job since the market crashed last year. She jogs in Central Park, has a bustling social register, and two cats. The last thing she needs is a mandatory Friday night club trawl—

Oops! Here it comes!

Oh *god.*

She's spent the whole night charming the party promoter. Listening to his nonsense while talking Claire up. "You should speak to my friend Claire," she's urged at least a dozen times. "You two sound like you have a lot in common." The party promoter is a little bit sleazy (and his friends are atrocious), but he's the kind of type-A personality she knows Claire's into. And he's been to MIT, which is almost Ivy League.

If she can just get Nick to give Claire his number, she can alleviate the guilt about that summer in the Hamptons. Which was unfortunate, but just happened, as these things tend to do. If she can just get Nick's number and pass it on to Claire, she's going to call it a night and walk away from this madness. Was she actually kissing the party guy back at that nightclub? *Never again!*

Oh no!

The bathroom door kicks open as Sophie maneuvers in the stall, and she hears male voices as she spasms and unloads.

"—hey ladies!"

"East Side girls, never look so fine—

"Hey ladies! Anyone in here?"

—never look so fine, never look so fine."

"Well there you go. A straight shot. Okay Big Guy, make it so."

"Thank god."

"Lotta guys smoking crack back there."

"Yeah. Would have thought the ladies would be packed. No wait! There's someone here!"

"Oh yeah. Sorry miss! Don't mind us! It's an emergency!"

"Keep smoking!"

"So you're going to burn those bunnies you brought along? I liked the chick in the red leather jacket. I liked the chick in the boots."

"The chick in the boots is a bitch."

"The chick in the boots is a *hooker*."

"Say what?"

"The chick in the boots is a hooker. Hang on." A disgusting burst of stall noise as Big Guy dumps his load.

"Ew!"

"You okay in there?"

"Hang on." The noise is repeated in a different key.

"Wow. You really are sick."

"You are one sick puppy."

"You okay in there, Big Guy?"

Paper-dispensing sounds. Some tentative wiping. A fabric rustle and a fly being zipped. Big Guy is on his feet, breathing heavily. The toilet flushes and the stall door squeaks open.

"Where were we?" he pants.

"The girl in the boots is a hooker? I thought she was in real estate!" Baxter exclaims.

The squeak of a faucet. Big Guy's washing his hands.

"Oh yeah. I was making conversation and said something like, 'I hear you put out for money.' And you should have seen the blood drain from her face."

"No way!"

"Uh, hate to say this, but it's very possible her reaction might be attributed to the incredible fucking rudeness of your question."

"Sorry dude. You can always spot a hooker."

"You can always spot a hooker? I'm using the singular, not the plural here."

"Sure. But I'll clue you in later. Right now there's this rich Midwestern dickhead who's about to seriously regret betting his Porsche on a bunch of rock bunnies."

"Fire in the hole!"

"We got fuck-all smoot. If I'd have known Buddy Boy was going to throw his Porsche away, I'd have rationed it. But since I didn't, I don't."

"How are you feeling?"

"Fucking awful. We got enough for two big lines each. And then the DOA."

"The DOA?"

"Level playing field, gentlemen. You know the drill."

"You're an intense guy, Big Guy. But I love you."

"Fire in the hole!"

Upstairs, the Shagpile guitarist, bass player, and drummer are singing—

> *"Forever and ever, you'll stay in my heart,*
> *and I will love you, forever and ever, we never will part,*
> *oh, how I love you, forever and ever, that's how it must be,*
> *to be without you, would only be heartbreak for me . . ."*

—while Demonica belts out a gospel-style *"Oh answer my prayer"* over the top of their perfect Motown tri-harmony. It's their last song. The ferry has circled Liberty Island, trawled back around the Battery and up into the East River, and is churning along past the Lower East Side. For some reason, the night has turned misty.

The Manhattan Bridge is somewhere ahead, and all you can see of Brooklyn is the cheesy neon clockface of the Williamsburgh Bank Building. The ferry windows have fogged over, and Zebra Hat Girl has lost her hat. She's on to her third can of Red Bull and vodka, and a handsome kid with Oasis hair and sideburns has his hand down the front of her strapless Halston top. The Sgt. Pepper crew are in various stages of undress, and you can see now that they're not Scottish or Irish, but merely tough local kids with theatrical 'tude who are drunk to the point of singing prep school cadence.

Lindy Minh and Naoko are back on the main deck, and Lindy Minh can't *believe* she's missed Demonica's performance. She's on the tips of her toes, craning her neck to see the band while emitting a stream of Buffy factoids and lore, and Claire has snatched Marissa's cigarettes and stalked outside to smoke them. Marissa finishes her beer and wanders outside in grudging solidarity while Shagpile closes the set with a big rock finish, and there's something oddly distinctive about the drummer's technique. Yojimbo's sure he's heard her before. But where?

He mulls this over as the house lights come on. The crowd are clamoring for an encore in a self-absorbed way, but are too drunk to actually applaud. The lush high crowd. Way past their bedtime. And here comes Troxler, Baxter, and Big Guy, yee-hahing and hollering with conspicuous energy, their glassy eyes as fogged up as the windows. Baxter looks particularly awful. His thinning hair is unkempt, and there's a savage confidence in his approach that just shouldn't be there given the unsteadiness of his gait across the dancefloor. In the harsh light, the three e-biz professionals look like off-duty cops or corrupt politicians. Bad men. They walk right past Lindy Minh and Naoko, climb up onto the stage, and squeeze around the back of the Sovtek amps, and Yojimbo can hear them behind the black stagecloth.

Hustling their way into the Shagpile dressing room.

THE SLUM LORDS

Big Guy and Troxler have palmed their DOA, and Troxler has spent a large part of the evening doing the old Francis Bacon trick of taking his drink to the bathroom and pouring it into the sink. He's in better shape than Big Guy and way more sober than Baxter, who has no self-control where drugs are concerned.

Big Guy's form is iffy, so Baxter takes point. The backstage area is a sealed-off section of the ferry, and it's big enough to accommodate ten rows of plastic seating. The chairs are strewn with band paraphernalia, and there are road cases and luggage stacked up in the walkways. The overall feel is late-night airport. The weariness of transit. The girls are slumped in their seats, removing makeup and sipping house booze out of plastic cups, and there's hardly any security behind the stagecloth. Just a couple of roadies and a guy from the label. The label guy is doing his routine, but he's obviously a junior flack minding bottom-rung talent. His voice has the faintest gay cast as he works the backstage vibe.

"911? You *killed* them!" he's saying. "*People* dying out there!"

Baxter picks up on this and cranks his gay voice on approach. Baxter's gay voice is razor-sharp, but he tends to bludgeon you with it. Once he's in the groove, it's bitchy queenspeak all night.

"Shush your mouth, girlfriend," he tells the label guy. "Nurse Betty has *arrived!*"

The label guy swings around, and Baxter's all over him. The guy has no chance. It's like that scene in *The Hustler* where Paul Newman touches the break and says, "Didn't leave you much" to Jackie Gleason, whereupon Gleason goes, "You left enough," and promptly sinks the whole table. Baxter and Troxler now have context to riff with, and they immediately start to parody the label guy's tone.

"You girls were fabulous!" Troxler husks. "I was in heaven."

"You *killed* me. I'm in heaven too."

"911? We're dying here!"

"Guys. You shouldn't be backstage," the label guy starts. "This area's for the band only—"

"Put a sock in it, Dorothy," Baxter growls.

"Ooh! The welcome wagon!" Troxler has discovered the band's drink rider. It's pretty humble, but the girls are at that point in the tour where the wild nights are long behind them. He sifts through the bottles of low-cal soda and water, and unearths the lone quart of Jim Beam.

"Mind if we join you?" he asks the guitarist.

"Help yourself." The guitarist shrugs.

Troxler gives her a quick burst of three-quarter profile and tosses the bottle to Big Guy. A team move. Big Guy has no line in clever gay mimicry, because Big Guy is a gym rat homophobe who lives in fear of being gay. He loves locker rooms. Loves to walk around naked. Would kill you in a second if you suggested there was more to his enthusiasm for the male physique than merely clinical interest, and he catches the bottle and hunts around for plastic cups.

"Thanks dude," he says offhandedly.

"Here. Let me," Baxter says to Demonica, and amazingly enough, she lets him unzip her costume. He gets to handle the latex, and can feel the second wave of DOA kicking in. The gay ruse is a good one, he thinks, swallowing hard. *Book of Ruses. Ruse Book. Big Red Book of Bonking,* as he finds the zipper and peels the latex from her shoulders.

"Your horns . . . give me the horn," he gasps.

"They're cute, aren't they? The SFX guys did them for the music video."

Baxter makes a gargling noise of affirmation.

"Hand me that towel, will you?"

Demonica's down to her microbra and G-string, but her changing room demeanor is hardcore NBA. She's a journeywoman. Her touring résumé runs the full gamut of performance, from singing backup with REO Speedwagon through to acoustic gigs at Lilith Fair, and she's seen more than her fair share of backstage hustlers. She's also done Hollywood, which means she's been exposed to a higher caliber of hustle. For a white-hot six months, she was in the box, careerwise, and then the phones stopped ringing and the electric smiles were switched off, and what she saw was a lot of one-night-stand hostility. Guys like Baxter saying, "Oh, you're still here?"

The deal with the cruise is contractual blowback from Warner. The final show in a reduced tour for the CD. After this, Demonica goes back to being Sarah Figgis from St. Paul, Minnesota. Screenwriter husband. House in Venice Beach. She's given it her best shot, and the band rocked the fucking Hudson tonight. The Statue of Liberty was a nice touch. A career highlight. A motif of the American Dream she's been chasing for fifteen years. She towels herself off while the drugged-up, grinning guy behind her has an intensity rush with her latex costume, and she can't help smiling at the idiocy of these things.

"Catch," she says, and throws him the towel. Then into a body-hugging Gaultier creation. She usually wears her sweats after a big night onstage, but the label has organized some kind of after-party bash, and she figures she may as well see her contract out in style.

"So what brings you backstage?" she asks Baxter. "You seem a little older than my core audience of computer nerds and frat boys."

"Homage," says Baxter, French-accenting the *age*. "This here is an authentic complimentary lighter from, uh" – he pauses to read it – "the Mondrian Hotel on Sunset Boulevard, and I have come backstage in the manner of your standard Pink Floyd fan to hold its flame aloft."

"How sweet."

"Except we're experiencing problems with the technology. The flint wheel is not producing fire. We have no fire. We are fireless."

"It's probably childproof."

"Well then. No homage for you. Something from the rider, perhaps? A drink? Some M&Ms?"

"I'll take an Evian if you can find one."

"Ah. An Evian. Evian spelled backwards is *naive*."

"You don't say."

"Makes you wonder what they're selling you."

"Water, I think would be the answer there. So are you getting me an Evian or am I getting it myself?"

"Let me confer with the help. Hey Big Guy! Who are you this evening?"

"This evening?" Big Guy pauses to think.

"How about 'drinks waiter'? How does 'drinks waiter' sound?"

"Like you're walking to St. Louis from now on, you fuck."

"Yeah yeah. Pitch me an Evian, will you?"

"Get it yourself. I'm on plastic cup patrol."

"Cups are here," the bass player says. She and the guitarist are new to the scene. They're in their early twenties and were scouted from the indie metal band they formed in college. In many ways, they defy belief. They're classic laid-back, weed-smoking California girls who are not only heart-stoppingly beautiful, but have that rare intuition where they can shred pretty much any rock style out there, and it breaks Demonica's heart to wave goodbye to this band, because it could have gone the distance. Could have been so much more than a stupid TV show.

"—happens. What can you do?"

"Not a damn thing," Troxler says. "I remember the episode you guys were in, too. Bit hazy on the plotline, but seem to recall the full vampire treatment. Bulging foreheads and shit."

"That was badass," the guitarist drawls. "Except it was like we were not in the scene? At all? Like maybe ten seconds? We had dialogue, and they cut it all out. It was *baffling*, you know?"

"No shit." Troxler has slewed the gay voice into weary backstage rockspeak. True to form, the guitarist is dismantling a cigar and has a bag of weed beside her. Frightening-looking stuff. Infantry green, with a high bud-to-leaf ratio.

"So what happens now?" he asks.

"Now as in right now, or now as in the future? Right now, I'm going to smoke this blunt and go to some party and get wasted on the Warner tick. They owe us, man. And we're collecting."

"No shit." *Baxter, your Porsche is mine*. Troxler smiles.

"Dude, you have a choice of Jim Beam or Jim Beam," Big Guy cuts in. "Or wicked-fucking-bud! Jesus! Where the hell did you get that?"

"Washington State."

"You fly around with that shit?"

"You kidding? The air travel stopped when the show was canceled. This is a bus tour, dude."

"I'll take a Jim Beam," Troxler says peevishly. "Any ice?"

"What's your friend's name?" Big Guy points at the bass player.

"Kim."

"Hey Kim—you know if there's any ice?"

"Classic bass player name."

"Excuse me?"

"Kim. Classic bass player name. Check out any band with a female bass player and the short odds say her name will be Kim."

"Whatever you say, man." The guitarist rolls her eyes.

Troxler's generalization has missed the mark because he's pitched a decade wide. He's thinking Kim Deal, Kim Gordon, but of course those women and their bands are old seadogs to the Shagpile guitarist. She's into new shit. Not old shit. And it's like, can somebody tell her why these suit-wearing dudes are invading her space right now?

"Some ice over here." Kim points to a bucket.

"On it."

"You want a drink?"

"Nope."

"O-kay." Troxler's cheeks burn as he follows Big Guy to the ice.

Kim is still in her Emma Peel bodysuit, and she's talking to the drummer, who is filling in for the East Coast leg of the tour. The regular drummer – as in the drummer for the pilot – was an actress/model with basic kit skills, and Kim just loves playing with the replacement because she's a serious musician and a legend in the business. Kim had posters of her old band on the wall in Sacramento. Huge kick sound. Big lazy fills. The drummer and Demonica go way back, apparently, and she's sitting in as a favor, which is seriously cool. She's changed out of her stage clothes and is wearing sneakers and jeans and an extremely old Brooklyn Dodgers jacket that looks like it might have belonged to her dad, and she's so no-frills that Kim wants to be exactly like her when she makes it.

"*Please* come to the party," she begs. "I can't believe you're not coming."

The drummer smiles. "Stick a fork in me, Kim. It's getting to the point where I'm lucky to make it through the set. I'm old. I gotta go home."

"But this is our last gig together."

"Yeah, and it was a good gig. A party is a party. You can have one anytime."

"So what, you're going to drive home?"

"Uh huh."

"At four in the morning."

"That's the plan."

"Where's home?" Big Guy asks.

"Cape May, New Jersey."

"An Alphaville girl!" Baxter pounces. "They're like the undead! They *just keep coming*!"

"Easy there fella," the label guy cautions.

"Who's your friend?"

"Not my friend." Troxler grins. "Just a colleague from the label."

"The label?"

"Sony Music. I have a card here somewhere."

"You guys are from Sony Music?" the label guy asks nervously.

"Not in any official capacity." Troxler's fishing through his wallet. "Big fan of the show."

"He has a *card*," Baxter says sarcastically. "A *business* card. Two colors on off-white stock? He's going to *whip* that card out of his wallet. Whip it out now! C'*mon*!"

"Settle," Troxler tells him.

"You guys are from Sony?" Demonica shoots the drummer a significant look. "And what brings you handsome fellows out on the East River this evening?"

"*Fromage!* We come in search of the little cheeses!"

"You'll have to excuse him. He's not well."

"Nous sommes manger le petit fromage!"

"Well done. No seriously, we have a friend in TV marketing who worded us up on the cruise. She did the Buffy books. Got us on the list."

"The list?" Suddenly, we're back on the label guy's turf. "You guys were on the list?"

"*Supposed* to be. We got to the wharf and it was a no-show. Had to fork out armfuls of cash before they'd let us on board."

"Really?" If there's one hard and fast rule about the music industry, it's this: People in the business never pay for entertainment. Access is viewed as a right, not a privilege. The unwritten rule is that the lowest-rung label representative would rather walk from a venue instead of paying to get in. Armfuls of cash? The alarm bells start ringing.

"So what? You guys are in A&R? Publicity?"

"Interactive," says Baxter, and buys them time to regroup. "DVD Division and iTV Labs. We build backchannels. Four-year program. Very high end."

"Oh right." Sighs of relief all round.

"So you're computer geeks," the guitarist drawls.

"Oh hardly." Troxler could get away with interactive, but his ego won't let him. The guitarist has wandered over, blunt in hand, and he's still smarting from her earlier dismissal. The girl is what, twenty-two? twenty-three? and yet he feels this need to impress her, so he takes the spade in both hands and digs them deeper in the hole.

"We create content. We produce and direct," he says.

"For Sony Music?"

"That's right."

"What sort of stuff? What kind of content do you do?"

"I'm afraid I can't tell you." Troxler smiles. "Signed a bunch of NDAs. You know how it is."

"Sure, so what kind of content have you *done?*" the drummer asks.

Troxler's book-jacket smile is unforced and natural as he surveys the group of women around him. His cheeks flush with just the right shade of immodesty, and he looks briefly at his shoes as though debating which power card to deal. What kind of content, you ask? What kind of big sexy product will blow you away? He needs a name. He needs to casually namecheck something Hitlerian in the lie department. A name so big as to blitzkrieg disbelief. And the names are there. The big steroidal names: *Schwarzenegger. Madonna. Springsteen. Stallone.* Names so big as to transcend humanity—except, of course, that names like these are invariably partnered with other big names – *Universal. BMG. Columbia. Fox* – and a mismatch in partnering could blow the whole routine. He not only needs a big-name Sony artist, but he's also going to have to supply a watertight collaboration schedule, and as this sudden workload bears down upon him, he makes the mistake of looking to Baxter for help.

"Just show the girl your freaking *card!*" Baxter squeals.

Troxler's search engine is stunned into action, and the best he can do is David Bowie. They've worked with Bowie. Some kind of . . . some kind of interactive game. He's dimly aware that the ferry is docking. Has docked. The ferry has docked, and he sees Bowie with the bad hair he had in *Labyrinth.* All gaunt with those mad, bulging eyes. *Bowie in a game! Bowie in a game!* He blasts a cross-court look to Big Guy, because Big Guy is the team specialist in watertight blowhardery. Big Guy, who deals in content and reads upward of ten newspapers a day and surfs the net and watches CNN and *has his whole fucking story locked down before he leaves the apartment;* and he's right there for the layup, below net with a couple of seconds on the clock, and oh no!—

"We've done *everything.*" Baxter yawns. "This is a boring conversation."

"I'm not finding it boring," the drummer says.

"I'm not finding it boring either," Demonica agrees.

"You have our full attention, dude," the guitarist chips in.

—Big Guy is crippled by injury! He has the sweats! The dry horrors! It's all he can do to keep his food down! The Shagpile girls are giving Troxler the fisheye, and his book-jacket smile becomes an awards-night losing grimace. Senator, thanks for coming. We played a good game, a great game, but the other team was better.

"See, here's the thing," he says weakly.

"*The Handsome Devil*! The new *Outer Limits*! The blue chick from that dumb TV show!"

"The David Bowie game." He glares at Baxter.

"Anything on TV where you want to supersize your content! Where you want the big Coke and fries with whatever the fuck you're watching!"

"Yeah baby," Big Guy says with some effort.

"*Handsome Devil*? You guys worked on *Handsome Devil*." The attention stays on Troxler for all of Baxter's interruptions. He's in the spotlight. He has no choice but to try and make the shot.

"Sort of, yeah," he admits.

"*Handsome Devil* is on the WB," Demonica points out.

"We consult."

"You work at Sony and consult to Warner? That would be a first."

"We just started at Sony. They bought us out."

"Congratulations. So when did you work on *Handsome Devil*?"

"God. When was that?"

"It's not about when it was, it's about when it will be," Baxter says. "We did the work a year and a half ago, but you're not going to be able to see anything for another couple of years. We're talking infrared keyboards. Satellite bandwidth. We are the Men in Black, ladiesh and gentlemen. We make . . . the imposhible . . . poshible."

188

The Shagpile fisheye pans from Troxler to Baxter, and Baxter is exultant in the spotlight. This is Fat City, as far as Baxter's concerned. His eyes are jacked wide and he's doing a bizarre interpretation of the Carson golf swing. For a few blissful seconds, it looks like there might be a margin for recovery. . . . But sadly not.

"—I thought you said you produce and direct."

"—*Handsome Devil* wasn't up a year and a half ago."

"—so what are you coding in?"

This last question from Kim the bass player. She's sucked back a headful of blunt and is staring at Baxter with genuine interest. Like she might actually have a handle on the technology. Baxter walks and talks a good home game, and is very hard to rattle when he's on his own turf, but even so. Troxler, Baxter, and Big Guy have their respective T1 lines to the bleeding edge, and the three of them know that iTV content – as in the kind of content you produce and direct – is light-years away from the major networks. Baxter's backchannel pitch is steeped in bullshit. But does the rock bunny know this?

"What do we code in? Whatever they give us," Baxter says. "Open Author. Microsoft Pak. Liberate. Whatever."

"You can't run video in any of those programs."

Baxter takes a deep breath. "Yes you can," he says.

"No you can't." Kim's voice has that California inflection, that no-holds-barred "anyone who disagrees with me is a dork" end-of-subject tone that straddles the terrain between incredulous and mocking, and Troxler recognizes this tone because it's precisely the tone he uses to humiliate his enemies after destroying them in battle. He closes his eyes. *The rock bunny knows.*

"Yes you can," Baxter insists.

"No you can't. You guys are smoking crack." Kim laughs. "They teach this stuff at Berkeley. The kind of interactive TV you're talking about is *so* far away from where we are now. *Handsome Devil*? I don't think so."

"Uh, guys," Big Guy says in an ominous tone.

"Besides, the show wasn't even *cast* a year and a half ago," Demonica says. "They didn't have Wolf Larson. They didn't have any of the girls."

"See, here's the thing—"

"So who the hell were you directing?"

"Guys."

"Hey. *Fuck you,*" Baxter snarls at Demonica, and Troxler can feel the slum foundation giving way beneath him. The crumbling brickwork and rotting timber. The hasty preparation and total disregard for craft. One of the reasons he has hung in with Baxter and Big Guy for so long is that their bunny-hunting routine has an improv skill level to it, and when they're on a roll, he feels the artistic gratification that comes from precise timing and razor-sharp repartee. He loves the teamwork when it works, and his internal scorecard has the hit-to-miss ratio standing at a solid 55 percent. No rehearsals. Just thinking on your feet. On a good night, the exhilaration is such that Troxler honestly imagines he could act or do standup, that he could climb onstage and legitimately claim the attention he never got from his dad, but as Baxter starts in on a now-familiar tirade, he sees himself in a hotel lobby. Banging out show tunes. Contributing a bit of homespun flair to the evening's ambience, while deluding himself that he's a serious artist.

The blunt-smoking girls are laughing at Baxter, while Demonica and the drummer feign astonishment at his sudden shift in personage, and Troxler just knows they've blown the cover of phony label reps before. That posing as a label rep rates pretty low on the scale of backstage hustle. The roadies have wandered over and are sizing up Big Guy, trying to figure out if he's sick enough to be taken, and Big Guy admittedly does look pretty awful. For the first time that evening, Troxler wonders whether his friend is okay.

"That's it! You guys are outta here!" the label dude exclaims.

Troxler turns slowly with B-movie portent.

"Guys," Big Guy says, making the time-out signal with his hands.

"—a little *old* to be dressing like fetish Barbie? Unless of course you have a sideline career you'd like to clue us in on—"

"Back off, man," Troxler snaps at the label dude.

The label dude and roadies back up immediately.

Kim casually passes the blunt to the guitarist. In the background, some kind of loudspeaker announcement from the Moonlite Cruise crew, inaudible above the sound of people disembarking, but probably thanking everyone for traveling with them and hoping to see them again soon.

Troxler glares at the label guy, but his heart isn't in it. He's doing a passable impression of his dad doing a passable impression of Tab Hunter acting angry, but without his dad's blue-collar rage to kick the next phase into gear. *Punchline,* he thinks. A punchline would be handy. He tilts his head into three-quarter profile and shoots a beefcake look of danger at the Shagpile girls and crew, and as he sifts through the quips and put-downs and one-liners, he's literally broadsided by Big Guy's meltdown on the court.

"Ew!" The guitarist's eyes fly open. "Did I just smell that?"

"Char-*ming.*" Demonica recoils.

Big Guy has collapsed across a row of plastic seats, and a terrible stench is coming off him. It should be funny, but it's not. He looks like he's taken a bullet in the chest.

"I would advise you ladies to evacuate the area," he says with quiet dignity. "Because any minute now, I'm going to kill someone."

"Wow. Are you all right, dude?" Kim asks.

"Yeah dude," Baxter echoes. "Are you all right? I guess we're going to have to hose you down."

"You're a dead man, Baxter."

"A hose for this unfortunate gentleman!"

The Shagpile drummer looks over at the roadies, who are young and lazy and easily distracted, and they're completely fascinated by the chaos backstage. They're supposed to help her with her drums, but why bother? She has a long drive ahead of her, and can pack and unpack a kit in much the same way a marine can strip and reassemble an M16 rifle, so she nudges Demonica and says "later" and carries her kick and cymbal cases around the front of the stagecloth. The drum kit they've rented is a lightweight sixties Ludwig, and she smiles as she pulls the cymbals apart, because that scene in the dressing room was *funny*. The things you see in an all-girl band.

A couple of Asian girls are loitering near the stage, and it looks like they might be steeling themselves for an approach. But no. They join the disembarking crowd and disappear onto the wharf. The sky outside is that pre-sunrise blue, and the drummer yawns involuntarily at the thought of the long drive home. It's nice to be packing her own drums, though. She likes the fact that she can drive away without having to schmooze and hang in there and worry about album sales and marketing and all the other things that constitute success in this business. That she completed her tour of duty and somehow made it out alive. She ties up the stand bag, then hefts the kick drum and slides it into its case. Finished. Her car's in a lot beneath the FDR, and she's tempted to slip backstage and get one of the roadies to help her, but it's a nightmare back there, and there's that thing with these young guys where they come on way too strong about her old band. She can tell they find her touring anecdotes hilariously outdated, like she was with Sabbath or Zeppelin or something. And they buy pot off the guitarist and smoke it on the job, and this lack of professionalism bothers her. So whatever. She'll make a couple of trips.

She throws the stand bag over her shoulder, picks up two road-cases, and staggers across the dancefloor, which is slick with beer. There's a curved metal staircase leading down to the main deck, and as she pauses at the top of it, she hears a vigorous sound of scuffling from the wharf. Moonlite Cruise security are finally having their revenge. A fleet of patrol cars are down there, and the cops on the wharf are of the late-night, leather-jacketed variety. They've cuffed Simon and a couple of his henchmen, and have the half-naked Sgt. Pepper team leader facedown on the ground. A group of police-women have culled a throng of female suspects, and are shining their flashlights through backpacks and purses. The party is definitely over, and the heavy-handed lateshow of security is one more down-side to an entertainment industry the drummer's glad she's left behind. The bigger the gig, the worse the cops behave. And New York cops. Don't get her started.

"Do you want a hand with your kit?" a voice says behind her.

"I'm okay, thanks," she answers reflexively.

"You sure? Your kick drum looks pretty heavy—"

"—and I'm a frail little thing, right?"

She turns, expecting to see your average fanboy, your standard hanger-on, jonesing for contact, lit up with sweaty post-gig awe. "Want a hand with your kit?" is the unsophisticated cousin of "Hi! We're with the label?" and she's just not in the mood, so she wheels around and is surprised to find this casually dressed older guy stand-ing there. Not a bad-looking guy either. Mid-thirties. Sweater and jeans. And, in sharp contrast to everyone else on the boat, clear-eyed and sober. He's smiling a little ruefully at her response to his offer, and she can tell this is not his regular scene.

"No. You don't look the slightest bit frail," he says. "But that stairwell looks tricky, and it's madness on the wharf."

"You're telling me," she agrees. "It's crazy backstage. Must be a full moon or something."

"It's crazy backstage?"

"It's *always* crazy backstage."

"Really?" The guy in the sweater looks like he's about to say something, but he changes his mind and smiles instead. "How long have you guys been together?" he asks.

"I really couldn't tell you. I'm just sitting in for a couple of gigs. You actually caught the final show. The band breaks up after this."

"You're kidding."

"Nope. Good band, too. It's a shame."

"It is a shame. So do you – do they – only play covers?"

It's the drummer's turn to smile ruefully. "You have no idea what tonight was about, do you?" she asks.

"Nope. In so many ways."

"You ever watch *Buffy the Vampire Slayer*?"

"Funny you should ask. I have friends in Australia who assure me it's the best thing on television, but I could never get into it. It just seemed . . . kind of dumb."

"Won't argue with you there. I think it was one of those things like *Seinfeld,* where if you sat down and watched every episode, the show would pay dividends on your investment."

"Right. You'd glean a complex understanding of the vampire problem plaguing some California high school."

"Oh, at least."

The drummer tosses her hair and changes position, realigning her body to take the weight of the kick drum.

"Aren't you supposed to have roadies or something to help load out your stage gear?" the guy in the sweater asks.

"Yeah, but I rented this kit from a friend in New Jersey," she says. "It's easier for me to drop it off tomorrow morning."

Yojimbo looks up at the sky. "It is tomorrow morning," he points out.

"Yeah, well. I guess I'd better get going. I have a long drive ahead of me."

"Right. So . . . do you want a hand with your kit?"

"Sure." The drummer smiles. "That would be great."

YOUNG MEN ON FIRE

The dextroamphetamine had burned itself out. The pleasant high had leveled gently. The ferry had docked. The party was over. Yojimbo had been standing around for a very slow half hour.

It was weird how quickly the cruise had passed. How it had throttled into gear and motored through the night. They had boarded the boat at what time, eleven-thirty? And now the sun was preparing to rise over the Brooklyn Navy Yard. Marissa and Claire had gone off to find Sophie, and something unpleasant must have happened while they were on the lower deck, because they left in a hurry without saying goodbye. Claire had seemed particularly furious, and there was a moment on the stairwell where she had turned and shot Yojimbo the blackest of looks. It was an abrupt, unsettling exit that confirmed what he had been thinking for some time. That for all of his brother's success-driven energy, the evening was, in fact, a sad and lonely affair.

He stood onstage as the drummer collected a second load of

equipment, and could hear Baxter's voice in the distance, taunting, provoking. The voice of a rich man belittling the help. God knows what they were doing back there, but half an hour was enough. He had kept his part of the bargain. It was time to call it a night and check into a hotel. And at six A.M., this meant an expensive, twenty-four-hour, middle of Times Square hotel. Three hundred dollars plus for a single room, breakfast buffet not included.

Unlike his brother and colleagues, Yojimbo wasn't particularly wealthy. He had a prestige job in Melbourne with a surprisingly humble rate of pay. He rented, didn't own, and drove a cool old Volvo, the kind that attracted admiration and disbelief from visiting Scandinavians who hadn't seen its like on the roads since the early seventies. The two suits in his wardrobe were department store purchases, and he always planned his travel well in advance. Checking into expensive hotels at the last minute was the kind of thing he tried to avoid, and the expense element bothered him. It was needless, just as his brother's garbled, defensive attempt at brinkmanship was needless. Martin had set the evening up to make a statement, but had failed to articulate it, falling back on a familiar routine of superior noncommitment. Presenting the information, but not directing it anywhere. *C'est la vie.* And despite his voyeuristic pleasure in watching a faster crowd overheat their engines, Yojimbo's overall take on his brother's New Cynicism was that the parties concerned should all grow up. Yes, the gates had closed on the easy money, and that was too bad, but to build a defeatist philosophy around it – to spike the kool-aid and propose a suicide toast to the symptom, not the cause – well, that was crazy. He had no respect for that.

A mood was developing and he tried to suppress it, concentrating instead on the Shagpile drummer and the odd-shaped boxes she was preparing to carry. Up close, she was tiny. She was one of those thin-shouldered, small-waisted girls who look incredibly good in tight jeans, and was dark-haired and striking with an aquiline nose and classic velvet-painting eyes. Her face was familiar in the sense that it personified the genetic elements of what a non-Latino would consider beautiful in a woman of Latin descent, but with a matter-of-factness of expression that negated all stereotypes. She didn't look fiery or hot-blooded so much as competent and practical. The pockets of her Dodgers jacket were packed with drumsticks and brushes, and judging by the way the fabric bagged out, the jacket was a longstanding travel companion. At a guess, he would have said she was in her early thirties, and, mental stereotyping aside, he had a distinct feeling he had seen her before. Album art would be the logical guess. Something iconic. Some kind of famous band photo from the none-too-distant past.

"You set?" he asked.

"Almost," she replied. "Moving a drum kit is a science."

"Anything else I could carry?"

"No. The floor and kick are the heavy ordnance. You're good."

"Is your car parked far away?"

"It's under the FDR, a couple of blocks uptown," she said. "It's close-ish. We pretty much just have to get across the wharf."

"Piece of cake. Nothing to it."

"Yeah, right."

They negotiated the stairwell, curved down to the main deck, and paused at the head of the gangway. A couple of fly-looking security guys were standing nearby, and seemed very pleased at having had the sense to put some distance between themselves and what was shaping up to be a minor riot on the jetty. The cops had established their stronghold in the parking lot surrounding the wharf, while at the prow of the boat, some heavy-duty scuffling had broken out between select members of team Sgt. Pepper and the pissed-off footsoldiers of Moonlite Cruise security. A thin morning fog steamed up from the water, throwing a veil of privacy over the combatants near the boat, and the two parties obligingly got down to business, throwing fast and tight punch combinations with a minimum of fuss. The surprising thing was that the Beatle fans could fight. They were drunk (and highly caffeinated), but held their ground like cadets, which was probably what they were, upon reflection. Military brats from some East Coast academy. Despite the absence of their team leader and the superior grouping of enemy ranks, they were plying their trade with unorthodox zeal, backing knee- and fistwork up with fingers, foreheads, and teeth. The violence was shockingly fast. Ambiguity was taken out of the equation on account of the fact that both sides wore uniforms. Nautical white versus blue, pink, and orange. The policewomen on the wharf had noticed the melee and were shining their flashlights Sherlock Holmes–style through the fog, while at closer quarters, a couple of young cops had adopted alert positions near the open doors of their cruiser.

"That shit is *fucked up*, son," one of the security guys observed.

"Nigga, you ain' tellin' me *nothing*," his companion agreed.

Yojimbo and the drummer exchanged glances. The cops were too far from the boat to contain the fight. They had blockaded the lot and were exerting force from the central jetty decking, but this was way above the eyeline of the kids near the boat. Down by the boat, it was booze and tunnel vision. Badboys being lads. A spectacular display of drunken ugliness, the kind of tabloidworthy shocker best left to the professionals, and yes, the professionals were swarming to the site. But there was something ad hoc about the whole operation. Cars were screaming in from local precincts, but the active detail had an organic feel that could, in no small way, be attributed to the large number of fat cops in attendance. Big fat cops from the stationhouse. Stubby-armed bruisers with hanging gut and low-slung hardware, exchanging salutations as they moved from car to car. Not a DEA sting, obviously. More likely an enthusiastic response to a call-in. A Saturday morning social, replete with the genial push-and-shove of traded insults and nicknames, and the drummer let out an unimpressed stream of Spanish and hauled her boxes to the head of the gangway.

"You wait," she said. "They'll have thirty cars here in the next ten minutes. Every cop with a low quota will be hauling ass crosstown. It's like Christmas to these guys, so you gotta be careful. They will arrest you, okay?"

"Okay. So what do you want to do?"

"Lemme go talk to those young guys by the cruiser. See if we can hustle up an escort or something."

"An escort. Seriously?"

"Sure." The drummer smiled. "Cops *like* me. Me and cops are like *this*." Beneath the Dodgers jacket, she wore a black T-shirt with "Brixton to the Bronx" emblazoned across the chest. Yojimbo fell in beside her and they moved quickly down the gangway, listening to the sirens rolling in from Thirty-fourth Street.

"A smorgasbord of law enforcement," he noted dryly.

They hit the wharf and veered away from the fight, the wooden planks jouncing as they walked down the jetty. The strobe of police light intensified through the fog, and the parking lot was full of cruisers. Two NYPD vans and a bus were driving in. The disembarking partygoers had been corraled by the policewomen, who were directing them through a complex alignment of orange witches' hats. The central decking was congested with club kids. Lindy Minh and Naoko were trapped in the crowd, waiting for the handbag search and pat-down, and they had retreated back into corporate boredom, smoking cigarettes with a highly scrutable displeasure. Lindy Minh briefly caught Yojimbo's eye, and then she shrugged him loose. The kids around her were restless, and she allowed the jostling to knock her attention away. There was no sign of Marissa or Claire, which was probably just as well. The black look on the stairwell was enough for one night.

"You sure about this escort?" he asked the drummer.

"Nope," she replied. "This crowd is going nowhere."

"Too many cops."

"Yeah. You know you're screwed when they send the buses in. Someone's signed off on a high-volume bust, so it's a 'more is more'–type situation. Arrest first, ask questions later."

"So what do you think? Wait it out here, or go back to—"

A cheer arose from the jetty behind them. Yojimbo shot a look at the boat, where Moonlite Cruise security had apparently been routed. An aftermath of celebration was in play among the Sgt. Pepper crew, who were composing themselves in victorious tableaux like the cast of *Les Misérables* after the barricades have held. The cruise ship and fog made a spectacular backdrop, and in a manner befitting the heroes of the hour, the prep school thugs were besieged by women. For some reason, a lot of girls were on the jetty. High up on the boat, a procession had appeared at the head of the gangway, and was transporting equipment to the wharf. Two guys led the group, carrying a Sovtek Marshall cabinet apiece, and Yojimbo recognized the singer from the band behind them, descending the ramp in a tight-fitting outfit. Bodacious was the word that came to mind, and the prep school boys put their triumph on hold and moved up the jetty for some close-quarter ogling. A chant went up: a fierce "crisps and lager, tits and hoo-hah" thing that was more affronting than admiring, and the entire regiment swarmed the gangway for their personal glimpse of *Rogue*. The Shagpile girls were obviously working on the premise that hired security was still in the picture, because they were smiling like cheerleaders as they greeted the crowd, and Yojimbo watched them catwalk down into the roiling pack of hooligans.

"That doesn't look good," he said redundantly.

The drummer's hand was on his arm, and he felt her fingers tighten. As if in a daze, he set the drums on the ground and started to walk toward the interface of conflict. His mind was oddly blank, oddly clinical. Ghost voices and actions rolled across him like shadow. The urgency of work. The kind of work that required a singular deadness of emotion. A narcotic flatline of emotion. The kind of dark, narcotic deadness that guys like him lived for. Impossible to quantify in terms of hip or ironic, but with its own quirky register of competence. Total and brutal were the adjectives used. And quiet. Absolute. He walked up the jetty toward the crowd near the gangway, and yes, the girls were under siege. They were no longer smiling. The two roadies hurried past him, carrying their amps away from danger as he pushed his way through a tight knot of thug molls, and then he was standing behind the Lonely Hearts Club Band in action.

There were six costumed prep school boys in total. Their marching band uniforms had come apart at the seams. They were obstructing the girls in a solid lineblock, acting out the dominant clichés of netporn in which the men outnumber the women and systematically degrade them while the women smile bravely at an unseen photographer, and Demonica was taking the lion's share of the attention. Her Gaultier bodysuit was designed to stun, and she was carrying a guitar case and a suit bag and was in no position to slap the probing hands away. She was looking around for security and losing her composure, and you could see that behind the makeup and stage smile, she was a tough, struggling professional who deserved a lot more than a cowardly mob grope by a bunch of rich assholes. As Yojimbo closed in on the lineblock, he saw this one smug-looking kid get himself up in the Shagpile singer's face and deliberately spill his drink down the front of her bodysuit.

Without thinking about it too much, he pushed the kid off the jetty. There was a yell and a splash and a minor arbitrage of numbers, an upswing in odds that he was able to consolidate further by driving the heel of his hand into a second cadet's nose, and it was as though the electricity of the drummer's touch had sparked within him a primal urge to fight and defend. The commitment was total. The second cadet had swung around to engage him, and he snapped his arm up in a reflexive nose strike with an astonishing speed that shocked them both. The kid was a hulking brute, moon-faced with a furious blush of acne scarring, and his tiny, vacant eyes filled up with tears. His hands flew to his nose, and after a slow couple of seconds, he turned and retreated through the crowd, fighting his way to a quiet place where he could give the pain his full attention.

The good news was that the big cadet's body had blocked the action from his friends. The jetty push and hand strike went below the Hearts Club radar. Of the four remaining thugs, three were very much in girl mode, and Yojimbo was close enough to swing one, maybe two preemptive blows before they registered his threat. His anatomical knowledge was sufficiently complex to afford him a wide range of specialist targets, and he was zoning in on the nearest kid in costume, when he looked up and saw his brother on the gangway.

This was better than good news. This was terrific news, in fact. The kind of news that could invert the conflict index, because Martin Troxler was unyielding in a fight. He was his father's son, and had mad skills where non-negotiable, rock-and-hard-place lumbering standoffs were concerned. The expression on his face was hard to read, and he was helping Big Guy stagger down from the boat. From where Yojimbo was standing, it looked like the content salesman had a towel wrapped around his waist. He was walking strangely, as though he had sustained a wicked injury or suffered an untimely loss of motor skills, and was obviously not a going concern if it came to a serious head-to-head with the prep school thugs. Baxter was also disembarking, but at a few brooding steps behind his friends, and he was rubbing his jaw and looking oddly down-at-heel.

The lineblock had halted all traffic from the boat. The catcalls had simmered into general abuse. A mean-looking kid in a hot pink costume had coaxed an angry stream of vitriol from the Shag-pile guitarist, who was finishing the end of a marijuana-filled cigar and contemptuously blowing smoke in the Hearts Club soldier's face—and the exhilaration Yojimbo felt at seeing his brother on the gangway was tempered by the surprise of watching him stiff-arm Big Guy through the female musicians. Something bad had obviously happened backstage. Troxler's face was a glaze of martyred dignity and anger – a lot of it directed at the Shagpile guitarist – and in a moment of clarity, Yojimbo realized that a last-minute, good-versus-evil, stupidity-absolving alliance with his brother was not on the cards. The communication lines, the trenchwork, the complicity of childhood – the very things Yojimbo was hoping to rediscover when he agreed to join his brother on this club trawl in the first place – these things were gone.

"Hey Marty!" he called out. *"Martin!"*

"Coming through!" Big Guy moaned.

Troxler and Big Guy crashed through the lineblock, shoving Hearts Club thugs aside as they stormed off the boat. The crowd fell apart, and the prep school kids did this sociologically interesting thing where they raised their fists and flew at the enemy before suddenly realizing they were no longer a mob. You could see their minds working for the first time that night. *I'm in if you're in. Are you in? Are we in?* Individuality firmed up behind their masks, followed quickly by vulnerability and fear, and they jockeyed back into a defensive cordon, fists up, but in no hurry to throw the first punch.

Which was fine by Yojimbo. He grabbed the guitarist and helped her down off the gangway, looking around for his brother, who was somewhere nearby. Farther up the wharf, the cops were starting to mobilize. Black NYPD uniforms were visible through the fog. The girls near the boat were lushed-out beyond all judgment, and stood helplessly on the jetty as the police frontline grew stronger. Like everyone else, they seemed to realize that the safest thing to do right now was nothing. Inactivity separated the wheat from the chaff, although which was which depended on the mill of the cops' perception. Standing still meant you were either smart enough to know not to run, or too drug-fucked to bother trying, and Yojimbo was pushing his way through the crowd, trying to get to his brother before the whole thing turned critical, when a mosh wave rolled through the bodies behind him, signaling the start of another fight.

The fight this time was a two-man affair, temporarily limited to shoving and abuse, but with explosive potential on account of its two protagonists – Baxter and the prep school boy Yojimbo had seen on the boat with his hand down the front of Zebra Hat Girl's strapless top – having invested their egos in an at-all-costs win, and if the timing wasn't so *shockingly wrong* and *heinously ill-considered,* he would have got himself ringside and watched the thing with interest. Baxter had no chance. The kid he was taunting was West Point material with some martial arts thrown in for good measure, and a blank pit-bull stare was creeping into his eyes as Baxter's insults grew more esoteric. The source of the dispute was Zebra Hat Girl. Baxter appeared to have made some kind of proprietorial move – turned up to collect his date at the end of the evening and found her in the arms of some bounder, some cad – and the anger he had manufactured was frighteningly real. He had adopted a grimly righteous Marquess of Queensbury boxing guard and was goading the kid in Oxford quad–ese, while the kid had his hands up in a variation on the tae kwon do praying-mantis attack stance, and seemed very much in control of his material. Zebra Hat Girl was in hysterics nearby, trying to stop Baxter and the prep school kid from fighting, and despite the fact that a distorted notion of chivalry was in play on her behalf, no one was paying her any attention.

The police had fanned across the central jetty decking, and were right on the verge of moving in on the boat, and the thing Yojimbo couldn't believe was that now, at a time where any kind of attention-seeking behavior was a red flag to the cops, the kids around him were competing to be seen. *Look at me!* they were screaming, *Look at me! Look at me!*—and a cold, dispassionate anger took Yojimbo by force. It was as though entertainment had evolved beyond the passive act of watching. The audience had driven the talent offstage and was thriving in the cheap florescence of nonstop karaoke, and as the cops stormed the jetty while the club kids preened and wailed, Yojimbo shouldered his way into the middle of the fight and pulled the plug on both sides.

Baxter was a euthanasia case, a mercy killing. He was seconds away from a serious beating, and it was nothing less than a great source of pleasure to glide beneath his aesthetic-yet-harmless boxing stance and lay him to waste with a blow to the stomach. Yojimbo floated in and sank a textbook jab to the solar plexus, and could hear breath whistling through teeth as the fight sailed out of his brother's friend. Prior to Yojimbo's intervention, the prep school kid had been blocking a flurry of weird little punches, and his dead-eyed stare swam back into focus as Baxter clutched his stomach and hobbled out of range.

Zebra Hat Girl increased the volume of her sobbing, and threw herself into the prep school kid's arms. Her leather pants were squeaking like bedsprings, and there was an odd moment of sexual tension where everyone in the crowd felt obliged to look away. For a few seconds, it looked like the Hearts Club dude might actually stand down. But no. A sour look of violence returned to his face, and he swatted Zebra Hat Girl aside and did this mad little karate dance, a Jean-Claude Van Damme bicep-popping flourish that looked truly ridiculous in his marching band costume. And then the praying-mantis attack position. Fingers bunched together like shadow puppets of ducks. The director filming this sequence had evidently positioned invisible cameras around the wharf and instructed the kid to glare at every lens, because the facial mugging was something to be seen. Eyebrows were lowered menacingly, muscles twitched in jawlines, nostrils flared coltishly, a lot of internal motivation was on display, and were it not for the fact that the cops were audibly intruding on the mise-en-scène, the big temptation would have been to get up and trade a few blows for the sheer hell of it. See the kid's karate and raise it some Chinese boxing or Korean zen do kai. As it was, Yojimbo made do with a series of rapid knuckle taps to the leering kid's forehead: nothing too flashy, but enough to knock home the message that advanced martial art was on the specials board this morning, and perhaps Sir might consider putting the duck hands away.

The police were on the jetty and arrests were being made. Wheat or chaff, it didn't matter. The crowd was going down. Zebra Hat Girl was jostled back into the standoff, and as the prep school kid ditched the mantis attack stance and scuttled away with a look of horror on his face, she did a slow, heavily telegraphed pirouette-before-fainting, and lushly collapsed into Yojimbo's arms.

"Arrest this clown!" Baxter gasped in the background.

"Excuse me! *Excuse me!*" one of the Shagpile girls was shouting.

Yojimbo swung around as the police crashed toward him, and they were predictably deep in a final show of rough trade. Anyone dressed in clubwear was a target, which was bad news for the Shagpile girls in their sexy post-gig attire, and the guitarist had been detained by a couple of hard-faced policewomen, one of whom was sealing a used cigar stub into an evidence bag while the other grinned aggressively at the "drugs not hugs" slogan stenciled across her guitar case.

Baxter was howling in the distance.

Zebra Hat Girl was a touch more hefty than she looked.

Demonica stepped in and tried to reason with the cops, but they were having none of it. The Shagpile guitarist was led away in tears. An incredible mess. Big Guy, naked from the waist down, was provoked to rage by the removal of his towel, and the towel may as well have been radioactive by the way the cops were shouting. Troxler had seized his own piece of the limelight and was having a stagey, heavily nuanced bellowing contest with a young Chinese cop who appeared to be pulling a live feed from the Scorsese channel, puffing his cheeks out like an incredulous mobster, except he was like five foot five and Chinese and having trouble with his consonants, and if there ever was a time to click your heels and wake in Kansas, that time would be now. A fat precinct sergeant steered two rookies toward him, and Yojimbo pulled out his wallet, exposed his credentials, and waved his ID in the fat sergeant's face.

"I'm a doctor," he said calmly. "We have a problem."

"Overdose?" The sergeant groaned, ignoring the wallet and taking his cue from Yojimbo's tone of voice.

"Heart condition. Could be bad."

"So what's she need?"

"Hopefully nothing more than this," Yojimbo said, retrieving an orange prescription bottle from his pocket. "But I need to get her someplace quiet. Can one of you help me?"

"Hugosian, you go," the sergeant ordered. "Get him up to the cars."

"No problem," one of the rookies said eagerly. "Follow me, sir."

It was as simple as that.

Yojimbo swung Zebra Hat Girl off the ground, and carried her up the jetty under the rookie's supervision. In his arms, Zebra Hat Girl seemed authentically stricken. Her hair had maximized and she was making odd little sounds. Yojimbo handled her professionally, moving quickly through the crowd, and the interesting thing was that he not only looked like a doctor, but had looked like a doctor all along. Once the medical ID was out on the table, a perceptional stethoscope appeared around his neck. The crowd parted to let him through. Even his brother stepped aside. He carried the girl up the wharf to where the drummer stood watching, and she registered his new authority and raised her eyebrows in surprise.

"Excuse me, officer," he said to the rookie. "Could you maybe help the lady get those boxes out of here?"

"Jeez." The rookie flushed. "I don't know about that." He shot a furtive look at the jetty behind him, and then studied the drummer at length. "Okay, quickly," he decided, only too happy to assist a pretty girl. He picked up the floor tom and kick drum and steered the group toward the parking lot, using the request as conversational leverage.

"So you were playing on the boat?" he asked the drummer.

"Yes and no," she replied. "I was sitting in with some friends."

"No shit, 'scuse my French," the rookie said. He had a deep, hooting voice that was very endearing. "So were there, you know, celebrities on board? Anyone I'd know?"

"Nah," the drummer said. "Minor TV personalities. Nothing too exciting. But listen—a friend of mine just got picked up. Do you have any idea where they're taking her?"

"Stuyvesant Town if it's nothing major," the rookie said. "That's where we're going when we finish up here."

A fleet of police cars blocked the entrance to the lot, and the bus was full of detainees. The bus looked new and luxurious, and had the forward-thinking but slightly sinister *COURTESY, PROFESSIONALISM, RESPECT* sign in huge blue letters on the side. Miserable kids peered down from the windows like terrified children packed off to summer camp, and the two cops guarding the bus were trading quips in the cheerful spirit of successful class warfare.

"Yo Hugosian! Some snooty bitch go Q on you?" a black cop shouted.

"Say it ain't so, Hugs." A second cop shook his head.

The rookie let loose a deep and nervous laugh, while the drummer, whose grasp of police jargon was apparently top-shelf, informed Yojimbo that "Q" was Chicago cop shorthand for open mouth and lolling tongue – i.e., death – and there was an awkward moment in front of the bus where the rookie felt obliged to justify his escort.

"This guy here's a doctor," he announced. "The girl has got some kind of condition."

"You don't say," the black cop said. "So what's it to be, doc?"

"An ambulance would be good," Yojimbo replied.

Zebra Hat Girl was moving in his arms. The noises she made sounded suspiciously like giggling.

"Puglesi and that Asian chick still here?" the black cop asked his partner.

"Nah. They split. So what, you want we should put a call in to Beth Israel? How bad are we talking?"

The answer was plenty bad on a number of levels, the main one being Yojimbo's reluctance to lie. He was a script and stagecraft man. Improv wasn't his thing. On-site EMT guys might cover for a drunk girl, but calling in an ambulance was a vastly different proposition, and as Zebra Hat Girl opened her eyes and threw a dazzling smile at the assembled policemen, help arrived from an unexpected quarter as Baxter exploded into view, bristling with the demented energy of a B-movie killer's crucial end-of-reel attack.

"Incarcerate this fool!" he bellowed. "Throw him in jail and make him some large black convict's plaything!"

"Excuse me?" the black cop said.

"Do your duty, sir! You're a complicated man, and no one understands you but your woman!—"

"Do we know this guy?" the cop's partner asked.

"Nope. Nice suit, though."

"—*can you dig it?*"

The fact that Baxter was still at large had a lot to do with the sophisticated refractory properties of his slimline Randolph shades. He did the Nicholas Cage crazy laugh and somehow managed to convey the maverick authority of a wild-card Hollywood detective. Racial stereotyping stacked the odds in his favor. For all the cops knew, a keen mind lurked behind the unsteady gait and horrid pallor, and if the sunglasses revealed one thing, it was that he didn't seem to be afraid.

"Can we help you? Mister?" the black cop inquired.

"I doubt it," Baxter drawled, cupping his hand around his lighter. "The fat girl comes with me. What you do with these two fuckups is your business, but may I advocate a hearty pistol whipping? Perhaps a quick trip to the plumbing section of your local hardware store?"

"Hold it right there!"

"Wait a second—you know this guy?"

"Oh sure," the drummer said. "He's the security *liaison.*"

The black cop froze and shot a look at his partner, while a gradual smile lit the rookie's face. The security liaison. Whatever the hell that meant. Baxter was also smiling, but in an infuriating way, shaking his head at the drummer's poor attempt at humor, and he did a brisk little rictus of audience warm-up, adjusting his mike and waving hello to the crowd, and was right on the verge of a slam-dunk comedy response when the two cops grabbed him and cuffed his hands behind his back.

"Okay wild man. You're taking a ride downtown," the black cop said.

"Oh really?" The look on Baxter's face was very strange. He didn't seem so much shocked as vaguely grateful. "Oh please, not more community service! Not another contribution to your pension fund!" He sneered. "I pay more tax in a year than you guys make in a decade!"

"Don't you hate it when they do that?" the cop's partner asked.

The black cop had Baxter's wallet out, and flashed the rookie a glimpse of smoot-frosted money.

"Mr. Baxter here will not be traveling coach," he declared.

The cop's partner – a rabbity-looking Latino guy with low income written all over him – made a subtle gesture that was hard to decipher, and wiped the grin off Baxter's face with a swing of his nightstick. Yojimbo and the drummer weren't meant to see it, but it was the rudest strike of the morning. A vicious thrust to the kidneys. Baxter took the hit manfully, then changed his mind and started screaming as the two cops roughhoused him around the front of the bus, and they dragged him to the police cars by his handcuff chain and hair.

Back in the parking lot, Troxler was enmeshed in a similar battle with the young Chinese cop, who, aside from being heavyset and accessorized with the thick gold jewelry of low-level mobsterdom, turned out to have the type-A personality to match. The war on drugs was being waged in the trenches, and it was very much in the new Mafia style. The Chinese cop had no respect for the cinematic integrity of Troxler's old-world fighting craft, and thus the old man's heavily telegraphed Bob Mitchum punches, handed down through the ages from father to son, were no match for the graceless flurry of a Joe Pesci–type attack. Yojimbo watched in horror as his brother was simultaneously beaten up, handcuffed, and thrown into a cruiser with the unceremonious vérité of no-frills TV, and his face was fear-bleached and paparazzi-ugly as he was pushed into the backseat by the top of his head.

Elsewhere, Big Guy was attempting to hail a cab without his pants. He had thick, chunky thighs and a curiously feminine tan line, and had apparently decided to cut his losses and walk away from his friends. The cops were leaving him alone, but so were the cabbies, and he was last seen brandishing his wallet and hobbling toward a Thirty-fourth Street bus-and-homeless shelter, his bizarre appearance unsmilingly appraised by a sinewy crew of teenage crackheads.

Loose ends were being tied up. In Republican terms, the action had been a resounding success and it was time to shuffle paper at the station. Hugosian the rookie let out a listless morning yawn, and revealed himself to be sharper than he looked.

"She's drunk, right?" he said, nodding at Zebra Hat Girl, who was wriggling like a seal in Yojimbo's arms. "You should get her in a cab before the other guys come back."

"That would be good," Yojimbo said.

"No problem. Real pleasure to meet you, miss," he continued. "Big fan of the band. I was real sorry when I heard you broke up."

"That's very sweet of you." The drummer laughed.

Smalltalk ensued until they flagged down a cab, and it was a relief to unload the giggling Zebra Hat Girl. The giggling had been a worry, deflating whatever air of medical urgency Yojimbo was able to convey to the police cars, and he had received a lot of unimpressed sign language and hornwork by the time a cab pulled over. The cabbie was a highly strung Indian guy who had seen something "frightful" on the road a little earlier, and he was less than thrilled to take a New Jersey fare. But the drummer persuaded him. Turned on the charm and haggled through the window while Yojimbo coaxed a Fort Lee address out of the insensible Zebra Hat Girl—and then the rookie's car was waiting, and the rookie had to go, and the cabbie kept arguing in that pedantic Indian way, until Yojimbo cleaned out his wallet and gave the guy all the money he was carrying.

"Here's sixty-seven bucks," he said wearily. "I have your medallion number. Just make sure she gets home safely, okay?"

"Can I give you a ride somewhere?" the drummer asked after the cab had left the curb.

"Yeah. To the same place you're going, if you're going to that police station," Yojimbo said. "My brother managed to get himself arrested."

"Oh my god." The drummer groaned. "That wasn't . . . he wasn't—"

"The security liaison? No. That was someone else. I take it 'security liaison' is cop jargon for someone who deals drugs to nightclub bouncers?"

"Something like that. Your brother's the blond guy in the suit, right? James Spader hair. Thinks he's pretty good-looking?"

"Yeah, that sounds like him."

"Right. So are you really a doctor? I only ask because your brother was pretending to be a label rep backstage, and—"

"—you wanted to know if it runs in the family. No. I'm really a doctor. I'm a doctor, I hardly ever go to nightclubs, and I try, wherever possible, not to lie to the police. My brother, on the other hand, runs with a fast, irresponsible crowd of rich assholes. How did you know he was my brother?"

"He looks like you," the drummer said.

"Yeah, I guess he does. It's weird. Last night was some kind of contest between us, and the thing I can't work out is whether he won or he lost. I have no idea what the rules were. What he was trying to achieve."

"Well, if what he was trying to do was to get himself arrested, then I think we can safely say he's won—"

"Right."

"—and he's a loser. I say this from the perspective of someone who has seen more than her fair share of guys behaving badly. I happen to be a world-class authority on guys."

"A *world-class* authority. You're going to have to forgive me, but I have no idea who you are."

"Mercedes Cruz. God, Guns and Guts." The drummer smiled. "I didn't get your name either."

"Jim Troxler," Yojimbo said. "It's a pleasure to meet you."

HEARTWARMING

Jim Troxler and Mercedes Cruz sat in the waiting room of the Stuyvesant Town police station, killing time until the shift change, after which the arrested parties would be processed and released. The waiting room was off to the side of the admissions desk, and was full of uptown dads and lawyers. A certain grim flashiness was on display. Cell phones were barked into. Appointments were canceled. Notes were scribbled and strategies mumbled. No one over fifty looked particularly distraught.

A small group of club kids was also in the room, and they were working the phones and staging their own competence routines, largely for Mercedes's benefit, if eye contact was anything to go by. Just as the adults stayed calm around their peer group, the kids from the boat strived to appear older and more composed in front of the bona fide rock star in their presence, and in both cases, the behavioral cues came straight from *NYPD Blue*.

The coffee machine was at the back of the room, and it was an ancient and uncooperative beast of a thing that dispensed fluid with a kind of mechanical disgust. After feeding it more quarters than seemed reasonable, Jim Troxler returned with two scalding cups that burned his hands through the cardboard.

"Careful, it's hot," he warned Mercedes.

"I know. I was trying to warn you, but you got up so quickly? See the desk sergeant and the other guy he's talking to? They get their coffee from the deli next door. Everyone does. No one drinks the station coffee. It's *dangerous*."

"Ah. You've done this before."

"You kidding? My brother and I lived in Alphabet City in the eighties. We got the street thing scoped out, yo."

"So what are you doing in New Jersey?"

She laughed. "It's *nice* there. I'm telling you. It's quiet. You got the beach."

"You don't miss New York?"

"Nope. You miss Miami?"

"God no. I was happy to get out."

"So why did you go to Australia of all places?"

"Intern exchange. They had a guy down there who invented a new kind of heart valve, which was a pretty big deal. And I qualified for the teaching program. So I went."

"So you're a heart surgeon?"

"In Australia." Jim Troxler smiled. "They use a different system in the States. I doubt they'd even let me scrub up over here."

"Are you serious?"

"Oh, you know. They'd probably let me, but I'd have to sit a bunch of board exams first."

"Oh *god*. The only good thing about playing music for a living is that you don't have to study. And you get lots of free clothes, let's not forget that."

"I seem to recall a stars-and-stripes jacket you used to wear."

"Yeah, and I had my very own guy to tease my hair before a gig. Guitarists have guitar technicians, I had a hair technician."

"Was he actually called a hair technician?"

"Oh yeah! Man, he was *serious*."

"Wow. That blows me out of the water. I can't compete with that."

"Are you kidding? You have a career. You're set up for life. You can grow old doing what you're doing."

"I would have thought playing in a big-name rock band would have been a great career."

"It's a great career for everyone else. The second you become big enough to pull the bandwagon, all these people jump on board. Managers, tour managers, lawyers, agents—"

"Hair technicians."

"Hair technicians. And they're there for as long as you're making money. Once you stop making money, they're off with someone else. It's these guys who have careers, not musicians."

"But you must have done pretty well out of the whole thing."

"Oh yeah. We didn't do too bad."

"So do you miss it? Do you miss touring and performing?"

Mercedes frowned. "Do you miss medical school?"

"No. Not at all," Jim Troxler replied.

"You sure?"

"Yeah. Well . . . no, that's not entirely true. Med school was okay."

"What was so good about med school?"

"Probably the same things that would be good about starting out in a band. The part where it all comes together. One minute, you're trying something you've tried and failed at a hundred times before, and the next thing you know, you pull it off."

"This is what you miss about med school?"

"Sort of. I like the fact that there was a time, long, long ago, when I was afraid to open up a body."

"Ew! *Cha cha cha!*"

"It's not that—did you just say *'cha cha cha'*?"

"*Cha cha cha.* That's disgusting, man."

"Uh, yes, but it's what I do. Surgeons are but mechanics of the human body. Somewhere along the line, you have to open them up."

"And you're good at this?"

"This is my field of expertise, yeah. Many hours have been spent mastering the discipline of surgery. Many bodies have been opened. *Cha cha cha.*"

"You got chops, is what you're saying," Mercedes grinned.

"Chops?"

"Chops is like, all the tricks you can do. It's a jazz term. The old cats up in Harlem, they go on and on about chops. You go to Sugar Hill and sit in with these guys, and they're like, 'Girl, you got chops?' and then you play and it's like, 'Girl, you got *chops.*' You know?"

"So it's like your drum fills and rhythms?"

"Yeah. You get some horn player who's checking you out, and he might play a Latin thing as a kind of tease, so you immediately switch your accents to let him know you're on to him. Chops is basically about being *good.*"

"Right. I can see that."

The clock above the desk sergeant inched its way to nine A.M., while in the waiting room, fathers and lawyers checked their watches incrementally. The shift change was bearing down upon the precinct. Uniformed cops were gliding past the front desk, and Jim Troxler was chagrined to see them carrying blue-and-white cups from the deli next door. Unlike Mercedes, who obviously had some experience in these matters, he had absolutely no idea what he was supposed to do. Would he have to bail Martin out? Was money supposed to change hands? Television was the reference point here, but he didn't watch enough TV to make a seasoned call. And besides. He was enjoying his conversation with the attractive musician. He could tell by the way she had volunteered to wait for the guitarist that her decision was partly motivated by a similar connection. That she was in no hurry to end the night and drive home.

"So is being a doctor the same sort of thing you see on *ER*?" she asked.

"Yeah. They get a lot of it right."

"It's exciting, right?"

"My stuff is not that exciting. Your stuff is exciting. My stuff is more about doing the same thing over and over with a high degree of accuracy."

"But you have all that business with the mask and the gloves and the nurses who hand you shit."

"Yeah. I get to say 'scalpel' and 'suction.' That sort of thing."

"That's so cool."

"No, going up to Harlem and sitting in with old jazz cats is cool. But I take your point. I guess the thing I appreciate most about my medical degree is that somewhere, in the course of eight to ten years, I got the procedure down cold. I can *do* surgery. I'm not bluffing or faking it. Put me in a theater and I can operate, you know?"

Mercedes smiled. "I *know*. I don't think there's anyone on the planet I couldn't play with, but the thing with success is that it gets to a point where it stops being about how good you are, and ends up just being *who* you are. Do you get this, or is this not a doctor thing?"

"Not a doctor thing. But I see where you're coming from."

"Right. After the band broke up, I had this thing where I was invited out to Paisley Park to hang out with Prince for a weekend. And I'm like, 'Guy's a great musician, cool.' So I go to Minneapolis and get the limo at the airport and all that cheesy stuff, and I go to the studio and there's all this free shit – you know, clothes and whatnot – and it's like, everybody wants to see me in the clothes. It's all about the clothes."

"So did you end up jamming with Prince?"

"Yeah, and he was fine. But there's this concentration level you need to work shit out properly, and it became obvious pretty fast that Prince works his shit out alone. So, you know. What was I doing there?"

"Being famous."

"Right. Wearing these clothes and running through stuff. And you know what really got me?"

"No. What?"

"I could tell that I was a bit of a disappointment to everyone. I turned up to play and I was really into playing, and these guys all knew I could play. But it was a fashion show. It was light entertainment. And by the end of the weekend, the fabulous crowd – you know, the entourage – were all going, 'tell the rock chick to lighten up.'"

"People have been telling me to lighten up all night."

"This is your brother and those guys?"

"Yeah. Which is funny, because I was having an okay time. You want to know something funny?"

"What?"

"Early on in the evening, I asked my brother's friend, the pumped-up guy, what he did for a living, and he gave me this lecture about how totally lame it was to ask people what they do."

"And then he shits his pants."

"The mind boggles. Anyway, we went to a couple of clubs and then onto the boat, and the whole night everyone was having what I guess you'd call 'spirited conversation' on a variety of topics, mostly television—"

"And nobody talked about what they did?"

"It's not that. You get people who talk about themselves all the time and it gets boring pretty quickly. In many ways, it makes far better sense to shoot the breeze about films or TV shows or whatever's going on in Hollywood this week, because you have better odds of engagement. No, it was the fact that my brother's friend actually articulated this thing about asking people what they do. Like it's a chess move the experts frown at or something. And it got me thinking to the point where I spent a large part of the evening listening to these guys in conversation."

"And?"

"And the conversation was skillful. The surprising thing was that all the people we met were good at it. Right across the board."

"So what are you saying?"

"What am I saying?" Troxler sighed and rubbed the stubble on his chin. "Let's see. When we were kids, Marty and I switched schools a bunch of times. Long story. Not particularly interesting. But we had that thing where we had to make friends fast. And I remember my dad telling us that the secret to making friends was that you had to establish 'common ground.'"

"Sounds like *my* dad."

"Right. Totally old school. 'Hi, my name's Jim. Love the Dolphins. Hate the Packers. My old man sells insurance. When I grow up, I want to be an astronaut. How about you?'"

"Right, and then I take you home to my parents' place and show you my practice pads and ice-cream containers."

"Uh . . . you lost me."

"No no. I take you back to my folks' place and show you my practice pads and the ice-cream containers I used to practice on before I had a kit. We're like, thirteen, right?"

"Yeah yeah yeah. You started out on ice-cream containers?"

"What? You think my parents are gonna buy me a kit? I don't think so."

221

"No. I guess not."

"Okay. So back to your story. You're going to be an astronaut and I'm going to be the drummer in a band."

"Right. What I guess I'm trying to say is that in my dad's old-school model, you had to invest yourself in conversation. 'This is me, this is my deal.' And maybe wanting to be an astronaut is kind of dumb, but at least it says something about who I am. The thing that got me about the boat cruise was that the talk was like teflon. You know, 'so, how about those vampires?' for hours and hours on end. And even when people were talking about themselves, I detected very little investment of self in what they said. What I did detect was a lot of very skillful maneuvering around a kind of third-party, pop-culture terrain, in which the idea is to convey keenness of intellect via relentless showbiz metaphors and references."

"Try being famous. It's like that times eleven."

"Really? I would have thought it would have been a lot of people standing around wanting to hear you talk about yourself."

"No! This is the funny part. They *don't*. It's all about clever references and how the vampires are doing. You can talk about yourself as much as you want, it's not like anyone's listening."

"That's too bad."

"Are you kidding? See, this is where I think you have it all over me, because you're actually surprised that people talk a bunch of crap backstage. These people you've been listening to? I know these people, because they've been peddling me their various lines of bullshit all my life."

"Yeah, but you're talking about people in showbiz—"

"No, I'm talking right across the board. I'm talking high-level creative management through to PR flacks and flunkies. I'm talking caterers and hair technicians and the guy who sells your T-shirts at a gig. I'm talking Chris and Tina from the Madison Wisconsin Wal-Mart, and I'm talking your brother and his crowd of rich assholes.

You get these people backstage, and they all have one thing in common."

"And that is?"

"They hate what they do."

"Uh . . . yeah?"

"Yeah. The thing you're trying to work out is why you're not getting much investment of self in conversation these days, right?"

"Right."

"Well, there's your answer. Take it from someone who has seen a broad cross section of life pass through her dressing room."

"Boy. You're tough. You're the toughest rock star drummer I ever met."

"Eh. Drummers get a bad rap."

"I bet."

"So let's talk about me, 'cause I'm terribly interesting. We pick up on me at seventeen with my piece-of-shit Sears kit. Final year at Stuy High. Career ambition? Wants to be the drummer in a band. So, you know. Checkout chick at Price Rite. Puerto Rican guys in their muscle cars. 'Hey, *chiquita*! What you *doo*-en?'"

"You went to Stuyvesant High? Isn't that like impossible to get into?"

"Spanish quota. Next thing, you'll be telling me I'm *smart*."

"You go on to college?"

"Nope. Went straight to Elektra. See, I'm living the dream. You come up and try to hit on me at Price Rite, you bet I'll invest my ass in the conversation. But the thing is, I'm seventeen. I still got some-place to go."

"This is starting to sound cynical."

"God no! No no no! I'm one of the few noncynical people left. I *should* be cynical. I mean, there was a period of time where my hair was the subject of national scrutiny. I've been on the cover of the *National Enquirer* and the *Star*, for god's sake."

"And I have to say, you do seem smaller in real life."

"Right. But I'm not cynical."

"Which is good, because I'm not cynical either. But I'm not sure I'm going to go with you on the idea that the people who talk a bunch of backstage crap are unhappy with what they do."

"Is your brother happy with what he does?"

"Workwise? Yeah. Although we did have a weird conversation on the boat. I have to say, I'm not sure about my brother."

"So can we come back to me at Price Rite for a second?"

"Of course."

"Okay. I'm swiping groceries through the checkout. There are nine or ten girls just like me, and we all have dreams of being, you know, the girls in a Puff Daddy video or whatever, where you just kind of hang around and look glamorous. No effort involved. You know, Snoop Dogg's out at Long Beach and he has all his bitches, and it's like, what do these girls do the rest of the time when they're not shaking booty at the camera? Do we know? Certainly, it's not a topic of discussion at Price Rite, because deep down, we all know it's just fantasy. But that doesn't stop us from wanting it, right?"

"Right. Except you're thrashing away at the Sears kit."

"Yeah. I'm a step up from the general checkout mentality in that I actually got a program to make things happen. But anyway. Before we can leave Price Rite, we have to jump forward ten years and check out the music video to a certain song I can't bring myself to name—"

"*Happy happy happy, I'm so happy happy happy.*"

"—which we will not go into under any circumstances, except to say that the hair technician has been around and they've talked me into wearing an outfit."

"This is the stars-and-stripes jacket?"

"Yeah. The point to all this is that we play some stadium and go backstage, and I'm immediately surrounded by all the archetypes from Price Rite, except they're now working in the music industry. And I'm like a magnet for these people. They want to hang out and be glamorous with me. So okay, let's hang. But do you think I'm getting investment of self or common ground or whatever on these occasions? No way. What I'm getting is a lot of girls in outfits simulating the kind of attitude and lifestyle they've seen me simulate in music videos. I cannot *begin* to tell you how weird this is."

"Yeah, but does this mean they hate what they do?"

"Yes and no. They love what they do, because it gives them the opportunity to believe that glamour exists. And this validates their day gig. Which is, you know, writing press releases and stuffing envelopes and selling shit on the phone."

"Hang on a second. Glamour doesn't exist?"

"Oh, come on. I'm sitting here talking to my new friend the heart surgeon. And my idea of 'heart surgeon' is probably as wack as your idea of 'rock star,' right? My idea of what you do comes from TV. And it's all about the clothes. I got my outfit, you got your outfit, right?"

"Right."

"Pretty glamorous, huh?"

"No. Not really."

The replacement desk sergeant had settled in behind his desk, and he was a muscular old guy with white hair and an equally white Chelsea leather bar mustache. He had an easy manner, and was laughing and cracking jokes with the uniforms in the style of the friendly cop in an interrogation scenario, which was hopefully a good sign. A couple of the senior cardio guys Jim Troxler knew in Melbourne exhibited similar traits, and while they were the hardest surgeons to get to know personally, they were terrific in the theater. Real blood-and-soil men. The first wave of lawyers had surrounded the desk in the mock-deferential manner of legal counsel approaching the bench, and the sergeant chewed gum with open-mouthed amusement as he leaned into their questions and answered offhandedly. Troxler skimmed the exchange on camera two, his primary feed being a tight, newscaster-style head-and-shoulders of Mercedes Cruz, lit up in animation on the metal chair beside him. She appeared to be enjoying herself.

"The way I see it, it all comes down to the work," she was saying. "And see, the secret I learned in eight-plus years of nonstop touring is that the work is not glamorous. In showbiz especially. And if you can get good with that, you're basically okay. It's when you buy into the *idea* of work that you're in trouble. The regular girl in last night's band, the one who played drums in the pilot? Is literally one of those girls from an MTV video. Looks great behind the kit and is fabulous in a photo shoot, but I've never seen someone so terrified of actually getting up onstage and playing."

"Wow."

"And this is where you have it all over me, because this girl would look great in a surgical gown. But I can't imagine anyone in their right mind letting her operate on anyone."

"No. You're right. You can't fake it in surgery. I think that's why they work you so hard at the beginning. To kill your illusions."

"Which is good, right?"

"Yeah." Troxler nodded thoughtfully. "I guess it is."

The desk sergeant was calling names. Club kids bobbed and slouched from the room, shouldering their way through the throng of lawyers, and Troxler and Mercedes followed at a distance. The procedure seemed straightforward enough – a charge sheet with the fine already circled, a cashier in the precinct house and an automatic teller across the street – but there was that exam-result trauma of waiting for the call, and Troxler's apprehension grew when he realized there were two groups of detainees. The light offenders got away with disorderly conduct, an early release, and a three-figure fine, while the serious hellraisers had been sent downtown to spend quality time with their arresting officers. Which meant cavity searches, rough treatment, and a longer wait in the Centre Street Tombs. The Shagpile guitarist was one of the first names to be called, and Mercedes collected her duplicate sheet, frowned at the cashier and the hefty fine she had to pay, and squeezed Troxler's arm in sympathy when the sergeant closed the list.

"Bummer," she said. "That's too bad."

"What does this mean?" he asked. "What happens now?"

"What it means is that your brother's looking at something more substantial than disorderly conduct or a straight possession charge. It means whoever's writing him up is thinking about it."

"And this means?"

"A longer wait and more money. I'm really sorry, Jim."

"That's okay," he said. "I had a nice time talking to you. It was worth every minute on the boat."

Her dark eyes flashed. "Really?" she said. "You had a *nice* time talking to me. How polite. How well brought up you are."

"Sorry?"

"Oh, you know. I'm just a girl from Spanish Williamsburg who got lucky in a band. I never hung around no surgeons before. Musicians, yes. Cops for some reason, don't ask me why. But no doctors. Doctors always seemed off limits, you know? Like, where do you go to meet doctors?"

"Well, hospitals, I imagine, would be your first port of call."

"Yeah right. Like I'm going to start hanging around hospitals."

"Like I'm going to start hanging around backstage."

"Hey. You offered to carry my drums. That's pretty backstagey."

"Is it now? Well lucky for me I did."

"Oh yeah? And what's that supposed to mean?"

Well yeah, exactly. What was that supposed to mean? The conversation had taken a personal turn, had veered from the realm of theory into the far more hazardous terrain of the heart, and the fear Jim Troxler felt was classic New York urban fear. Mercedes Cruz was staring at him with the wistful smile of a track runner contemplating a race already run, and her eyes were bright with hope and disappointment. Interest had been kindled at the wharf, the wait at the police station had supplied a pretext for connection, and now the time had come to cast pretext aside. It was as simple as that. Mercedes had even done the spadework for him, setting him up for a straight call, and the thing with straight calls is *hardly anyone makes them these days.* Pretext is everything in city-based hookup, to the point where straight callers tend to be viewed as people uninspired enough to have no business calling, and the urban fear we're talking stems from this. Once the guitarist was released, there was no reason for Troxler or Mercedes to take things further than a handshake at the door. Except attraction. But did straight attraction count?

Jim Troxler. Thirty-six. Cardiothoracic surgeon. Tired to the point of narcolepsy. Fixed Mercedes in his gaze and called it neat. No phone numbers on napkins. No clever chicanery. Just a blind leap off the cliff face . . . he took a deep breath and leapt.

"Are you seeing anyone at the moment?" he asked.

"No. Are you?" Mercedes grinned.

"No."

"So what? You asking me out?"

"Yeah. If you're not seeing anyone."

"*Esso!* You have any idea how long it is since a guy asked me out?"

"No."

"Oh *god.*"

"Which means what? You get asked out all the time? You don't get asked out all the time? I'm embarrassing myself? I'm not embarrassing myself—"

"You're not embarrassing yourself. You'd be the perfect guy to go out with. You're smart. You're handy in a fight. But there's just one thing. Don't you live in Australia?"

"Oh yeah. There is that."

"That's one hell of a commute."

"Yes it is."

"I mean, if it was Baltimore or Washington, I could see it."

"You'd date a guy from Baltimore?"

"He'd have to do the commuting. We toured there a bunch of times. It's a pretty rough town."

"You ever tour Australia?"

"Yeah. It's nice. But I'm not about to start flying there every second weekend."

"I guess not."

"So." Mercedes paused to shake the hair out of her eyes. "How long are you in the States for?"

"I'm not sure," Jim Troxler said. "I've taken four months off, but it could stretch out indefinitely. I was also thinking about doing some traveling while I was here. You know, check out Savannah, check out New Orleans."

"Eh. The south is overrated."

"Are you kidding? I'm *from* the south."

"Florida? Oh please."

"Good beaches down there. Better beaches than New Jersey, I'm willing to speculate."

"What? You're inviting me down to Florida?"

"No. I asked if you were seeing anyone. We've established that you're not, so I'm trying to work up a plan of action. It's you who keeps jumping the gun here."

"I do that."

"But if you *wanted* to come to Florida . . ."

"Ha! So now who's jumping the gun?"

"Yeah, well. In normal circumstances, I'd blow off Florida completely, but uh . . . this situation with my brother? We're both in a difficult place right now. Our dad's dying of cancer, and we've been doing a spectacular job of not dealing with it. Except we've run out of time. We have to go down and face him."

"Oh shit."

"Yeah. It's a tough one."

"I'm so sorry. How . . . long has he got?"

"I'm not sure. Mom and Dad don't take direction very well, so they're kind of sketchy on the details. One of the things I have to do is talk shop with the doctors. Try and get a handle on timeframes and things."

"You're kidding. You don't *know*?"

"Well. It was cancer of the prostate, so the odds were pretty good. They had him on Lupron, but the cancer blew out to his hips and his spine. Chemo didn't catch it, so we're in the palliative phase. He's on a morphine drip, but he's also apparently chugging whiskey on the sly. He's one of those 'laugh in the face of death' kind of dads."

"Wow."

"Yeah. Marty takes after him."

"Right—and you don't."

A throwaway remark, accompanied by what Troxler could imagine was an Alphabet City street scope. He opened his mouth to say something lightweight, but was brought down to earth by what he saw in her eyes. The eight-plus years of nonstop touring. The number of times she'd been burned on the job.

"Yeah. I do," he replied evenly. "But in a different way."

"Which is?"

"I pull silly hours at work."

He left it at that, and saw her street smile harden. Watched her toss her hair and almost not think it through. But she stayed with him, and he helped her along with his calm surgeon's gaze.

"It's not just me," he continued. "It's a big part of hospital surgery. You get addicted to procedure. It's one of the things *ER* almost gets right, but actually has no clue about. I always laugh when I see TV doctors getting hooked on meds, because the real junkies are the OR cowboys upstairs."

"The OR cowboys. And this is you?"

"This is me."

"No kidding." Her face softened. "I hear you. I pulled insane hours for a while there, too. So what are you gonna do about it?"

"Right now? Bail Marty out and somehow get him on a plane. Go home, try to work things out with Dad. Suggesting you come down to Florida was, in retrospect, a pretty stupid idea. But having said that, I'd like to see you again. I'm serious."

"How serious?"

"Very. Deadly."

Mercedes smiled. "This isn't because I'm a rock chick, is it? 'Cause if it is, I have to warn you, I've retired. These days, I'm a glorified housewife. I take care of my brother and I part-time manage this bed and breakfast in Cape May, which is actually pretty cool."

"Your brother's . . . retarded?"

"No. My brother's a *guitarist*. Same kind of thing, except he wrote all the hit songs in the band, so we get royalties. It's our bed and breakfast. We own it."

"Really?"

"Yeah. On the subject of glamour, there you have it. Paris. Milan. A bed and breakfast in New Jersey."

"Wow."

"You still want to ask me out?"

"God no."

She laughed. "That settles that, then."

"Well . . . maybe not."

"Hey, I meant to say this earlier. It was nice what you did for that girl. Putting her in that cab."

"Yeah, that was an ugly scene. I should probably go and ask the desk guy what they've done with my brother."

"If he's not here, he'll be at central booking, way downtown. I'd offer to drive you, but my car is full of drums and I have to get Kelly back to the hotel. And besides. I think you'll find they won't release him until Monday."

"... *what*?"

"I could be wrong, but the way I think it works with central booking is that you have to see a judge before they let you out. And judges don't preside on the weekends. So they throw you in on Friday, you have to wait until Monday. I think that's how it goes."

"You're *kidding*. How do you know this?"

"Puerto Rican guys from the neighborhood. You know, friends of friends. Let's just say the Tombs is not off limits to my people."

"Your people?"

"Actually, if you want to get technical about this, my people are fourteen-year-old white girls from Westchester. But I'm Puerto Rican, yes."

"Do you think they'll let me visit him in there?"

"If you wave your doctor pass around. It did the job on those cops last night."

"Of course. Hey—it looks like we're on."

The lockup cells had been opened in the basement, and a different kind of door scene was playing its way up the stairs. The hysterical, the weak, the drawn and pale, the repentant—these were the A list as far as the cops were concerned. Ironic poise or cool defiance could wait around all morning. It was ruined mascara and a serious case of the shakes that caught the gate spook's attention and punched your ticket upstairs, and the opening bars of the reunion symphony were all high strings and honking reed. Lots of hugging. Uptown dads untroubled by the ruckus, just glad to know their little girls were okay. For all their trappings of rebellion – the dyed hair, the piercings, the studded belts, the tattoos none of the kids on the early release list came close to flaunting bad behavior in front of their parents, and the whole thing seemed such a sad pose. Even Kelly the guitarist was contrite. She came out with a gaggle of club girls behind her – real stoners, by the look of them – and the three hours of lockup had obviously gone confessional. They were promising to stay in touch. One of the girls seemed on the verge of throwing a Judd Nelson, *Breakfast Club* air-punch, and Troxler took his precinct coffee and dumped it outside, ruminating morosely on the subject of Mercedes.

He'd expressed interest. She'd expressed interest back. A geographic problem existed, but this was not insurmountable. The dextroamphetamine and jetlag had him lushed-out to a point where he may as well have been on drugs, and yet he felt weirdly lucid. An odd thing had happened to him. He had met this girl. She was smart and non-cynical and as far removed from his world of surgery as he was from her world of music, and it startled him to realize how long it had been since he dated someone outside the medical profession. He was in his mid-thirties with an efficient, functional lifestyle that revolved around his work, and somewhere in the course of nailing surgical procedure, he had become his own man. And yet the supreme irony of his life was that he, a cardio specialist, had never had the big switch thrown on his own heart.

And now this.

How serious was this? Very? Deadly? Jim Troxler was an idealist who dealt in absolutes – the absolute of life and death – and even these were subject to the whims of market force. Time was the index, and you did the best job you could under the parameters of time. You developed routines, protocol, ideology. But even then, you could often tell how an operation was going to go, simply by studying the face of a patient. You could pick the survivors. The people who weren't going to take no for an answer. And it was for these people Jim Troxler worked hardest. More times than he could count, he had walked into a ward, caught the first glimpse of a patient, and *known* this was a keeper. Had known that nothing less than operational perfection beyond the call of duty was required. At the Royal Melbourne, he was, in the vernacular, the hospital's "gun cabbage man," "gun" meaning "extremely good at" and "cabbage" being a CABG, or coronary artery bypass graft, a tricky life-saving operation he performed three times a day. An assistant would make and cauterize an incision, saw through the sternum and clamp it open, and then Troxler would step in like an auto electrician and literally rewire the human heart. His preferred technique was to remove a section of vein from the leg or the thigh and graft it straight into the aorta, replacing age-worn or fat-clogged circulatory valves with state-of-the-art synthetic engineering, and his status in the OR was such that each new rotation of female scrub nurses had to be warned at the outset to leave him alone.

He did the work. The work mattered. The doctor-patient relationship was oddly gratifying, and supplied him with a rich tapestry of life that he could study at leisure. Had Lindy Minh or Naoko booked themselves in for surgery, he would have had no trouble talking to them. A big part of his job was putting his patients at ease. He was a hands-on participant in the business of life and death, and yet there was nothing dangerous or unpredictable in what he did. Nothing was left to chance, right down to the organic suture thread he had recently started using, where you could calculate to the minute how long it would take to dissolve in human tissue, and this was why his brother's club trawl was such a shot in the arm. He climbed the stairs and walked back inside the station, and found Mercedes settling up at the cashier. The stoner girls were loitering around, and a couple of the dads were showing interest. Hipster dads, all of a sudden. Oh, you've played with Prince? Great, yeah. *Purple Ruin.* Troxler flexed his surgeon's hands and smiled at the diversity of nonpatients around him; at the genetic resemblance between the club kids and their fathers; at the powerplay of status between the cops and the lawyers; at Mercedes accepting a business card from a silver-haired old fox in a pinstripe suit, as she looked in his direction and made a dumbshow of amusement. He walked past the front desk and took her gently by the elbow, leading her away to a quiet part of the room.

"Wait for me," he said.

Her face became serious. "Where?" she asked.

"Downtown. I want to go and look in on my brother. Make sure he's okay. Will you wait for me?"

"Sure." Mercedes nodded. "Outside central booking? I'm pretty sure it's on Centre Street. Do you know where that is?"

"I'll find it. I'll catch a cab."

She opened her mouth to say something, and then stopped. "Okay," she said. "I'll meet you outside the main entrance in what? An hour?"

"An hour sounds about right."

"Okay. I'll see you there at ten-thirty. Do you have cab fare? I can give you twenty bucks."

"There's a cash machine across the road. I'm good."

"So what, you still want to ask me out? The intercontinental thing is not a problem?"

"The intercontinental thing is a huge problem, but maybe I'm ready for a change. Maybe a bed and breakfast in New Jersey is what I'm looking for right now."

"Get outta here."

"I'm serious. You want to know something? Of all the people last night, you were the only one who asked me what my name was. Everyone else talked around it. Is this a New York thing?"

"It's a New York thing."

"And in Cape May, there's what? Local shopping? A couple of bars?"

"Lots of old people in big, rambling houses. It used to be a resort town. It's really nice."

"So take me there. Let me find out what the deal is with Marty, and then let's go there. Let's spend the weekend checking it out. There's an airport nearby, right?"

"In Atlantic City."

"So I can book a flight down to Florida from there."

"Right. This is pretty weird."

"It is weird. All I ever do is talk to doctors and patients. I take a bit of karate, but I've never used it on anyone. And I've never met anyone I've wanted to, I don't know, hang out with as much as you, especially not backstage at a gig. I get all kinds of people coming through my office, but it's always on my terms, so the weird thing is that my brother has actually done me a huge favor by forcing me outside my usual sphere of influence."

"In a roundabout way. You could have got beat up or arrested."

"Yeah, but I didn't."

"So now you get the girl and drive out to New Jersey. That's the plan?"

"That's the plan."

"Eh." She shrugged playfully. "I can see that."

"You can?"

"Sure. Roll credits over receding Manhattan skyline. Drive out in a shitbox yellow Bug with a killer sound system. Too bad we don't have a Porsche or a little red Corvette."

"A shitbox yellow Bug will do just fine."

OUTGOING

The cops took some persuading, but they agreed to let Jim Troxler visit his brother in the Tombs. It was against regulations, but he met the unspoken dress and occupational code. The bad news was that Mercedes had been right about the weekend traffic being locked up until Monday. The charges against Martin would be read before a judge, which meant he would have to spend two nights behind bars.

The male section of the basement housed a couple of large cells, which were already half full by Saturday morning. A ballpark assessment of the average prisoner was that he was in here for drugs and hitting the straps of withdrawal. The ambience was jittery. Most of the guys were in the grip of addiction, and were sitting around hugging their stomachs and groaning. The rage would kick in later with the natural order of containment, but for the moment, a quiet conversation could be held.

Martin Troxler was sitting on a low metal bench, putting out an experimental vibe of hostility. His face was bruised, and he had a slight cut under one eye that he had made no attempt to clean up. A suit-wearing badass. Mess with him at your peril. His watch was missing and they had taken his laces, but apart from that, he looked slick enough to be mistaken for someone important in middle-management crime. Baxter was beside him, trying to uphold a dangerous, mobworthy smirk, but his mouth was swollen and he looked more like a frightened tax accountant. The DOA had crashed, and various aftereffects were swimming through his nasal cavities, exerting pressure on his head fluid and making his eyes bulge grotesquely. He saw Jim Troxler in the hallway and alerted Martin with an elbow nudge that provoked a sharp hiss of anger. Judging by the way they walked over to the bars, they were concealing a lot of pain from the other inmates.

"Hey Marty," Jim Troxler said.

"Yo Jim," said Martin. "So what have you got?"

"In regards to?"

"Getting us out of here."

"It's been real, but we're over it," Baxter muttered. "Had enough. Want to go home now."

"I can't get you out," Troxler said, surprised by the question. "You're in for the weekend. They didn't tell you this when they brought you down here?"

"Not directly. Too busy slapping us around."

"We have money," Baxter said. "I have plastic upstairs."

"Money's not going to do it. I've already asked."

"Fuck."

"Okay. Do we need to call a lawyer?"

"You can call a lawyer if you want, but I think they're going to tell you what the cops told me. You have to see a judge on Monday, end of story."

"See? I told you."

"Fuck."

"So what does this do for you? You'll have to wait around a couple of days. You going to tell Mom?"

"No. But I'm not going to wait around either."

"What are you going to do?"

"Well here's the thing," Jim Troxler said. "I met a girl on the boat. I really like her and she seems to like me, so we're going to drive to New Jersey and see what happens."

"You old dog."

"Wait a second," Baxter said. "This is the Italian chick in the baseball jacket, right? I have a feeling I've seen her before."

"Puerto Rican, not Italian. And yeah, you saw her backstage after the band finished up. You guys were pretending to be label reps or something?"

"Oh my god." Martin whistled through his teeth. "She was in the band?"

"It gets better."

"Oh yes it does. Hey Buddy Boy, you hearing this? A rock bunny."

"Yeah right." Baxter snorted. "And which rock bunny are we talking? What position did she play?"

"She was the drummer."

"Ah. The *Energizer* bunny." Baxter laughed. "Sorry dude, I'm afraid some verification will be required before the Boxster changes hands. Perhaps you could furnish us with evidence. Do a Rob Lowe, shoot some tape?"

"You sleazy fuck," Martin hissed.

"Are you out of your mind? We're in the lockup, they took a urine sample, all bets are off."

"You sleazy *fuck*," Martin snarled with real anger. "There is no *way* you are squirming out of this one. A bet's a bet. You proposed it, you put your car up, you lost. My brother gets your car."

"Right now? Oh sure. Hey, take my car!"

"I mean it."

"Take my fucking car! Enjoy!"

Jim Troxler watched the two friends as they argued, and there was nothing to be gained by joining in. The overhead light was oppressive, throwing down a fierce, non-theatrical wattage designed to punish those accustomed to hiding in shadow, and Martin Troxler and Baxter looked wretched in this light. Their suits were shiny and fussily tailored; exactly the wrong kind of cut for a two-day stretch in the Tombs. Even in crime, his brother was slumming. The rest of his cell housed the legitimate drug trade in their sweats, and they were nothing if not authentic in their baggy jeans and do-rags, their pipe-burned lips curling with disgust as they watched the two would-be gangsters blow their cover by arguing. A couple of hard-looking inmates were glaring at Baxter as he upped the ante by shouting "Porsche" instead of "car," and Jim Troxler looked over at the duty cop, who shot him a bleak little headshake of amusement and wandered off to the guardroom at the end of the hall.

"Listen, we don't have much time," he told his brother. "A lazy hundred says I've booked a plane ticket for you."

"Oh, of course." Martin sighed. "So have you?"

"Actually, I haven't."

"But you want me to fly down anyway."

"Yeah."

"And what's the deal with this girl? You're shacking up for how long?"

"I'll be down on Monday. Let's just fly home and get this over with. We can discuss strategy after I've talked to the doctors. When was the last time you were down there, anyway?"

"May. I couldn't stand it. I couldn't handle mellow Dad."

"Yeah, well. I got your back, Marty. We'll tag-team his ass. You can be my bridge partner. We can drink his cheap booze."

"Or not."

"Or not. This isn't just about him, you know."

"Oh, I know. It's just I'd rather remember the old man as Racetrack Dad or Insurance Salesman Dad. Even Bartender Dad had an evil kind of charm. The thing you're going to find when you're down at the house is that it's impossible to reconcile these memories with the little old guy pumping your hand and smiling at you."

"I'm sure."

"No you're not. You've been ducking it, just like me."

"Of course I have. Because I *know* what we're in for. You don't think I've swung by the cancer wards and checked out the prostate guys? The thing with what Dad's got is that it's one of the few cancers you can beat. The survival odds are good if you get to it in time. But – and this is what's so wonderfully fucked up about it – you have to nuke or remove the testicles to eliminate testosterone, because testosterone is how the cancer spreads. The guys on the wards at the Royal Melbourne? Big, truck-driving Australians with their testosterone nuked to shit by drugs and therapy. Jaunty hat wearers the lot of them. And if I was the old man, I'd be chugging whiskey too."

"No kidding."

"I want to remember Racetrack Dad. Racetrack Dad was cool."

"He was cool." Martin smiled. "Totally insane, but with a certain *je ne sais quoi*."

"Right. So maybe he knows what he's doing. Maybe we give him the benefit of the doubt."

"Maybe we do. This is not the place to have this discussion."

"So let's have it in Fort Lauderdale. Let's have it on the strip. Any of those bars we used to drink at still around?"

"The strip? The strip has fallen into the hands of tourists, my friend. I do my drinking elsewhere. Like in New York?"

"So wherever. Maybe we go to the Rotary."

"Ah yes. The Rotary." Martin's eyes were hooded in the overhead light. A glimmer of interest was visible, but not much more. "That *would* be fun," he said. "We could camp out. Have the place to ourselves."

"Have a serious conversation about where we go from here."

"A *serious* conversation. So tell me about this girl. Not quite the type you usually go for, is she?"

"Yeah, listen—"

"A *drummer*. Traditionally, the dumbest member of the band. So what, you're envisaging this as a weekend fling, or do you see it more as a 'bring her home, meet the parents' type affair? And didn't you just score a residency or something? Some kind of terribly impressive and hard-to-get job in Melbourne?"

"Not yet. I'm up for one next year."

"So it's academic. You and the rock chick."

"I'm here for four months, Martin," Jim Troxler said sharply. "I'm here for the duration. I'm moving into my old room, I'm grocery shopping with Mom, I'm sitting down with Dad and talking things through. I'm not flying back next week. I'm *here*. And while I'm here, I'm going to take some time out and get my life back on track, because I'm not sure I like where it's heading right now. Okay? Fuck the residency. I've spent my whole life trying to not be like Dad, except I'm just like fucking Dad. And you're even more like fucking Dad than I am. We're in a fucking lockup and you *still* have to win whatever argument it is we're having. I'm on your side, but you still have to cream me in argument, even in the fucking Tombs, and I wonder why this is. Why *is* this? 'Cause you're in the Tombs and I'm not?"

"Well gee whiz, metaphorically speaking—"

"—Metaphorically speaking, you put yourself in here. All *I* did was not. You can piss and moan about the old man and your workload and the book you rushed through production. You can mitigate your circumstances all you want. But at the end of the day, it's not me or the big irony crowd you have to deal with. It's these 'keep it real' guys behind you. Think you can wow them with catchphrases until you see a judge on Monday?"

The duty cop was far enough from the cell to greenlight an approach from the back of the room, and Baxter was contending with the joint malevolence of three very large men, all of whom "loved the suit." A preemptive scuffle broke out. Baxter was trying to show some prisonyard steel, but none of the inmates appeared to be buying it, and Troxler turned from the cage and was about to call the cop back over when Martin caught him by the wrist and pulled him closer to the bars.

"Don't," he said quietly. "You'll make it worse."

"Okay." Jim Troxler nodded.

"Don't worry about me. I'll see you on Monday. And Jim?"

"What?"

"Don't buy me a ticket. I have frequent flyer miles."

It wasn't quite the scenario either brother had hoped for, but there was something firm and resolute about their handshake through the bars. Jim Troxler locked eyes with Martin and had a feeling that two days in central booking might provide the right kind of adversity to settle the differences between them. One of the detrimental things success does to character is remove the adversity that helped build it in the first place, and this lack of adversity had made Jim Troxler as complacent as it had made his brother smug. The rigors of surgery had trained him to be an accomplished croupier in the casino of risk, but it was time to start playing with his own money. And, interestingly enough, his brother had staked him in on what was shaping up to be the first big game of his future.

"Hey," he said. "I owe you one."

"Oh, come *on*," Martin snorted. "I was going to fly down the whole time."

"I'm not talking about that."

"You're talking about what, then? The moral high ground? Getting yourself laid? They aren't mutually inclusive, you know. Nice guys *do* finish last. Despite evidence to the contrary."

Troxler couldn't help laughing. "Well then. You're the man to help me out. There's this girl from New Jersey. And this terribly impressive and hard-to-get job in Melbourne. And I'm burning out at the job. Really. I'm good at it, but I'm doing it for the wrong reasons. I need to rethink my position, and you've helped start the process. So I owe you for that. Maybe I can do the same for you when we're down in Fern Grove."

"Maybe you can. But can you go now? It's going to get embarrassing really soon, and I could live without you seeing it."

"Okay. Anything else you want me to do?"

"Nah. Talk me up to the rock chick if you think she's a keeper. We disgraced ourselves pretty badly backstage."

"I'll talk you up, I promise."

"So, what? You seriously think this girl might be a keeper? You'll tank your medical career for a drummer in a band? You're going to need some *coaching*, my friend. You're going to need a pit crew, backup drivers, the works. We could bring the old man in as a consultant. The old man was always good at taming the wild chicks—"

"Hey Marty." Jim shook his head. "Don't go there."

Martin Troxler smiled grimly and drifted away from the bars. It was hard to tell whether he was genuinely engaged by the floorshow of violence around him, or merely role-playing his way through it like everyone else was role-playing. At the back of the room, an assortment of dealers and addicts had Baxter surrounded and were competing, *Jeopardy*-style, to shout ghettospeak and threats with the mad panache of those given to airing their grievances on midday television. The Poetry of War in the sense that everyone yelling sounded wounded or deranged. The cameras were rolling, but the footage was ugly. Baxter in his suit, trying to make himself heard, but there was none of the poignancy of celluloid Nam, because the shit was in his face and had the power to really hurt him. Nothing droll or postmodern about it. The mythic war in America had turned frighteningly real, and like all wars, it was scripted by idiots. The narrative language was banal. The action graceless and cluttered. It was third-rate TV filler with one significant exception: the good guys were on the receiving end. The good guys were under attack. The good guys were being dope-slapped and called stinky-ass bitches and having their space invaded and their shit fucked up but good, and the look on Baxter's face was one of total disbelief. Like, "How the hell did *this* happen? What the hell did we do to bring this shit on?"

It was difficult to watch, and so Jim Troxler stopped watching. He turned and walked down the hallway, allowing the noise to recede behind him, and by the time he had followed the cop upstairs and signed himself out, his mental picture of the evening had receded as well. For all the attitude, irony, and money thrown around, the only take-home thought he had concerning his brother's way of life was that slumming seemed harder than doing the work. A whole lot harder. Much much much too hard.

He braced his stomach against the workings of his nerves (a combination of amphetamine blues and old-fashioned prom-night fear) and walked outside the main entrance, scanning the street with an anxious tightening of his heart, and then grinning with relief when he saw the Volkswagen parked there. A yellow Bug. Shitbox yellow. A practical, nonostentatious little workhorse of a car, and Mercedes was leaning against the passenger door, smiling up the stairs as he trotted down to meet her.

ABOUT THE AUTHOR

Howard Hunt has edited magazines in Melbourne, Sydney, and New York. This is his second novel.